She could actually hear
the quiet sound of his breathing

as they watched the mare nuzzle her baby.

Jonah was obviously exhausted. Light from the lantern emphasized lines of weariness in his face, cast shadows into the hollows beneath his high cheekbones.

What was it, Carrie wondered, that made this man, with his dark skin and his black hair, look more magnificent than the yellow-haired heroes in all the storybooks?

Unconsciously she moved her hand closer to his. And then suddenly she leaned forward. "Oh, look—Jonah, it's trying to get up!"

"Watch." Jonah didn't move a muscle. His voice remained unemotional, as if he had not just participated in a miracle.

Inside the stall, Carrie watched the long-legged creature stand shakily and begin nudging his mother's belly. "Oh, my," she whispered. Jonah's hand closed over hers, and it seemed the most natural thing in the world....

D0190690

Praise for Bronwyn Williams's previous books

Beholden
"...as welcome as a cool breeze on a scorching day.
I can't resist a fast-paced, well-written story."
—*Rendezvous*

Entwined
"Her intricately woven story is deftly done,
and her depiction of her hero and heroine is masterful."
—*Affaire de Coeur*

Seaspell
"A terrific read. I loved it!"
—Author Pamela Morsi

Longshadow's Woman
Harlequin Historical #553—March 2001

Bronwyn Williams

Longshadow's Woman

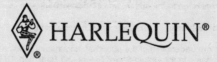

HARLEQUIN®

TORONTO • NEW YORK • LONDON
AMSTERDAM • PARIS • SYDNEY • HAMBURG
STOCKHOLM • ATHENS • TOKYO • MILAN • MADRID
PRAGUE • WARSAW • BUDAPEST • AUCKLAND

If you purchased this book without a cover you should be aware
that this book is stolen property. It was reported as "unsold and
destroyed" to the publisher, and neither the author nor the
publisher has received any payment for this "stripped book."

ISBN 0-373-29153-1

LONGSHADOW'S WOMAN

Copyright © 2001 by Dixie Browning and Mary Williams

All rights reserved. Except for use in any review, the reproduction or
utilization of this work in whole or in part in any form by any electronic,
mechanical or other means, now known or hereafter invented, including
xerography, photocopying and recording, or in any information storage
or retrieval system, is forbidden without the written permission of the
publisher, Harlequin Enterprises Limited, 225 Duncan Mill Road,
Don Mills, Ontario, Canada M3B 3K9.

All characters in this book have no existence outside the imagination of
the author and have no relation whatsoever to anyone bearing the same
name or names. They are not even distantly inspired by any individual
known or unknown to the author, and all incidents are pure invention.

This edition published by arrangement with Harlequin Books S.A.

® and TM are trademarks of the publisher. Trademarks indicated with
® are registered in the United States Patent and Trademark Office, the
Canadian Trade Marks Office and in other countries.

Visit us at www.eHarlequin.com

Printed in U.S.A.

Available from Harlequin Historicals and
BRONWYN WILLIAMS

White Witch #3
Dandelion #23
Stormwalker #47
Gideon's Fall #67
The Mariner's Bride #99
The Paper Marriage #524
Longshadow's Woman #553

Please address questions and book requests to:
Harlequin Reader Service
U.S.: 3010 Walden Ave., P.O. Box 1325, Buffalo, NY 14269
Canadian: P.O. Box 609, Fort Erie, Ont. L2A 5X3

Chapter One

With a graceful gesture, Carrie resettled her best straw hat, angling the brim against the sun. Sighing, she once more addressed the mule in the only language the beast understood. "Move along there, you lop-eared son of a bitch!"

If there was one thing Sorry hated more than pulling a plow, it was pulling a cart. It had cost Carrie more in time and aggravation than she could afford just to get the wretched old bag of bones hitched up. At this stop-and-go speed they wouldn't make it to the jailhouse until tomorrow, and she didn't have a day to waste.

Her husband was going to pitch a fit if he got home and saw the damage Sorry had done to Peck's paddock gate before she had time to mend it. Nothing was too good for that ugly gelding of his. His own private paddock, a fancy new stall, the very best oats, not to mention fresh water that had to be hauled all the way up from the creek daily, and Darther wasn't one to do the hauling himself. That's what he had her for, as he delighted in reminding her.

As for Carrie, the mule and the chickens, they could

starve as long as that damned racehorse of his didn't suffer the least discomfort.

Blessed horse. She was going to have to shed the habit of swearing. Emma said it wasn't ladylike, but it was hard not to fall into bad habits when every other word out of her husband's mouth was foul. Nor had her uncle been any better. Carrie had a vague memory of a softer voice with a far different accent, but it was wedged so far back in her mind that sometimes she thought she must have dreamed it.

"Step it up, Sorry, we're never going to get there at this rate," she pleaded.

But pleading didn't work. Reasoning didn't work. The damn-blasted mule just stood there, ignoring the heat, the flies—ignoring Carrie. The only thing that got through his thick skull was the language he was used to hearing from Darther.

"Listen here, you wall-eyed bastard, either you start walking or I'm going to carve your dumb ass into a thousand pieces and feed every scrap to the crows!" Bishop Whittle would be scandalized if he could hear her now.

Sighing, she slapped the reins across the mule's thick, dusty hide, causing him to lurch into motion. Her feet flew up, the straw hat slipped over her face again and she nearly lost her grip on the reins. "That's better," she grumbled, shoving her hat back on her sweating head.

Within minutes they had settled back to a torpid stroll. Where Sorry was concerned, locomotion came in fits and jerks, or not at all. "Come on, sweetheart," she cajoled, "we have a long way to go, and the slower you move, the longer it'll be before you can get shed of this old cart. I'll give you a turnip if we make it back before dark.''

Which would never happen at the rate they were going. Not that she was afraid to be out after dark. Still, she didn't like the prospect of driving home alone at night with a prisoner. By the time darkness fell she intended to be secure in her own home, with the chickens shut up for the night, the mule fed and watered, and her prisoner, if she managed to rent one, safely locked inside the barn.

Twitching away the flies, Sorry continued to amble along the dusty wagon road. Carrie managed to curb her impatience. At least they were moving. It could be worse. According to Darther, all mules hated all females. Something to do with what he referred to as their half-ass breeding.

If anyone should know about jackasses, it was Darther. Theirs was *not* a match made in heaven. The first time she had suggested hitching that ugly gelding of his to the plow and clearing the cut-over field, he'd given her a wallop that had landed her on her backside. She had been new to marriage at the time, and hadn't known what to expect.

Now she did.

From the top of a tall, dead pine, a red-tailed hawk watched her progress. Dust rose in pale drifts behind the cart, overtaking it as a fresh breeze sprang up from the cloudless sky. It hadn't rained since early July. All that was left of her kitchen garden, of which she had been so proud only a few weeks ago, were a few leathery beans no longer than her little finger, despite all the buckets of water she had toted up from the creek. She'd felt like giving up when the deer and rabbits had got to her cabbages, leaving only two rows of green stalks.

But giving up wasn't in her, because Carrie had another dream. And this time she had the grit and determination to make it come true. As a child she'd had those same qualities, but back then they'd been called stubbornness, and no one had wanted to adopt a stubborn, headstrong little girl who was neither smart nor pretty, even though she had tried her very best to be quiet and obedient.

One thing had never changed, though. Once she made up her mind to do something, she refused to give up. And Carrie had set her mind on making her husband's land prosperous again. The first step was to grow herself a cash crop. With the seed money she would get from that, she would clear more land and grow more corn, until not one square foot of dirt was wasted. One field had been cut over by a previous owner years before, but the job had never been finished. The stumps were still there, and now the underbrush had grown back again, but it was conveniently close to the creek. Come spring, once she got it cleared and turned, she could hill it and plant it by herself, and tote water during the dry spells. That was the first part of her dream. She couldn't allow herself to look farther into the future.

During Darther's absence she'd been making good progress. A gambling man, her husband was seldom home if there was a horse race, a dog race, a cockfight or a card game anywhere within a three-day ride. He would come home, more often drunk than sober, and stay just long enough for her to sponge and air his fancy suits and launder his shirts and smallclothes, and then he'd be off again. As the racing season neared, he'd be gone sometimes for weeks at a time.

Once he left home again, Carrie was in the field every day at cock-crow, digging and prying, playing tug-of-war by pitting that stubborn mule against equally stubborn stumps. It was backbreaking work, even with two good hands, but she was determined to have every damned stump—every *blessed* stump—dug up, dragged off to the side and burned. She'd been whacking away at gum roots when she'd missed and nearly chopped her thumb off. The fact that her hand had been filthy at the time hadn't helped, but one way or another she intended to be ready to plant come spring, and nothing as puny as a bad hatchet cut that refused to heal was going to keep her from doing it, either.

It was Emma, her elderly widowed neighbor, who had told her about the prisoners who were sometimes leased out for farm labor. "County allows so much a day for feed. As long as a man's not wanted for murder, you can take him out on parole and save the county his keep. I don't think it's on the books that way, but as long as you sign papers saying you'll return him in as good condition as when you took him out, they'll look the other way. Let him escape, and I reckon they can lay a claim against you for misuse of county property."

They'd been idly discussing ways of getting the job done, seeing as how Carrie's hand was so slow to heal. She couldn't afford to hire anyone, even if she could have found someone willing to work on her husband's farm. "Darther left me a little money last time he was home, but I spent it on meal and sugar and cracked corn. Wonder what kind of prisoner I could rent for the price of three dresses, two straw hats and a pair of shoes with holes in the bottom?"

She'd been half teasing, and Emma had laughed. Thank goodness one of them was able to laugh. "You'll manage," the older woman had said. "I've got some money laid by. You can pay me back from your first crop. For interest you can give me half a bushel of corn for my chickens.''

Carrie had thought about it all the way home that day last week when she'd gone to take her friend a basket of fried rabbit and turnips. It had been Emma who had befriended her nearly three years ago when Darther had first brought her to this godforsaken place to cook and clean and service his needs whenever he was sober enough to attempt the marriage act.

It had been Emma who had told her all she knew about that particular part of a wife's duties. More importantly, she'd taught her all she knew about planting. Carrie still had much to learn, but driven by dreams, desperation and determination, she refused to waste another planting season. By now she knew better than to expect any help from her husband. Even if he was home long enough, and remained sober enough, he was hardly inclined to soil his hands with honest labor. Racing and gambling were all the man ever thought about. He was convinced that Peck, half Arabian, but so ugly no one ever suspected him of being a runner, would one day make him a fortune.

Peck was fast, all right. Carrie had watched him being put through his paces out on the road, but even if the big, ugly gelding won a fortune, Carrie would never see a penny of it. Darther would plop it all down on the next race or cockfight or hand of cards, and lose every last penny. Not only was he a loser, he was a stingy loser. He might come home sporting a new silk vest with his fancy frock coat and checkered trousers, but just let her ask for money to buy something useful, like a new cow, or a plow that wouldn't fall apart at the first use, and she'd end up on her backside with a swollen jaw. Drunk or sober, her husband had a treacherous temper.

When Darther had accepted her in payment of a debt he was owed by her uncle, she had been so eager to escape her uncle that she'd allowed herself to be used that way. She had even begun to dream all over again. She had seen him around the store a time or two before that, and noticed his fine fancy clothes. He'd boasted a lot, too, only back then she hadn't known it was only boasting.

"Darther has racing interests," her uncle had said, making it sound terribly important, as if he owned a track, or at least a flock of Thoroughbreds. "The man knows more about horseflesh than he knows about his own family."

If he even had a family, he'd never admitted it. "Raised up in New York," he'd once boasted. "Been to every racetrack on the Eastern Seaboard." She had later learned that he was what was called a carpetbagger, a species not well respected in the South. But that was long after she'd married the man. When they had crossed the border into North Carolina after the hasty marriage ceremony, she'd been picturing a fine house surrounded by green fields where elegant, long-legged horses gamboled with their foals.

Oh, yes, Carrie was good at dreaming. It was all that had kept her going in the years since the Indian raid. She had learned to create a separate reality inside her head that made life more bearable.

Things *would* get better. Someone *would* adopt her and take her into their home. The uncle who finally sent for her would come to love her, and she would be a comfort to him in his old age.

None of her early dreams had worked out, of course. Her uncle, a storekeeper in Virginia, had turned out to be a mean, slovenly man without an ounce of kindness

in him. And Darther, so dapper with his well-fed body
and his fancy clothes, had turned out to be more nightmare than dream. The lovely plantation she had visual-
ized on the ride south had been the last straw. She had
taken one heart-stricken look at the pigsty her bridegroom called home and felt the last of her dreams crumble around her feet.

Her honeymoon had been no better. The painful, embarrassing experience that even now she couldn't bear
to think about, had ended the next day when a weasel-
faced man called Liam had turned up with the news that
some breeders were coming down from New York to
look over the crop of two-year-olds, and that there might
be some action up in Suffolk.

The dust hadn't even settled behind them before Carrie had braced her shoulders, set her jaw and gone to
work. She now had a roof over her head that didn't leak,
a chimney that hardly smoked at all, a real iron range
big enough for a kettle and a stew pot, and a kitchen
garden, never mind that it fed mostly deer and rabbits.

Best of all, she had a good friend and enough rich,
flat land, if she could ever manage to get it cultivated,
to grow herself a fine cash crop. Last year's hog was
gone but for a side of bacon hanging in the smokehouse.
Her cow was gone, too, and she really missed fresh milk
and butter. She'd had a nanny goat briefly, but the thing
had butted her off the stool one too many times. Carrie
had sold her when she'd eaten the bottom off a whole
line of laundry. Now she had only a flock of chickens,
but she managed to snare enough squirrels and rabbits
for meat, which she shared with Emma.

She'd have herself some fine, collard-fed venison, too,
if she could ever locate the ammunition for her husband's Springfield rifle. The gun rested proudly on a rack

of antlers over the door. He'd told her more than once that he'd skin her alive if she ever touched it, and she had to believe him. His pappy's Springfield, a fancy gold watch fob, and Peck, that ugly old gelding, were the only three things in the world her husband valued.

When he'd left home this last time she'd watched him out of sight, then deliberately climbed up on a chair and lifted the gun down from the wall. Staggering under the unexpected weight, she had propped it beside the door. Living more than a mile from the nearest neighbor, and that neighbor only Emma, who could scarcely do for herself, much less for anyone else, she felt better having protection at hand—or at least the appearance of protection. Now and again someone would wander in, looking for Darther. She always told them he was away, but because she didn't want strangers hanging around waiting for him to come home, she made sure they saw the rifle and tried to look like the kind of woman who knew how to use it.

And now, here she was, getting ready to take a prisoner home with her. What she needed was a big, mean dog, only she didn't know where to get one. Wouldn't much trust him if she did. Still, even empty, the rifle should be enough to keep her prisoner in line. He would have no way of knowing the thing wasn't loaded. Emma said he'd be wearing leg irons, too, so if he gave her any trouble, she'd just club him with the barrel.

Catching a glimpse of a brick building, which could only mean they were nearing Currituck Courthouse, Carrie dealt with her misgivings one at a time. The county wouldn't allow a dangerous criminal out on parole. Besides, he'd be in irons. As for what Darther would say when he found out, she would think of something. She could tell him she intended to plant a pasture for Peck;

that should do the trick. Until it was knee-high, he probably wouldn't know the difference between corn and
pasture grass.

Meanwhile, she had her own future to see to.

To pass the time, he counted. Counted the fleas
crushed between a grimy thumbnail and forefinger.
Counted the bricks in the wall, the bars on the window,
the number of times the jailhouse dog yapped outside
the door.

Counted the years of his age, that numbered twenty-
nine—not as many as he would have liked, but as many
as he was apt to see.

Counted the ships that had sunk beneath him, which,
unfortunately, totaled three. Counted the shipmates lost
at sea, too great a number to recount without pain, even
though he had had no friends among them.

With a mixture of grief, anger and resignation, Jonah
Longshadow counted the years it had taken him to save
enough money to buy his land, fence it and stock it with
a blooded stallion and a few good brood mares. He
counted the number of foals he would never live to see
and wondered who would eventually claim all that was
his.

And when he was done counting all that, and counting
the days his body could go without food, he turned to
counting his chances of escaping the hangman's noose.

The number was less than the number of hairs on a
goose egg—less than the number of legs on a fish.

Hearing footsteps approaching his cell, Jonah suffered
the indignity of eagerness. There might even be more
than a crust of stale cornbread today. Yesterday's chunk,
no bigger than his thumb, had been soaked with something that hinted of ham and cabbage. He suspected ei-

ther the caretaker or the jailer himself ate most of the food prepared for the prisoners, allowing them only enough to keep them alive for a trial.

The water he could abide. Even with a few wiggling worms, the kind that would turn into mosquitoes, it filled his belly. A man could live for a long time without food as long as he had water.

It was the jailer this time, not the young caretaker. He came empty-handed, and Jonah's belly growled in protest. He sank back onto the matted straw that smelled of dog and crawled with fleas and waited to be told that the judge had finally arrived, had tried him without a hearing and sentenced him to hang for the crime of being a stranger, a half-breed. For being a survivor. With a streak of bitter amusement, he hoped it would be today, while he still had the strength to stand and face his executioner.

"On yer feet, Injun, got some good news fer ye."

The sun was at its hottest by the time Carrie finished her business and turned toward home, her prisoner following along behind. Hobbled by leg irons, he couldn't walk fast, but then, Sorry was in no great rush. She only hoped the poor wretch would be worth the two dollars he had cost her.

An Indian. She still couldn't believe she had rented herself an Indian, after what had happened to her parents. But he'd been the only prisoner at the time, and she was determined not to go back empty-handed.

The jailer, a potbellied man with a drooping moustache and eyes that seemed to weigh her and find her wanting—which was nothing new in her life—had given her a small key, but warned her to keep the leg irons in place at all times. He'd told her to shoot the thieving bastard if he tried to escape, to feed him once a day and to keep a close eye on him. "Injuns are a tricky bunch, breeds are even worse. If I didn't have to be gone all next week, I wouldn't let you take him, but Noah'd likely end up either starving the poor devil or letting him escape."

Carrie didn't know who Noah was, nor did she care. All she wanted to do was get home before dark. Before she changed her mind. She had expected a prisoner to look meek and subdued, not like a wild animal, ferocious and furious at being held in captivity.

She had every intention of feeding her beast—her prisoner. Wild or not, she had paid two whole dollars for him and she fully intended to get her money's worth, even if it meant breaking him to the harness herself. She might be a dreamer, but she was also a realist. She fed her chickens so they'd lay eggs. She fed Sorry, hoping to get a few hours of work out of the lazy beast. A man, even a miserable, flea-ridden creature like the one trailing behind the cart, his ankles hobbled by a short, heavy chain, wrists bound by a lead rope, would need food to keep up his strength.

According to the jailer, he had been imprisoned for robbery, but for all anyone knew, he could be a killer, too. She might have been smarter to put off clearing her field for another year, or at least to wait until her hand healed and she could do it all herself. But she'd already started the task, and it wasn't in her to give up. Another year and the brush would be even thicker. If this was what it took, why then, she'd do it, second thoughts or not.

He was filthy. When he'd gotten close enough for her to get a whiff, she'd been reminded of the hides she'd nailed to the side of the barn to cure. Not that she was much cleaner herself after a day on the dusty road, but at least she'd started out the day with a washbowl and a chunk of lye soap.

It occurred to her that she didn't know his name, didn't even know if he had one. Well, of course he had a name—everyone had a name, but she hadn't dared look him directly in the face, much less ask for an introduction. When it came right down to actually handing over money to rent a human being, with him not having any say in the matter, she'd been unexpectedly embarrassed. It was too much like buying a cow, or a horse.

Even so, she'd seen enough to know he looked mean and arrogant, as if being filthy and imprisoned was something to be proud of. Touching the rifle for reassurance, she tried to ignore the hatred she could practically feel burning into her back through layers of faded calico and coarse muslin.

Passing the small farmhouses between Currituck Courthouse and her turnoff in Shingle Landing, people stared and whispered at the sight of a man being led behind the cart like a cow. One little boy threw a rock and yelled something hateful. A woman taking wash off the line stopped to stare and call out a warning. "You be careful, there, girl—he don't look none too trustable to me."

He didn't to Carrie, either. All the same, she cringed at hearing him discussed as if he were a dumb animal. She knew what it felt like to be passed around like an unwanted parcel, discussed as if her ears were no more than handles on a pitcher. She'd been only a child when it had happened to her. Her prisoner was a full-grown man—a thief, possibly worse. The jailer had let on that he was no better than a savage, didn't even speak the King's English. She'd heard the poor wretch muttering something under his breath in some heathen tongue while the jailer was tying him to the back of the cart and testing his knots by jerking them as hard as he could.

Carrie slapped the reins across Sorry's rump, wiped the sweat from her eyes and wished she hadn't already finished the jar of water she'd brought with her. There'd been creeks along the way where Sorry could drink, but Carrie wasn't about to get down on her hands and knees and drink beside her mule. She could wait.

But what about her prisoner? She peered over her shoulder to make sure he was still following along behind the cart. It wouldn't do either of them much good if he passed out from thirst without her noticing and she dragged him all the way home.

Sweat trickled between her breasts. August was so blessed hot! She was worn to a frazzle just from riding. She couldn't imagine how he must feel, having to walk, especially with those heavy chains around his ankles. If his back itched, he wouldn't even be able to scratch with his wrists bound together with the lead rope.

Once her conscience started to nag at her, it refused to let up. Finally, when she could bear it no longer, she hauled short on the reins and climbed stiffly down off the high seat. Her left hand was throbbing, her bottom sore as a boil from the oak bench seat, but it was her conscience that bothered her most. It simply wasn't in her to be cruel to anything, man or beast. The man might be a filthy, thieving heathen, but she hadn't forgotten what the missionaries had taught her about being a Good Samaritan and doing unto others. She had to admit that even with a sore bottom, she'd sooner ride than have to walk all the way home, swallowing dust.

With a reassuring glance at the rifle, she signaled the man to come forward. Bishop Whittle would have been proud of her. He'd been real big on doing unto the least of them, and all that. A criminal would probably rank pretty far down on his list of leasts, but all the same...

"I reckon it won't hurt if you ride the rest of the way on the back of the cart."

If gray eyes could be said to blaze, his did. The words hung there between them, like that long, frayed lead rope. And then the man turned his back on her.

Carrie couldn't believe it—the arrogant bastard actually turned his back! Indignant at having her good deed thrown back in her face, she snatched up the lead rope and gave it a hard yank. "Don't you turn your back on me, you sorry, thieving—"

Jonah called on the pride that had brought him so far. The pride that was now battered almost beyond resurrection. Raising his manacled wrists, he jerked on his end of the rope, catching the stupid woman off guard. When she fell forward, landing face down in the dirt, he felt a fierce stab of satisfaction.

Which might be the last thing he felt, he told himself as she lunged up from the road and reached for her rifle. Furious at having been dragged along a public road, he was in a vengeful mood. From under a thatch of matted, vermin-infested hair, he glared at her, making no effort to hide his hatred. This small, drab creature with her sun-reddened nose was not responsible for a single stroke of his ill fortune, but he was in no mood to be reasonable, much less charitable.

They were evenly matched. His hands were bound, his legs in irons, but he was taller, stronger, and far craftier. She was a small woman with one hand wrapped in rags, but she had two distinct advantages. White skin and a Springfield rifle—even though the gun was almost too heavy for her to lift. Braced against the side of the

wagon, she could hardly manage to hold it steady, but
her eyes never left his. Grudgingly, he allowed her credit
for a measure of pride, no matter how foolish.

He was a Kiowa warrior. She was merely a woman.

In the torpid heat of a late summer afternoon, they
stood there for one endless moment, linked by misery,
frustration and the birth of an awareness neither of them
was willing to acknowledge. The mule, as pathetic a
creature as Jonah could recall seeing, even here in the
east—began to graze on the dried grass at the edge of
the road. Jonah told himself he could stand in the middle
of the road as long as she could. Unfortunately, he hadn't
eaten in far too long and he needed to make water.

So he did something to break the stalemate. Lifting
his head, he closed his eyes and loosed the fierce, wild
war cry that had once echoed across the plains.

Startled, the mule threw back its head and brayed,
adding to the cacophony. A pair of crows erupted from
the top of a dead pine. Jonah had the pleasure of seeing
the woman's face grow pale as milk from a starving
cow.

It had been more than ten years since Carrie had heard
such a cry. She had almost managed to block it out, to
the point of renting a man who was part Indian. Now it
came roaring back like a relentless nightmare. On that
dreadful night so long ago she had barely escaped with
her life. Hundreds of others, including both her parents,
had been slaughtered, victims of the Minnesota Massacre, a wild rampage that had lasted more than a week.

Taking two steps forward, she jabbed him hard in the
belly with the rifle barrel. "Don't you *ever* do that
again," she hissed, as wild color rushed up to replace
her pallor. "You can walk till you drop in your tracks

for all I care, then I'll drag you the rest of the way and feed what's left of your miserable carcass to the hogs!''

Carry didn't have a hog, but as a threat, it was about the worst she could think of. She only hoped he believed her. Having seen him up close—seen his eyes, which didn't match the rest of him, even as they simmered with hatred—she was even more conflicted than when she'd stopped to offer him a ride.

The man was a prisoner, she reminded herself. An Indian, no different from the ones who had murdered nearly an entire settlement. He might not have been a part of that particular event, but he'd done something awful, else he wouldn't have been in jail. Given half a chance, he'd probably wrap the rope around her neck and strangle her.

Just as well she'd had second thoughts about letting him ride with her. She was sorely tempted to turn around and drag him back to the jail. He could rot there for all she cared. The trouble was, she needed him—needed someone, at least, and he was the best she could do. Unless she was willing to wait another year to get her first field planted, it was this man or nothing.

With a show of boldness she was far from feeling, she tested the knot, nodded, and climbed back up in the cart, wincing as she settled her tender backside onto the hard, splintery seat. Her hand throbbed all the way up to her shoulder—she had a hardened criminal on the other end of a rope, and she was just now starting to wonder if she'd have the courage to let him off the leash long enough to do any work.

This might not have been one of her better ideas.

Just before she slapped Sorry into motion again, she turned and glared over her shoulder. ''Out of the kindness of my heart, I was willing to let you ride. Well, you flat out used up any kindness I had to offer, so you can just damned well crawl, for all I care.''

As if he could understand a word she was saying. All the same, she said it because it needed saying. At least God, if He happened to be listening, would know her heart was in the right place.

Over her shoulder, she spoke again in a loud voice, enunciating each word clearly. ''And just so you don't go getting any crazy notions, I can shoot the toenail off a one-legged crow at a hundred yards. I'll shoot you dead if you try to run away, you understand me?''

Jonah understood every word the woman spoke, but he had long since learned the advantage of keeping such knowledge to himself. The woman was weak and foolish. She lied. She was also afraid of him, but Jonah did not make war on women.

Uttering not a word, he weighed his options. He had been away from his farm for twelve days. His horses were pastured. There was grass. There was a creek for water. One of his mares was due to foal soon. He needed to be with her, for she was a foolish animal, but first he must retrieve the deed to his property and the bill of sale for his stock before his parole ended, which would be when the circuit judge arrived. Even then, his chances of convincing a judge of his honesty were low. He had paid for everything he possessed, but there was no way he could prove the money he had used had not been stolen.

Overpowering his captor would be easy, but would accomplish nothing. They'd been traveling somewhat west of north. By now he was beginning to recognize a few familiar landmarks. When they passed the one-lane road that led to his own property, he focused his mind on the thought that one way or another he would reclaim his freedom. He had not come this far and survived this much to give up now. He had no way of knowing where the woman was taking him, but he knew it could not be too much farther. She had not brought along food.

So he walked behind the cart, breathing in the sweet, dusty air of freedom. While his mind turned over various ways he might prove his innocence, his gaze rested on the straight, narrow back of the woman. When she lifted her ugly straw hat he saw that her hair was thick and pale and shorter than his own. Only children had hair so short. She was not a child, but she was young. Even with two good hands she would be no match for the willful mule. The mule knew it. The woman still held onto her illusions.

He studied her bandaged hand and wondered how grave the injury was. Though her arms were pink, he thought it was from the sun, not the telltale signs of an inflammation streaking up from under her wound. He had seen people die from such an inflammation.

Jonah didn't particularly want his captor to die. He had heard the jailer tell her she must feed him. By remaining her prisoner now, he could build his strength and have a far better chance of escaping.

Shortly before they turned off the main road, she stopped to allow the mule to drink from a broad creek, beckoning for him to do likewise. He refused to be grateful, even when he was able to use the opportunity to step behind a massive gum tree and relieve himself. When the rope between them pulled even tighter so that he could barely lift his hands, he muttered under his breath. His trousers securely buttoned again, he moved back into the clearing just as the woman emerged from behind another tree, adjusting her skirt. For reasons he didn't even try to understand, Jonah felt like laughing.

She had turned off the main road a mile back, following a smaller road until they turned off once more. Jonah fixed in his mind the landmarks. Eventually they came into a clearing. Passing by a cabin that was scarcely larger than his jail cell, she stopped outside a barn that looked as if it would take only one hard wind to collapse.

"You'll sleep in there." She pointed first at the prisoner and then at the gaunt, tin-roofed structure with a collapsed shed at one end.

Jonah could have told her he would be far more comfortable sleeping out under the stars, but that would require speaking her language. Silence could work to his advantage. He was still attached to the cart, though he could easily have freed himself, but to what end?

Instead, he waited for the woman to unhitch the mule. When she turned to look at him, a frown on her face, he saw that she was even younger than he had first thought. Turning abruptly, she picked up a stick, marched across the clearing and drew a line in the dirt surrounding the house. Turning back, she said, "I'm going to untie you now, but you're not to step over this line, you hear?"

To emphasize her words, she pointed to him, then to the house, and shook her head vigorously. "Not go to house? Do—you—understand?"

He understood lines. The U.S. Government drew lines in the earth and called them reservations. Jonah would not cross her line. Wooden houses stifled him. They were ugly and drafty and too often smelled of unwashed bodies. Bitterness coloring reluctant amusement, he nodded solemnly.

"Then I reckon we'd better get you settled first and

then see about cleaning you up. I don't hold with fleas and lice, not even in the barn.''

Jonah would rather not ''hold with'' them, either, given a choice. He could feel the miserable devils crawling on his scalp and the skin of his groin. At this moment, he couldn't have said who he hated more, the man he'd been forced to become, or the woman who reminded him of it.

Chapter Two

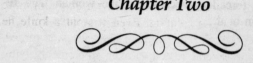

Carrie led her prisoner to the barn holding her rifle under one arm, with the lead rope wrapped around the wrist of her bandaged hand. Inside, it was barely light enough to see, but she didn't dare put down the rope or the rifle in order to light the lantern. The man glanced around, his gaze going immediately to the new stall Darther had had built for his gelding. There was a cot just outside the slat wall where Liam slept when they were here. According to Darther, Liam, who usually reeked of whiskey and lineament, was both jockey and trainer. So far as Carrie was concerned, he was just another mouth to feed. She liked him no better than she did her husband, but evidently, he was part of the bargain.

So when the prisoner moved toward the cot, she jerked on his rope. "Not there," she said, and then swore because talking to a heathen was like talking to that blasted mule. Neither of them understood a word she said.

Grabbing a hoe, she scratched a line in the earthen floor, dragging him with her as she moved. Then she pointed to the line and shook her head, indicating that he was not to go beyond the mark.

When he nodded his head she decided the poor wretch was not entirely without understanding. Next she would have to fix it so he could go outside to relieve himself without being able to run away. The privy would have to wait until she could think of a way to give him more slack. Rope was no solution. Even without a knife he could hack through it the minute her back was turned, using any of several rusted, broken implements lying around the barn.

He could simply jerk the end from her grasp, come to that. The rifle was all that kept him from freeing himself and taking off into the woods. Which meant that she was going to have to keep it nearby at all times.

Selecting a length of chain from among several hanging on the wall—hoping there were no weak links—she secured her prisoner by padlocking one end to his leg irons and the other to the hasp on the open barn door. Having to hold the heavy rifle and work with her good hand was an awkward, not to mention painful, process, but at least he had the freedom to step outside when he needed to.

"There now, I reckon that ought to do it, long's you don't trip over the chain," she said, and then shook her head because it was useless, trying to talk to him. Which reminded her that she still had Sorry to deal with.

Throughout the entire process the man hadn't uttered a sound, but his eyes had followed her every move. She almost wished he would complain, even if she couldn't understand what he was saying. He was beginning to remind her a little too much of the starving pup that had turned up at her back door one day last winter. One look and she'd lost her heart. Shaggy tan fur, big golden eyes, just begging to be loved.

Begging to be fed, more likely, but she'd taken him in and made a fool of herself, crooning, whipping up the eggs and buttermilk she'd been saving for a big pan of cornbread. The miserable mutt had lapped the bowl clean, spattering goo all over her floor. Then he'd peed, snapped at her hand, and run right between her legs and out the door, leaving fleas, dog hair, and a mess for her to clean up.

That poor wretch in her barn looked as if he hadn't eaten in weeks. If anything, he was even dirtier than the pup had been, and while his eyes were gray, not yellow, they sure as shooting weren't begging for love. She couldn't afford to get softhearted, not when she was dealing with a hardened criminal.

Chained to the wall, Jonah watched her leave. Then he lifted his head, closed his eyes and swore fluently in three languages. He'd have done better to have gone back to the damned reservation instead of trying to make a new life for himself here in the East.

Closing his mind to the weight of the heavy leg irons, he tested the extent of his freedom, moving around the cluttered barn, studying the selection of tools available. All were rusted. Most were broken, but useful enough for his purposes. The woman was a fool. Perhaps he'd been a bigger fool not to have tied her up with her own rope, dug the key from her pocket and escaped.

Choosing a short length of baling wire, he set to work sharpening it to a fine point on the grindstone. The locks were ancient. Two twists of the sharpened wire and the first popped open, and then the second. He removed the hinged iron bands from his ankles and examined the raw and bleeding flesh. She had offered to let him ride on the back of the cart. Proudly, he had refused, but pride would be poor comfort if his feet rotted and fell off.

When he heard the cabin door open and close, he moved swiftly. By the time the woman appeared, he was back in irons, sitting meekly on a pile of straw. At least it was clean straw. Dusty, but with the sweet smell of the meadow, not like the straw pallet in his jail cell that had reeked of things he'd rather not think about.

"I brought you something to eat and a blanket." Her voice sounded more hesitant now that she'd left her rifle behind. From the open doorway she eyed him warily before kneeling to place a thin woolen blanket and a plate of cornbread glistening with drippings just inside the door. "And here's a bucket of water." She reached behind her and swung the rusted pail inside. "You can drink your fill and wash with what's left. Tomorrow I'll take you down to the creek and you can scrub."

She'd forgotten to mime and speak in those insultingly loud, single-syllable words. Not that she didn't still treat him as if he were of somewhat lesser intelligence than that miserable mule of hers. Which, he thought with bitter amusement, was probably true.

Without moving, he continued to stare back at her through the fast fading light. She was small for a woman, lacking the soft layer of flesh most women kept even in the starving times. Under the shapeless garment that hung from her shoulders, she appeared more child than woman. Either way, it made little difference, as both were capable of inflicting cruelty on anyone they perceived as being different.

The smell of fresh cornbread and bacon drippings knotted his gut painfully. His belly hadn't been filled since he'd been taken from his own land, but he'd be damned before he would shame himself by crawling in the dirt and falling on her bread like a starving animal.

"Well." She hesitated, as if reluctant to leave. He wanted to shout, Go, woman! Leave me one small shred of dignity! "We'll start pulling stumps come morning. I'll bring you more food and show you where the creek is so you can bathe first. Um…the blanket. I know it's hot now, but it gets cool just before morning."

He made a sound in his throat that was something between a curse and a growl. It served the purpose. The woman fled, and he felt like laughing. Only, he felt more like weeping.

She had not brought him a cup. He scooped water from the bucket with his hands, then gave up and drank directly from the pail and poured the rest over his head. The bread was good, almost as good as that he remembered from his youth.

His youth…

Lying back on the bed of straw, his belly uncomfortably full, Jonah Longshadow stared up at the hayloft overhead and wondered at the curious pathways that had led him so far from his lodge on the banks of the Red River. He had come into this world a part of two distinct cultures, unwanted by his father, a white soldier who had raped his Kiowa mother. As a child he had often been taunted by other children for his white blood. As a youth he'd been watched by his elders. He had felt compelled to prove himself by counting coup on the enemies of his mother's people. Increasingly bold, he had cheated death many times, for as a warrior, he was fearless, having little to lose.

But as a horse gatherer, he excelled most of all. By the age of eighteen, he was spending most of his time raiding the wild herds that roamed the area. Four years later, in the spring of 1875, he had just returned to his lodge after a week spent stalking a notorious ridge runner, a magnificent stallion that kept watch over his mares from the high ground. That night soldiers from Fort Sill had swept through, rounding up every warrior in the territory. Jonah, whose name had not been Jonah then, had been taken along with more than seventy others.

Pride had kept him from pleading his case, for as a warrior, he had worn the red cloth sash of the tribe's elite Koitsenga—the Society of the Ten Bravest. Along with the other men, he had been put in chains and dispatched to Fort Sill. There, they had been placed in an unfinished icehouse and thrown chunks of raw meat once a day until they were eventually transported by way of wagon and railroad to Saint Augustine in Florida. Expecting to be executed once he reached his destination, Longshadow had instead been sentenced to indefinite imprisonment. The difference had seemed slight at the time, but that was before he met Lieutenant Richard Henry Pratt.

Pratt was like no other white soldier in Longshadow's experience. The man had fought against the Kiowa, yet he bore no malice, choosing to educate his prisoners rather than punish them for defending their homeland. He'd had the prisoners construct their own barracks, then moved them out of Fort Marion's dungeons. Putting them to work as bakers, sailors, fishermen and field laborers, he had even allowed them to keep their small wages. During the time when they were working on their barracks, he'd enlisted the help of a few white women to teach them to read, write and speak English.

Warily at first, but with increasing eagerness, Longshadow had allowed himself to be taught. Somewhat to his astonishment he'd discovered that he was a fair

scholar, partly because of an insatiable curiosity, and
partly because he had recognized education as a powerful tool. With the world around him changing so rapidly, a man needed all the knowledge he could absorb
in order to survive.

After three years, Lieutenant Pratt had persuaded his
superiors that the prisoners were firmly reconciled to the
white man's way. They had been granted their freedom.
Most had returned to the reservation, but a few of the
once-fierce warriors had elected to stay in the East.

Longshadow had been among those who elected to
stay. His mother was dead. If he went back, he'd be
expected to live on the reservation with its invisible bor-
ders. The Kiowa way of life was finished. From his tu-
tors he had learned about the Jesus Road and the Plow
Road. The first he hadn't understood; the second held
no appeal. Instead, he had chosen the sea. Over the next
few years he had saved the money he earned as a seaman, recognizing the power of the white man's gold, for
even then a dream had been growing inside him. A
dream of one day breeding fine horses. But it would take
more gold than he possessed, which meant more years
of work until he could save up enough to buy breeding
stock and the land on which to keep them.

As a prisoner he had sailed for a company that traded
in the West Indies. Upon receiving his full pardon, he
had returned to the sea, for of all the options, that one
was most acceptable. Life at sea reminded him of the
past, when his world had been wild, free and vast. And
although he read, wrote and spoke English, he kept that
knowledge to himself, having quickly discovered that
most of his crewmates resented an Indian who spoke
their language more precisely than they did. Although
he liked Pratt, and would trust the man with his life—

had done as much—he found it hard to trust other whites.

So after promising to return the favor by helping some white person in need, he arranged with Pratt to collect his pay directly from the ship owner and deposit it into an account in Longshadow's name. Each time he returned to port, Pratt gave him an accounting, congratulating him on his good sense. While other members of the crew drank and gambled away their pay almost as quickly as they earned it, Jonah watched his savings grow. He studied the written account from the bank, visualizing the horses he would one day buy—a good stallion and two, possibly three sturdy mares.

For four years he had carried the dream, as one after another, three ships had foundered in the fierce storms called hurricanes and gone down. Each time, Longshadow, along with at least a part of the crew, had survived. That was when his mates had taken to calling him Jonah, saying that no ship he sailed on was safe.

Jonah recognized the name. It had come from the Jesus Book. He had rejected that path, but he accepted the name as a reminder that, just as the Feather Dance had not brought back the buffalo, neither his own god, who was called Tiame, nor the white man's Jesus, had kept him from being punished for sins he had not committed.

Carrie braced herself to confront her surly prisoner and herd him to the creek. If she had to work with the man, he was going to have to scrub himself clean. She put up with her husband's stench because she had to, else he'd knock her to kingdom come. For all his love of fancy clothes, Darther hated bathing. He always reeked of whiskey, sweat and cigars.

But she didn't have to put up with a blessed thing

from her prisoner. She'd paid her two dollars—he was hers to do with as she saw fit. And as long as she was going to be working at his side, she saw fit to clean him up. Once he knew how good it felt to be rid of his own stench and the vermin that infested his hair and his body, he would likely insist on bathing at least once a week.

She herself bathed every single day from either a bowl or a washtub. Once a week in the summertime she dunked herself all over in the creek and scrubbed, hair and all, with her best soap that had crushed bayberries added to the fat, ashes and lye to sweeten the scent. She did her best dreaming sitting in water, letting it lap around her, washing away the cares of the day.

With a towel over her shoulder, the Springfield under her arm and a chunk of plain soap—not the scented kind—in her apron pocket, Carrie let herself out early the next morning. The fog lay heavy across the clearing, sucking around the pines and gum trees. By the time it burned off, she intended to have at least five of the biggest stumps dragged out of the ground and all the way over to her burn pile. It would take more than a sore hand to slow her down, she told herself, setting her jaw in determination.

Scattering a handful of cracked corn to the chickens along the way, she sang out a greeting. "Rise an' shine!"

Rise an' shine… Carrie had been hearing those words in her head for as long as she could remember, saying them aloud even when there was no one to hear but the chickens and that aggravating mule. For the life of her, she couldn't remember if they'd come from her own family or from one of the missionaries who had given her a home after the massacre. All she knew was that saying them made her feel better. As if she weren't entirely alone.

Besides, "Rise an' shine" sounded far better than her uncle's, "Git your lazy ass down here and git to work, gal!"

Darther didn't even bother with that much. If he was awake at daybreak, which was rare, because he usually stayed up half the night when he was home, drinking with Liam and planning ways to win the next race, he would kick her out of bed onto the floor. Kick her hard, too.

"Oh, how I hate that man," she muttered. She tossed out the last of the corn, dusted her hands off and yelled toward the barn. "Rise an' shine in there! Come on, time's a-wasting!" He might not know what she was talking about, but at least he would know he couldn't sleep all day.

Jonah was awake. He'd been awake for hours, lying on his back on the itchy blanket for no better reason than that he liked the oily wool smell of it. It reminded him of the blanket he had slept under as a boy before he had left his mother's lodge.

Gritting his teeth against the pain, he clamped his leg irons on, reattached the long chain, and stood, shaking straw from the blanket and folding it neatly. If he didn't present himself, she would come in after him, armed with that damned Springfield, no doubt. He'd like to grab the thing and—

No, he wouldn't. No scrawny, ignorant white female with colorless hair and the brain of a rock was worth losing his last hope for freedom. Clearing himself was going to be risky enough as it was, without the added offense of murder.

When she appeared in the open doorway, they eyed

one another silently for a moment. She was not quite as shapeless as he'd first thought. Her hair was pale, not colorless. Looking as though it had been hacked off with a dull knife, it curled about her face, at odds with the firm set of her jaw, which was at odds with her small nose and large, wary eyes.

Jonah waited for her to speak, wondering if she would forget that he was only an ignorant savage and speak to him as if he were a man. He thought perhaps she was not cruel, only fearful.

She said, "Mornin'. Looks like another day with no rain in sight," and unhooked the other end of the chain from the door frame. And then, as if remembering who he was, she said loudly, "Bath. Creek. You come now."

And you go to your white man's hell, he wanted to say, but didn't. His time would come. He had learned patience in a hard school.

The creek was broad, but shallow, the water dark and clear. Judging by tracks on the worn bank, it served as a watering hole for deer and smaller animals. Someone—the woman, most likely—had knelt there to wash, or to draw buckets of water. Trees overhung the banks, shedding a few yellowing leaves to drift slowly downstream.

Jonah turned to her and lifted a brow before it occurred to him that such a gesture might indicate a thinking being rather than a slow-witted half-breed.

"Here. It's soap." She handed him the chunk she had been holding. "You're supposed to wet yourself all over and rub with this." She mimed the action, which he found both irritating and amusing. "And don't try to run away, because I've got ears like a bat."

And the intelligence of an earthworm, he thought, letting amusement overcome his anger. With the lead chain wrapped around the wrist of her bandaged hand, she struggled to hold the heavy rifle in the other. Would she actually shoot him in the back if he waded across and climbed up the other side? Somehow, he didn't think so. He wasn't at all certain she could lift the weapon to take aim.

Awkwardly, she looped the chain around a hanging branch. She did not release her hold on the gun, neither did she release his leg irons. He could easily have freed the chain, but what good would it have done? Hobbled, he could hardly escape. There was still the Springfield, but even if she managed to take aim, he had a feeling it might not be loaded.

It was because he craved it, not because she forced him to do it, that he stayed, Jonah told himself. He eased down the muddy bank into ankle-deep water, closing his eyes as the abrasions under his irons caught fire. The pain burned right down to the bone.

"Well, get at it," she snapped. "We don't have all day."

Pain and pleasure, pleasure and pain. Either of which, Jonah reminded himself, was better than merely existing as he'd been forced to do in that miserable hole of a jail.

"Use that soap," she called out.

He looked at the ungainly chunk in his hand. As much as he hated the smell of it, he needed it to wash away the worse stench of the jail. Still dressed in the thread-bare shirt and canvas trousers he'd been wearing twelve days earlier when the sheriff's men had come to take him away, he thought of how he must look. A once-proud warrior, a member of the Ten Most Brave—prisoner now to a small, witless woman.

He turned away, facing the direction where the winding creek disappeared in the woods. How far away was his own property? If he followed the creek, would it take him there?

He could sense her uneasiness, almost feel her eyes boring into his back. Did she truly expect him to scrub the places where he needed it most with her looking on? Was she so shameless?

His battered pride stung at being seen in this condition by an enemy, he wanted to strike out. To see her grovel, this miserable woman with her pale hair and her pale, sun-speckled face and her damned rifle. Clearly, she trusted him no more than he trusted her, but there was not one thing he could do about it for the moment.

Still standing only ankle-deep, he turned to face her. Crossing his arms, he smiled. It was not a nice smile. He watched her face grow red with anger. Saw her lift the heavy rifle and brace her feet apart as she tried to balance the barrel across her forearm. Jonah knew the woman was afraid of him. The thought pleased him enormously. Without lowering his gaze, he slowly uncrossed his arms, caught the back of his shirt in both hands and tugged it over his head.

Her eyes widened. The rifle barrel wavered. Still holding her wary gaze, he dropped his hands to the buttons of his canvas trousers. Deftly unfastening the top three, he allowed his trousers to slip over his narrow hips.

The barrel of the gun struck the dirt a moment before his trousers crumpled about his ankles. Jonah felt like laughing aloud. Didn't the foolish woman realize that he could not remove them as long as his legs were bound together by this damnable iron bracelet?

She gasped and turned her back, but not before he had seen her eyes widen on his body. He might have enjoyed the small triumph even more had it not been for his

burning ankles and various itches that made him want
to shed his skin like a snake.

Bending, he scooped a handful of mud and gravel
from the creek bottom and began to scour his belly. The
woman had quickly turned away after one horrified look
at his nakedness. Now, enjoying his brief moment of
privacy, he scrubbed and scratched and nearly purred
with the pleasurable sensations.

"Hurry up, you're taking too long," she called without turning around.

He had taken as long as he dared, but nowhere near
as long as he wished. Reluctant to dress in the same
filthy clothing, Jonah grunted to gain her attention.
When she cast a quick glance over her shoulder, he held
his bundled shirt in front of his privates and gestured
with the remnant of soap that was left.

Grudgingly, Carrie nodded. There was no point in putting buggy clothes on a clean body, so she told him to
go ahead and scrub his clothing, but to be damned quick
about it. She added the swear word to be sure he knew
she meant business, the same as she did with the mule.

Turning away to avoid catching another glimpse, she
pretended a great interest in the few remaining blossoms
on a honeysuckle vine, but she couldn't dispel the image
of that magnificent male body. Merciful heavens, the
man was a—he looked like a—and his skin wasn't red,
it was sort of almond-colored. Or maybe butternut.

*He was so taut, not flabby like Darther. What would
it be like to—*

*Stop it, Carrie Adams, don't even think about such
things!*

Sensing when it was safe to turn around, she noted
that he was fully dressed again, although the wet clothing clung to his body in a way that looked uncomfort-

able. Realizing that she was staring, she nodded abruptly toward the path and they set out once more, the prisoner going first, Carrie and the Springfield marching along behind. She tried to concentrate on a mental list of all the things she intended to accomplish before day's end, but her gaze kept lingering on his wet hair, glistening like coal under the early morning sun. Even in chains the man was arrogant. The way he moved—the way he held his head. Those wet clothes...

He's just another mule, Carrie, no more, no less! Five stumps. Think about those, not about the way he looked standing there in his bare skin.

And she tried, she really did. All the way back from the creek she focused her mind on the task ahead. At the rate of five stumps a day, the field would soon be cleared, and once the stumps were gone, her hand would be healed, and she could hitch up the plow and turn under the brush, allowing the roots and grubs to die over the winter months.

Think about that, Carrie, not about—

But oh, my mercy, he was so pretty to look at. It wasn't the first time she had seen a man's body. She had seen her uncle once when she'd barged into the kitchen while he was in the tub. At least she'd seen his knees, his bald head and his bony shoulders.

And Darther, she thought with a shudder, who was pale as whey, with rolls of flab, with his little bitty thing hanging down like a dead worm.

She shifted the rifle to a more comfortable position, wishing she could trade it for something smaller, and tried not to think about male bodies, naked or clothed.

Back at the barn, she gestured to the mule, and then to the harness she had devised for pulling stumps from the ground. Her prisoner nodded, made a few minor adjustments, and then hitched up the mule. Sorry, the miserable traitor, didn't once attempt to kick or bite, and Sorry purely hated being hitched up to anything.

At least he did when it was Carrie doing the hitching. *Damn-blasted mule. Damn-blasted sneaky Indian.*

She glared at her prisoner, and because she was later than usual getting started—or because she hadn't taken time to eat her usual breakfast of black coffee and cold biscuits, her mind began to wander once more.

Behave yourself, Carrie! He's a prisoner, a thief and probably worse. You need him because with only one good hand, there's no way you're going to get that field cleared, so don't even think about his—about the way—about his thing!

Pointing to the lane that led off behind the cabin to the cut-over field, she gestured for him and the mule to go first. Without a word spoken, the blasted mule picked up and walked, sweet as pie, trailing the makeshift harness behind. Carrie kept her gaze focussed on the distant trees and forced herself to concentrate on how to direct a man who didn't speak English. Didn't speak anything, so far as she could tell.

Even if he wasn't all that bright, he probably understood a few words, a few simple commands. So she took a deep breath and spoke aloud, hoping the sound of her voice could drown out the image of a beautiful naked man standing ankle-deep in her creek. "Best way I know is to dig out under the spreading roots enough to saw through the biggest ones," she said gruffly. "Once Sorry pulls the thing over, we can saw off the taproot and haul the stump out of the ground. Oh, lordy, you don't understand a word I'm saying, do you?"

Shaking her head in frustration, she pointed to the biggest of the five stumps she intended to tackle today.

"Dig," she commanded, and pointed at the spade she had left in the field the last day she'd worked, too weary even to drag her tools back to the barn.

They were so late getting started that the heat was already miserable, making her think longingly of the cool, clear creek. The one thing she truly liked about summer was that the days were long enough to include a soak in the creek. With no close neighbors, it was safe enough as long as she kept an eye out for snakes. It was a chance to scrub all over without having to haul and heat water, bail out the washtub and then mop up the kitchen floor afterward. A chance to sit and dream for a few peaceful moments—to try to remember the stories she had read when she'd gone to the missionary school. She did like reading stories. Over those early years she'd been well schooled, although she'd since forgotten most of what she'd been taught.

Now even the pleasure of sitting in the creek and trying to remember her favorite stories was ruined. She wouldn't dare linger knowing her prisoner was nearby, even if he was locked in the barn. From now on, she wouldn't even be able to go near the place without picturing him standing in the edge of the water, with his smooth, muscular body, his mocking gray eyes, and those dark, mysterious places that made her bones feel weak as tallow.

And damn-blast it all, her hand ached! Every three days she poured turpentine on it and packed it with sugar again, the way Emma had showed her, but bandaging one hand with the other was difficult. If her prisoner had been an ordinary criminal instead of a savage heathen— if she hadn't seen him naked—she might even have asked him to help her, but that was out of the question.

"Git to it," she snarled, much as she would have addressed Sorry.

By the time the sun had passed overhead she intended to have three of the five stumps out of the ground. Using gestures and a few simple words, she explained how they would go about it, then propped the rifle against a nearby stump within easy reach. While her prisoner sawed through the first of the newly exposed roots, she dug out around the next one. When the roots were all cut through, she cussed Sorry into position, fastened the harness to the stump and whapped him on the behind. "Pay attention," she said when the mule set his weight against the heavy stump. "This is the way we do it."

With the first stump hauled to the edge of the field, they moved on to the next. The mule was powerful, she'd grant the miserable bastard that much. It took a lot of swearing to get him to moving, but once he did, things happened fast. Small roots popped and snapped, earth broke, and one stump after another surrendered.

Once, in a moment of triumph when a deep taproot gave way, she glanced up and grinned at her prisoner. He looked startled, then embarrassed. And then, of course, she was embarrassed, too, and so she swore at the mule. Snatching up his lead chain, she led her prisoner to the next stump.

Jonah was used to hard work. Back on the reservation it had been the women who had done most of it, freeing the men to hunt and trap and make war and ponder on the changes that were coming to their world and how best to deal with them. But he'd worked, even then. Mostly with horses. He understood horses far better than he understood men, either red or white. Both as a prisoner and as an ordinary seaman, he had worked, but he'd worked hardest of all after retrieving his money from the bank and buying his own land here in the East.

Breeding horses was a noble thing. It was not drudgery. His people were convinced that if a man followed the plow, the drudgery would take away his manhood and he would become like an old woman, withered and good for nothing.

Jonah feared the yellow-haired woman might force him to follow the plow. So far she had not. He did as she directed, but he did no more than that. He could have made things far easier for her, but he did not.

The second day, she drew another of her lines in the earth, outlining the section she intended to clear of stumps and eventually plant. He told himself that she would have to do most of it without his help, for by the time winter passed and the earth grew warm again, he would have long since cleared his name and returned to his own land.

Or failed in his attempt and been returned to jail, to be tried or hanged without benefit of judgment. The white man's justice was not always logical, or even just.

Sawing through the thick, damp roots, he thought about what he must do, and knew he could not wait much longer. Soon he must escape long enough to retrieve the papers he had hidden on his horse farm and return before he was found missing. If he was caught trying to escape before his work parole was over, he would be shot down before he had a chance to prove his innocence.

Timing, Jonah told himself, was important. Meanwhile, he must allay the woman's suspicions and allow his ankles more time to heal. When the time was right, he would set out as soon as darkness fell, running hard for as long as it took, uncovering his papers and running

all the way back before the sky grew pale again. Once
he had proof of his innocence in his possession, he might
even work in her damned field one more day. She had
fed him well. She had even forgotten herself so far as
to give him one of her rare smiles.

As tired as she was by the end of each day, Carrie
felt like celebrating, seeing the progress they were making. Even Sorry was easier to manage with the prisoner
nearby. It was almost as if the two of them spoke a silent
common language. As if they had some secret understanding. Like to like, she told herself, unwilling to admit she could possibly envy a mule, just for having
someone to talk to.

Carrie hadn't been able to visit Emma since she'd
brought her prisoner home. She could hardly leave him
behind, but she didn't dare take him with her. Poor
Emma had seen enough misery over the years, having
outlived a husband and a whole slew of children. Living
alone, with the rheumatism so bad she could hardly hob-
ble around on damp days, the last thing she needed was
to come face to face with a wild Indian in her own home,
even though renting him had been her idea in the first
place.

Although Carrie had to admit that cleaned up, he
didn't look quite so fierce. He still wore those same old
ragged clothes, but then, her own weren't much better.
His hair, the color of polished mahogany, was long
enough to be tied back with a piece of string, while hers
had been hacked off with a butcher knife back in the
spring, when she'd caught a fever and Emma had said
she had to stay cool. Instead of the neat braids she had
always worn, her hair had grown in thick and curly,
reached a certain length and stopped growing. Emma

said it was because of what she ate—or rather, what she didn't eat.

She ate as well as she could when half the time Darther forgot to leave her enough money even to buy salt, much less bacon and flour. She needed a damn-blasted cow, was what she needed. She'd taken her nanny goat to Shingle Landing and traded her for a supply of tinned milk, but tinned milk didn't make butter.

Once her corn crop came in, she vowed, she would get herself a fresh cow and six more hens, and maybe a pig. Maybe even two pigs.

She got through the day without cursing more than once, when Sorry deliberately stepped on her foot. It was something she was working on—not cursing. Something *else* she was working on, she amended. Today they had cleared out all but the last few stumps and dragged them over to the edge of the field to burn. Carrie watched the sky, unwilling to risk setting a fire unless rain was in the offing. According to Emma, her cabin had once been a tenant house, the big house having been burned when Colonel Draper and General Wild had led their Union forces on a rampage though Camden and Currituck counties, burning more than a dozen homesteads.

Carrie thought it must have been something like the Indian raid that had taken her own family. Years had passed, the sharpest pain had faded, but the memories would be with her until the day she died. Looking back, the home she remembered as a child had seemed large, but it couldn't have been too much larger than Darther's small cabin.

At any rate, a small cabin was enough for her needs, as long as the land was still fertile. Emma said it had once grown cotton, the bolls as big and as white as snowballs. Carrie didn't want to grow cotton. She couldn't eat cotton, wouldn't know how to harvest it even if she could grow it. But corn...

It was going to be so beautiful. Row after row of tall, green stalks. Enough to grind for meal, to save for seed, to feed her stock and still have some left over to trade for cloth, salt, side-meat and calico. And then, she would clear more land and grow still more corn.

The air was lavender with dusk as they headed home from the field. Sorry plodded along behind her prisoner like a faithful hound. Carrie could have chosen to be jealous, but instead she felt only satisfaction with the amount they had accomplished. It would have taken her until Christmas to get this much done alone, even with two good hands.

She was smiling when she happened to notice the way her prisoner was walking. He was exhausted. They both were. His stride was hampered by the heavy irons, but it was more than that. Her smile gave way to a look of concern. He was limping. If he was injured—if he could no longer work, she would have to return him, and then she'd be right back where she'd been before, only now she owed Emma two dollars which she was fairly certain the jailer would refuse to refund.

Biting her lip, she shifted the heavy rifle to her other shoulder. She no longer even attempted to keep it turned on him. It was almost impossible to manage when they were working together, anyway. They both knew that.

He was definitely limping. It had to be the leg irons. The heavy things allowed him to walk, but not to run. If the jailer hadn't warned her not to remove them, she'd have been tempted to unlock them before this. He could work twice as hard if he could clamber in and out of stump holes more easily. But in that case, she'd be the one who was handicapped, with the gun in one hand and a bandage on the other. Besides, she suspected he knew she would never shoot him.

By then they had reached the yard. Uncertain how to proceed, Carrie came to a dead halt. "Whoa, there—you, too, Sorry."

Jonah winced from the indignity of being addressed in the same manner as she addressed her mule. At least she hadn't sworn at him the way she did Sorry. The mule was neither deaf nor stupid, but somewhat slow to make up his mind whether or not it suited his interests to obey.

Scowling, she stared down at his feet. Pride would not allow him to acknowledge his pain, just as pride would not let him reveal his understanding of her language. Caught in a trap of his own making, he had endured days of pain and humiliation, wondering why the stubborn woman couldn't see the truth before her eyes—that a man couldn't work in irons. That if she wanted to get her money's worth before his parole ended, she'd do better to release him, sit on a stump with her rifle pointed at his head, and let him get on with clearing her field. If he had to follow the Plow Road, he'd as soon get it done as quickly as possible.

"Leg, um—hurt?" She pointed to his ankle, her pale eyebrows knotted in concern. Jonah had heard the jailer tell her she must return him in good condition. She was obviously worried about her investment.

He knew she carried the key in her pocket, along with the napkin in which she had wrapped two chunks of bacon and cornbread, which they had devoured at noon, sitting in almost companionable silence in the shade of the hedgerow. For a few moments he had felt almost as if they might be…not friends, yet not quite enemies.

To his astonishment, she dropped to her knees before him. When he felt her hand on his foot he stopped breathing, but he couldn't restrain a soft oath when the irons dug into his raw flesh as she folded the two halves back on their hinges.

Seeing the blood caked with dust until it looked like mud, she crooned in dismay. "Oh, my mercy, oh, sweet Jesus, you're torn all ragged."

Closing his eyes against the fresh pain, he willed his mind to escape to another place, another time. For once, it didn't help. With harsh, shallow gasps, he waited for the pain to recede. Yesterday he had torn strips from his shirt and tied them around his ankles to pad the irons, but the cloth had only stuck to his blood and dried, tearing away still more flesh when he moved. Crossing her line in the dirt floor of the barn, he had found a jar of hoof dressing and plastered both ankles with that.

"You'll have to let me wash it and dress it with turpentine and sugar. Emma—that is, my friend who knows about these things, says that's the best medicine."

Still on her knees, she gazed up at him, her eyes dark with concern. Jonah felt as if he'd swallowed a fish bone. It had not yet pierced his gullet, but he was afraid something irreversible had just happened.

Her hand was still resting on the top of his dusty bare foot. Her own feet were bare, too. He had seen her wearing boots but once. They were worn through on the bottoms, good only for trapping rocks and sharp pine seeds against her naked feet.

His own feet were bare because the men who had come to arrest him had not allowed him to take away anything, not the papers that would prove his innocence, not his boots, not even the freedom papers he had received from Lieutenant Pratt.

"I'm sorry," she whispered. "I know you can't understand me, but I'd never have had this happen, not even to a wild animal. I saw a wolf once that chewed his foot off to get free of a trap, and..."

A wolf. He was no more than a wild animal, caught in a trap. He didn't know whether to laugh or cry, but he did know that if she didn't take her hand off his foot, he might do something they would both come to regret.

Leading the mule into the small fenced paddock, Carrie forked him a ration of hay and then led her prisoner toward the cabin. He was no longer shackled or chained, which meant that if he were going to escape, it would be now. He could knock her on the head, grab the rifle from her hands and take off through the woods.

Yet, something she'd seen—or fancied she'd seen—in those clear gray eyes of his, told her he wouldn't try to escape. Not yet, at any rate. Without thinking, she had knelt in the middle of the lane to examine his injuries, just as she would have stopped to examine any wounded creature in her care. But the instant she'd touched his warm flesh, the strangest sensation had come over her. She had looked up—he had looked down—and for one brief moment something tangible had passed between them. Her only comfort was that he'd been as startled as she was.

Now she tried to think of a way to make him understand what needed to be done. "Now listen carefully," she said in slow, measured tones. "I will help you." She placed her hand over her heart. "You must not try to escape." She pointed to the road and shook her head vigorously. "If you run away, you'll die." And then, all in a rush, she blurted out the fearful consequences. "You'll end up with the blood poisoning and die out there in the woods all by yourself, and then the jailer will come after me and hold me responsible, and I'll end up in jail in your place."

But of course he couldn't understand a word she said. Shaking her head, she said, "You sit." She pointed to the three-legged milking stool she'd brought inside when the cow had gone dry and she'd traded her to a farmer in Snowden for a rooster, two hams and a side of bacon, and said, "You sit."

He sat. They were both dirty after a day in the field, but he had rid himself of vermin. She'd broken off branches of wax myrtle and told him in words a child of three could understand how to use them to keep the fleas from his straw bedding. Evidently, he had taken her meaning.

"This is going to hurt," she muttered. Lifting his foot in her hand, she felt again that peculiar awareness—like the quivery feeling of the air just before a lightning storm. Embarrassed, she glanced up to see if he had noticed anything.

He felt something, all right. His lips were clamped together and his eyes had the strangest expression. Maybe this was the way Indians looked when they were hurting. She'd never seen one up close before, not since the night they had come a-whooping and a-hollering into the settlement near Redwood Falls. Those had been Sioux. The sheriff had called this one a Kie-oh-way heathen. It had been more than ten years, but he looked different from the Indians she remembered. He was taller, for one thing, and his features were...

"Well. Enough about that," she said decisively, earning a puzzled look from the man whose ankles she had just cleaned, treated and wrapped with strips of an old bed sheet. She was tempted to see what he would do if she asked him to help her rebandage her hand. Some things were hard to do one-handed, and the old bandage was in tatters after a day's work. "I don't reckon you could...?'' Shaking her head, she answered her own question, "No, I reckon not."

Jonah had learned long ago to lock away all emotion. He could not afford to think of the woman as anything more than a means of escape. A means of eventually clearing his name so that he could return to his land and his horses. She made it difficult, however, first by treating him with such disdain he wanted to shake her until her teeth flew in all directions—then by treating him not only with kindness, but with sympathy. It was enough to undermine his determination.

He told himself she was crazy. For all she knew he could be a murderer, yet she had brought him into her house and tortured him with her careless kindness. She had stared at his naked body that first day. She knew well that he was a man. She had scrubbed his wounds with her lye soap and mopped them with turpentine until his eyes watered with the pain. She had shared her food and water with him, sat beside him to share a patch of shade, yet she considered him less than an animal. A wolf caught in a trap. Not only deaf, but stupid.

The woman was crazy.

Chapter Three

Together the next morning they set fire to the pile of stumps, some of which were dry, a few still damp from the earth. When flames whipped through the heap and spread to the bigger stumps in the middle, they turned to one another with a look of shared triumph. Then, almost as if they were embarrassed, Jonah began gathering dead branches to toss on the fire, and Carrie began stepping off the length and breadth of the clearing for perhaps the hundredth time. The ground was hard, baked dry by weeks without rain. Scrubby vegetation had flourished once the tall trees had been cut down, allowing the sun to reach the ground. Those would have to be cleared next. Even as they worked, they both watched the burn pile carefully to see that the flames didn't spread. When a finger of flames spilled out and began creeping through the dry grass, they both rushed to beat it out with tote sacks wet from the nearby creek.

With the fire once more under control, they stared at each other, sweaty, sooty, and triumphant. And there it was again. That shimmering awareness that made the world go utterly silent for one endless moment.

Silently, Jonah called himself a fool for staying as

long as he had. He had meant to slip away at the first
opportunity, but here he still was. Now, in exchange for
food, a clean place to sleep and the occasional smile
when the woman forgot herself, he was going to have
to follow that damned plow and turn the earth so that
she could plant her corn. He had not meant to linger so
long.

She didn't even know how he was called. The sheriff
had called him *Kie-oh-way.* He had heard him call her
Adams. Miss or Mrs. Adams? There was no man in her
bed or at her table, but a man's coat and shirt hung from
a hook on the wall. Perhaps she had once had a man and
he had died. Or perhaps he had thrown her away, as a
Kiowa did if one of his wives displeased him. He could
easily see how this woman could displease a man.

Yet he could also see how she might please a man....

"Now this," Carrie informed him the next morning,
"is what we call a plow."

"It is also what I call a plow," he wanted to say, but
held his tongue. It had angered him at first when she
forgot he was only an ignorant savage and spoke to him
as if he were slightly more intelligent than her mule.
Now it amused him.

Using pantomime to illustrate her words, she said,
"What I aim to do is harness it to Sorry so that he can
do the pulling, the way he did with the stumps." Placing
the worn straps over her own shoulders, she mimicked
pulling the plow. "But you'll have to steady it, else it'll
skitter over the top of the ground and fall over. I'd do
it myself, but the thing's got two handles and I've only
got one good hand."

He was curious about that. Her hand was still bundled
up in a grimy rag, reeking of the turpentine she had used

on his ankle that had burned down to the bone. She held it against her breasts now and then, as if it pained her. More than likely what pained her was holding that damned Springfield, which she insisted on carrying with her into the field, even though they both knew he could have easily escaped many times.

"I don't reckon you know what the devil I'm saying, but I was ever one for talking, and you're all I've got to talk to." She pointed to the rusty plow. "Plow. Now, you try saying it. *Plow.*"

It was all he could not to laugh, but soberly, he repeated the word. "Plow."

"Oh, that's real good! We'll have you talking in no time, you see if we don't." Her smile was as warm and encouraging as a pat on the head, as if he'd just retrieved the stick she had thrown.

So he followed her into the field, appreciating the way she walked in spite of his irritation, amused at the way she squared her hat on her head, then lifted it to fork her flyaway hair from her eyes. It was a man's straw hat, ugly, but useful for one with skin so fair it reddened each day from the sun and faded by nightfall, leaving behind light brown speckles. She began each day with the sleeves of her dress covering her arms, but before the day was half over, she would turn up the sleeves and unfasten the buttons at her throat.

Gazing past the mule's bony haunches, Jonah watched the way she moved, fascinated at how much a man could learn about a woman from the way she walked, the way she bent to chop at a stubborn shrub. Buoyed by hope and determination, she strode into the field each morning like a warrior riding into battle. Although he had to admit there was nothing at all warrior-like in the movement of her hips or the way her bosoms bounced under the thin covering of calico.

By the end of each day she drooped like a flower that had been plucked and cast aside. Plodding in from the field, it was all she could do to keep the rifle from dragging on the ground. He would have offered to carry it for her, but he suspected she might misunderstand his motives.

Irritating woman. Were all white women so contrary, or was it only this one small individual? The women of St. Augustine who had taught him to read and write had not affected him this way.

The problem, Jonah told himself, was not this particular woman. He would have reacted the same way toward any woman between the ages of fifteen and fifty, having been without the comfort of a woman's body for so long. His blood still grew heated when he thought of the way he had dropped his clothes before her, standing ankle-deep in her creek. He had done it out of anger, out of resentment, wanting to shock her, to frighten her.

Instead, he had been the one who was affected. He'd had to turn away quickly and lower himself into the water.

Steering the white man's plow, he told himself that evening, was not as bad as he'd feared. He understood the mule. The mule understood him. They worked well together. As for the woman, that was another matter. She walked beside him every step of the way, from one end of the clearing to the other, sometimes moving ahead to chop down a bush, or falling behind to crumble a handful of freshly turned earth in her hand. They would stop at the far end, drink from the jar of water she'd left there in the shade, then set out again.

"This is the first time I've tried planting a cash crop,"

she confided. "Corn—well, everybody needs corn. Last year I had to buy corn. There's still some left in the crib, but it's old and buggy, and I have to grind it, and the grinder's gone to blazes. It's good enough for Sorry and the chickens, but with a decent harvest, I can take my corn to the mill and get it ground, and pay the miller with part of the crop. That's the way we do it," she said gravely, as if imparting a valuable tenet of her white man's wisdom.

Jonah reminded himself of his promise to Lieutenant Pratt, that he would help the first white person in need he encountered. The Adams woman needed help all right. She was weak, injured and alone, yet no one came to her aid. There were houses within a few miles of her cabin, yet no one visited. She had mentioned a friend, but the friend had not come to help her plow her field. It was becoming increasingly obvious that she was an outcast. Jonah knew what it felt like to be an outcast.

"You might have noticed, I've been raking up leaves and piling them up out behind the chicken house." She had fallen into the habit of conversing with him as if he were an ordinary, reasonably intelligent man. He had already learned two things about her. She was kind-hearted…and she was lonely. "Emma says if I can get me some oyster shells and dump them on the heap and then set it afire with some trash wood on top, it'll make the sweetest kind of fertilizer. She says the land here-abouts is sour. It needs shelling, if I can find a Currituck fisherman willing to trade me a load of shells for corn or a few jars of wild honey."

She chattered the way he sometimes talked to his horses, only he rarely used words. His horses understood his thoughts, and he theirs. It was a gift he'd been given as if to make up for being two halves and never a whole.

Soon he must leave, he promised himself, not for the first time. The hardest work was finished. She would use a planting stick in the month of the dogwood, and her corn would flourish. The land was rich, some of it was boggy, but all was fertile. He had read books on such matters once he had decided what he would do with his life.

"Lordy, I'm starvin', aren't you?" she said, mopping her damp, sunburned face.

"Lordy," Jonah echoed solemnly, wondering why it was the white man called Indians redskins, when it was the white men themselves who turned red as his old Koitsenga sash from sunlight and whiskey. His own skin was more the color of a freshly tanned hide. Sun only deepened the color. Whiskey, he never touched, having seen what it did to his shipmates and too many of his own people.

They had taken to sharing the evening meal. She had not allowed him inside her house again since treating his ankles, but when she came outside to lock up her chickens and bring him his supper, she would often bring her own and join him, sitting on a plank bench outside the barn while he squatted on the ground nearby. Now and then she would speak, and he would nod and grunt in response, or lift his shoulders as if he didn't understand, and she would shake her head and sigh her impatience with him. He had come to enjoy the game, even though he was beginning to feel guilty, yet how could he break the silence now? It had gone on too long. She would be angry with him for tricking her.

Angry enough to shoot him? He was all but certain the rifle was not loaded. Even loaded, it wasn't much of a threat, for the barrel was so heavy she could hardly support it with her one good hand. She might shoot out one of her precious glass windows, but he no longer feared she would kill him, no matter what he did.

So why didn't he simply walk away?

Jonah couldn't answer. It was not the accommodations. The barracks in St. Augustine had been newer, cleaner and more comfortable, except for the mosquitoes. The food she provided, usually beans, sometimes greens, sometimes only cornbread soaked with bacon grease or honey, and on special occasions, a strip of fried side meat, was obviously the best she could offer, for she ate the same thing. It was filling and satisfying, but he would have enjoyed a meal of buffalo or venison, or even fish.

"Moon. See, coming up over yonder woods? It's called a moon."

The woman was not an idiot. Why did she insist on sounding like one?

But he knew why, of course. It was because she thought he had less intelligence than one of those stumps he had cut free of the earth and burned. It made him angry, and that very anger was a reminder that he had stayed too long. He had given the woman her money's worth. The sooner he retrieved his papers, the sooner he could clear his name and get back to his own land.

And perhaps someday before he was too old, the gods willing, he could find a woman of his own. Another outcast, perhaps, who would not look down on him for his mixed blood.

The Adams woman had not gone to a church-house since he had been with her, yet he knew she had a day of the week when work was forbidden. A day to rest, according to the Jesus Rules. She had used her last Rest Day to pull up the withered bean vines outside her door and scrub the privy. While she raked the dirt around her house, with the chickens following after to peck at any bugs uncovered, Jonah had worked on repairing the barn and enlarging the fenced paddock. Then he had propped his feet on a tussock under a giant oak tree and allowed the warm, sweet air to flow over his body. Freedom had a taste—a flavor and a scent all its own.

Increasingly worried about his horses, Jonah knew he could not wait much longer. The mystery was why he had waited this long. He made up his mind to go on her next Jesus Day. He had fallen out of the habit of running since his imprisonment and his sailing days, but his ankles were nearly healed now. He was fairly certain he could run at least half a day, maybe longer, without needing to stop. He could take the mule, but stealing a mule was a hanging offense.

On the other hand, he would rather hang for something he did than for something he didn't. Either way, he concluded, he would be back with his papers before she brought his supper.

When her Jesus Day came around, the woman was up before sunrise, harnessing Sorry to the cart. She set a napkin-covered basket in the cart, handed him a plate of bread, side meat and greens, and explained that she was going to visit her friend. "I'm going to trust you," she said, her small, pink face so earnest he wanted to take it between his hands and reassure her. "I'm not going to lock you up, because I can't think of a way to do it without using those miserable old irons, and I wouldn't do that to a mad dog. But I cooked you some greens last night because a body needs greens to stay healthy, and I'll bring back a jar of Emma's peach preserves. You can have that to look forward to."

Wearing a different dress from the one she wore every

day—a faded yellow that bared her arms and throat, she stared at him as if waiting for a response.

He was tempted. By Daw-k'hee, the good mother earth, he was tempted.

But he only nodded his agreement. Watching her drive away a few minutes later, he set aside his conflicted feelings and concentrated on fixing directions in his mind. He had noted certain landmarks on his way north from the jailhouse. His sense of direction was well honed, both from instinct and from experience, but he had never traveled from this place to his own land. Asking directions would be risky.

Carrie's hand was not healing. "Honey, I'm going to have to open it up again," the old woman said, shaking her head. Carrie knew the procedure. Dreaded it like a bad toothache, but she knew it had to be done. So she washed Emma's butcher knife, sharpened it on the stone, then held it in the candle flame until the edge glowed red.

She cried. Couldn't help herself, and with Emma, she didn't even try to pretend. She cried not only from the pain, but for what her life had become, for what it had been before, which was both better and worse—and for the glimpse of something more wonderful than anything she could have imagined.

Something she would never have.

While she sat with the basin on her lap, allowing the blood and pus to flow from her ragged hatchet wound, she told the old woman about her prisoner. "I know it's only because I'm there alone so much, but it's almost like having another friend. I don't even know his name, but he's got the clearest gray eyes. I've seen him smile, mostly when he doesn't know I'm watching. And Emma, he's got the whitest teeth.''

"Mmm-hmm. A woman can't help but think, as long as that's as far as it goes.'' It was clearly a warning, and Carrie took it in the spirit in which it had been offered. Her own mother would have probably done the same.

Emma Tamplin was a small woman, barely four and a half feet tall. Having once been wed to a successful farmer who had gone to war when the Yankees had invaded the south, she had lost everything—husband, home, children—everything except for her dignity, her wisdom and her kind heart.

All of which Carrie had come to value enormously. Trying hard to ignore the throbbing of her hand that went all the way up to her shoulder, she said, "I know, I know—I'm being foolish. But Emma, following him in the field every day, watching the way he works so hard— Why, if Darther ever put in a single day's work, I swear, I'd fall over in a dead heap, but my prisoner works like it was his corn we'd be planting come spring.''

"Any man worth his salt would rather be outside in the fresh air than rotting away in jail.'' Emma's husband had died in a Yankee prison. To this day she couldn't bear to see things penned up if she could possibly help it. "I'm going to poultice you with my special salve, if you'll hand me that there jar over there on the dresser.''

Carrie happened to know the greasy salve was made of ground mouse dung and butter, with a few herbs mixed in, but if Emma believed in it, then Carrie did, too. An hour later, her arm no longer throbbing quite so fearfully, they sat on the tiny front porch and talked about this and that. Emma never complained, which made Carrie ashamed of all her own complaints.

"I know it's not right, but sometimes I wish he would forget where he lived and not come home at all," she said, cradling her hand in her lap. She'd been airing her latest grievance against Darther, who'd refused to give her money to buy a cow because he had a chance to buy into a certain surefire winner.

"Racetrack trash, that's what he is. I heard all about racetrack trash when I was at Uncle Henry's. That's all they ever talked about—who was losing his shirt, and who was winning big, and where the next race was going to be. They weren't even real races, not the kind where ladies go and wear nice gowns and fancy hats."

"I don't know your husband personally, child. I do know he's not made a single friend in these parts in all the years he's been here, but there's bound to be some good in him somewhere, even if he is a Yankee. He had the good sense to marry you, didn't he?"

Carrie didn't bother to reply. Emma knew how hopeless things were. She had seen Carrie's bruises too many times to believe they were all caused by her own carelessness. Besides, they almost always coincided with one of Darther's infrequent visits home.

"Living alone can be peaceful, I'll not deny that. Still, I'd give anything in the world to hear my Luther ranting and raving over the fools who're running our government now, or fussing because I can't make bread the way his mother used to do. Sometimes even harsh words are better than no words at all."

Carrie couldn't think of a thing to say to that. Harsh words were about all she'd heard ever since her Uncle Henry had sent for her, and Mrs. Robinson had put her on the train with a change of clothes in a paper sack and a dollar bill pinned inside her pinafore pocket.

A little while later, pleasantly full from the biscuits

she'd baked and brought with her, served with Emma's wild peach preserves, Carrie hitched Sorry to the cart and set out along the narrow road. There was a shortcut through the woods she took when she was afoot, but today she'd felt like riding. She had actually expected that blasted mule to behave, seeing as how her Kie-oh-way had him trained now. The man didn't even have to swear at him, he just looked him in the eye before they set out to do a job, and the mule turned sweet as pie.

As if sensing her inattention, Sorry came to an abrupt stop, laid back his ears and brayed. Startled, Carrie nearly dropped the reins. "You stubborn, no-account crazy bastard, you do that again and I'm going to whomp your hide till it's raw, you hear me? Now, git to movin'!" She cracked the whip in the air, and the mule moved another few steps, then halted again.

The man was a witch. Carrie didn't know if mules and witches spoke the same language, she only knew that her hand was hurting again from being cut open, drained and poulticed, and then having to drive a contrary mule. What's more, she was starting to get that crampy feeling in the pit of her belly, which meant drinking a slug of whiskey, which she despised, and going to bed with a hot brick wrapped in a towel.

She finally gave up and let the beast have his head. He knew the way home as well as she did. He also knew he wouldn't be fed or watered until he got her there. She was in no mood to put up with stubborn animals, four-legged or two-legged. "No wonder Darther calls you Sorry," she muttered. "You're the sorriest son of a bitch ever to suck air."

She was going to have to stop swearing. Emma didn't like it. Mrs. Robinson would be shocked. All the missionaries would be shocked. Her own parents would have been shocked. Sometimes Carrie even shocked herself, and not always with the words that came out of her mouth.

But dammit, things were different now. If she had to deal with a stubborn mule who knew when she was feeling miserable and went out of his way to aggravate her—with a drunken sot of a husband who cared far more for his horse than he did for his wife, and an Indian prisoner who couldn't speak the language, she had to make up her own rules.

Bumping over the rutted cart trail at a snail's pace gave her time to think, time to wonder about things such as whether or not her Indian had a wife waiting for him at home, wherever his home was. Wondering if he had a name. Well, of course he had a name. It was probably one of those heathen-sounding names no white man could wrap his tongue around. She felt guilty for not having asked, and guilt, added to all the rest, made her feel even more miserable. Every now and then, usually when she had her monthly bellyache, she would get to feeling this way. Out of sorts. Weepy for no reason at all.

By the time she pulled into her yard, she was close to tears again. What if she lost her hand? It happened more often than not when a wound refused to heal, and hers had refused for weeks, probably because she kept flexing it and breaking it open again and again.

What was she going to do when her prisoner had to leave? In spite of Darther, she had come so far, encouraged by Emma and by her own dreams. In spite of everything that had happened in the past, she was doing so well, with her own home and a field almost ready for planting come spring.

Not even the familiar sight of her neatly raked yard

and her snug little cabin could cheer her as she neared the end of the road. Home. Her first real home in so long, with the water-oaks turning gold and the gum trees turning purple. Emerging into the clearing, she braced herself to do what needed doing before she could rest. The chickens still had to be fed. The mule had to be unhitched, watered, fed, rubbed down and penned up.

Her prisoner would probably want to be fed, too, with whatever she could scratch together for a meal.

He wasn't outside. He wasn't in the barn. She knew very well he wasn't in the house, because she'd warned him the very first day that she'd shoot him if he came messing around.

But since then she'd taken him inside to dress his ankles. Maybe he thought that meant he could come and go at will. "Well, we'll just see about that," she muttered, glaring at the chain he used to wear, which was neatly coiled on a nail on the inside of the barn door. "If that damned heathen has run out on me, I'll shoot his sorry ass," she swore, feeling tearful and oddly discouraged, considering all they'd accomplished. Here she was so close to getting her field ready so that all she would have to do come spring was spread manure, poke holes in the ground and drop in her seeds, four in each hill. One for the soil, one for the crow, one for the mole and one to grow. Emma had told her everything she would need to know about planting and laying by food for the winter, and curing everything from mites on her chickens to bugs on her vegetables. She had even tried to explain away these monthly miseries, but knowing they would pass didn't make her feel any better when her belly hurt and her hand hurt and she felt so discouraged she could cry.

Carrie had just hung the harness on a nail inside the

barn when she heard a noise overhead in the hayloft. Dust sifted down through the cracks, drifting through the shaft of late afternoon sunlight that slanted in through the wide opening. There wasn't a single thing in that loft but hay left over from last year and Darther's store of whiskey.

"Oh, lordy, I don't need this," she muttered. Bracing her fists on her hips, she tipped back her head and yelled, "You up there—Kie-o-way, or whatever your blasted name is, you just get yourself down here right this minute, you hear me?"

She felt like crying. She felt like kicking something. Blast it all to blazes, she *knew* her emotions were all over the road, but she had trusted the man! And then, the minute her back was turned, he'd had to go snooping around until he'd found Darther's jugs that Liam had toted up there last April when they'd won that big pot and spent every red cent of it on Buffalo City moonshine instead of the fresh cow she'd been begging for.

Since then, every time they came home from a successful trip, the two of them would bring down a few jugs and spend the first night celebrating. She would hear them all the way over to the house, laughing and singing and carrying on—shouting and *whoo-hawing* at one another. It got so she'd find herself wishing the next time one of them climbed up after another jug he would fall off the edge of the hayloft and break his miserable neck, and then she'd have to go and pray over her own wicked thoughts.

Hearing a rustling sound overhead, she set her foot on the bottom rung of the ladder. It might be rats. Usually they got to the grain and left the hay alone, but maybe they were holing up for the winter.

It wasn't rats. She'd have seen signs of them, because

she watched diligently for such things. Besides, she had two good rat snakes that kept the barn pretty well clear of rodents. Either her prisoner was up there, drunk as a crow in a barrel of mash, or Darther and Liam had come back and chased him off.

Or worse.

Carrie didn't dare think of what *worse* might mean, she only knew she had another mess to deal with when all in the world she felt like doing was falling into bed and sleeping her miseries away.

There was no sound coming from Peck's stall. No saddlebags tossed down on Liam's cot. Liam's mare wasn't out back in the paddock, which meant it couldn't be Liam and Darther up in the hayloft drinking themselves sick.

Which meant…

Well, shoot. She almost wished Darther *had* come back home. And that said something about her state of mind that didn't bear close examination, she told herself as she began to climb the steep, narrow ladder to the loft.

Chapter Four

It was dark as pitch in the hayloft. And dusty. Carrie sneezed, swore, and sneezed again. "All right, you might as well show yourself, I know you're up here."

She waited. No response. But of course, if he was sprawled out in a corner, dead drunk, he wouldn't answer. Couldn't answer even if by some miracle he was sober enough, as he barely understood plain English. "Speak up, else I'll go off and leave you here to fall down and break your miserable neck!"

For two beans and a straight pin she would do just that. Save the county the cost of hanging him. Save herself the aggravation of watching him walk behind her plow, with his dark hair shining in the sun, pulled back so that it was neater than her own. With his narrow little behind and his wide shoulders and his hands, so square and steady on the splintered wooden handles.

She should never have peeked that first day at the creek. She had tried so hard not to think about the way he'd looked standing there in the morning sun, strip, stark naked. But the harder she tried not to think about it, the more she thought about it, the image stuck in her mind like a cocklebur in a sheep's pelt. The only other man she had ever seen naked from head to toe was her husband. It was hard to believe they were the same species.

Evidently, they had something in common after all. Drink.

Disgusted, disappointed and thoroughly out of sorts, Carrie stood there, uncertain of what to do next. She told herself that soon he'd be going back to jail, where they would probably hang him. She couldn't allow herself to think about him as a man—as a real person. It hurt too much. "Then stay there," she muttered, turning back to the ladder. "Drink yourself into an early grave. Fall down the ladder and break your fool neck, see if I care!"

"Aah-choo!" The loud sneeze was quickly followed by three more. One hand on the ladder, Carrie froze. Hearing a brief scuffling sound, she squinted in the darkness and saw—or at least thought she saw—something moving in the small pile of hay that had been scraped into a corner to make room for Darther's jugs of moonshine.

Whispering.

Whispering? He was talking to himself when he couldn't even spare her so much as a single word?

"Damn your sorry hide, if you can still crawl, then you'd better get yourself down this ladder! If I have to come after you—!" She'd give him one more last chance, and then she was leaving him to his fate. She had run plumb out of patience. And bellyache or not, she had a full day's work planned for tomorrow. "You listen here, I don't care how sick you are come morning, you're going to be out in that field at first light, you hear me? I paid for your services, and I'm damned well going to have them!"

Someone sniffled. Someone swore. Voices whispered

fiercely, and then two small forms emerged from the darkest corner up under the eaves. Carrie's mouth fell open. And then, "Lord ha' mercy, what in the world...?" she crooned softly.

Feet dragging, they moved closer. Two...*children?* Little boys, from the looks of them. It was too dark to see more than one shapeless lump with two heads and two sets of feet. They were clinging together as if they were afraid of being swallowed up by a bear.

By now the sun was completely gone, with only the afterglow to see by. It wasn't enough. "Can you climb down the ladder?" she asked, wondering what she would do if they couldn't. "Who are you? What are you doing hiding in my barn?"

And where on earth was her prisoner?

They were terrified, she could tell that right off, but they managed to separate into two distinct shapes and follow her down the ladder. She went first in case they fell, although what she would do if that happened was beyond her. Land on her back and break their fall, was about all she could think of. Separately, they climbed down, nimble as monkeys, but once they reached the bottom of the ladder, they hooked up together again.

Flapping her skirt, Carrie shooed them over near the open door where she could take a closer look at what she'd discovered. She leaned closer, then backed away. "Lordy," she muttered after getting a powerful whiff. They must have been playing in a hog wallow. They were hardly more than babies, the taller one scarcely as high as her waist, and she was not a tall woman. There was just enough light left to see that they were skinny as stick dolls, dressed from somebody's ragbag. One wore a man's shirt, ragged and filthy, that hung to his ankles. The other wore something that looked like a potato sack, with a wide-brimmed felt hat pulled down almost to his nose.

"Who are you?" she asked again, more gently this time. From the way they were shivering, you'd think they were freezing. They were obviously terrified, poor babies.

"Brudda," the one in the shirt muttered, and the one in the hat nodded vigorously. Beyond that, she couldn't get a word out of them.

"You're brothers. Did you run away from home?"

Shirt nodded. Hat shook his head.

Carrie reached out instinctively, but when they backed away she allowed her arms to fall at her sides. "Are you lost then?"

This time Hat nodded and Shirt shook his head. If someone was missing a pair of boys, surely she would have heard about it, wouldn't she?

Not necessarily. She went into Shingle Landing no oftener than she had to, and didn't really know a soul there. Holding her breath, she moved as close as she dared, trying not to breathe, trying not to scare them into running. It was hard to see much under all the layers of dirt. They could have been redskins, for all she could tell. Maybe her prisoner had brought his family to stay with him, she thought with a feeling of helplessness laced with hopelessness, tinged with plain old jealousy.

But as dirty and matted as it was, Shirt's hair looked almost as pale as her own. She couldn't tell about his eyes, as neither of them had lifted their face after that first terrified moment. They stared down at two pairs of small, muddy feet. Hat ran a finger under his hat and scratched vigorously. Shirt dug at his groin.

Wonderful. Just what she needed, another dose of fleas, or worse, and two more mouths to feed. "Well," she said on a long sigh, "As long as you're here, I guess you might as well stay the night. I'll fetch you something to eat, but don't you touch anything in here, understand? Stay off that cot and don't even think about that stall in the corner, it's—it's haunted. If you have to use the privy, it's around back, and if you're wanting to move on, then just go."

She waited. Shirt nodded. Hat shook his head. She didn't know if that meant they were staying for supper, staying the night, moving on, or that they wouldn't go beyond the boundaries she'd set. Come to think of it, at this point she didn't much care if they used the stall for a privy and wallowed all over Liam's cot, leaving their dirt and a whole passel of ticks and lice. But if they did, she knew who'd be the one to pay the price, and it wouldn't be those poor ragged young'uns, she told herself as she hurried back to the house.

She also knew too well what it felt like to be a child alone, hungry and frightened.

Half hoping they'd be gone, she brought out two plates and a pail of water. They met her at the door and fell on the beans and cold biscuits laced with molasses like a pair of starving hounds. On the way back to the house, she unhitched Sorry, forked him some hay and added a measure of corn, but the chickens had already gone to roost unfed. She would just have to make it up to them come morning, else they'd hold back on laying, and she desperately needed the few eggs they produced.

Not bothering to eat her own supper, she stoked up the fire, shoved her brick into the oven and heated what was left of the yaupon tea. Emma had showed her how to cure the leaves from the bushes that grew everywhere. When the green brew was simmering, she poured out a cupful, dribbled in honey and added a dollop of shine for her belly. Darther always marked his house jug before he left, but by the time he got home again, he was usually too drunk to check the level.

Besides, she needed it more than he did.

What on earth was she going to do with them? Run them off, the way she did the occasional stray dog, or the foxes that came sniffing around her henhouse, or the deer that marauded her kitchen garden? They'd be better off leaving before Darther got home, and so would she. She was going to have enough to explain without two children.

Tomorrow she would think what to do, she promised herself, drifting off under the influence of half an ounce of whiskey and too many unanswerable questions. Tomorrow she would have to go back to Currituck and tell the sheriff she'd lost his prisoner. If the boys were still here, she would take them with her. Maybe someone in Currituck or Shingle Landing would know who they were and where they belonged.

But long before morning came she was awakened by a ruckus out in the barn. Her first thought was, *fox in the henhouse,* but that was no chicken doing all that shouting. Her second thought was that her prisoner had come back. Fumbling in the darkness to light a lantern, she reluctantly dismissed that thought, as well.

Damn and blast his sorry hide, to think that the very first time she had trusted him enough to go off and leave him here alone, he had run off, leaving her to face the sheriff and try to explain. She *hated* being wrong about people, just purely hated it! She'd been wrong about her uncle, wrong about the man she'd married so hopefully—and now this.

Adjusting the flame so that it wouldn't smoke up the glass, she hurried outside. If the Kie-o-way wasn't the one upsetting those two babies out the barn, then Darther must be back. And if he'd won a big pot, he'd be roaring drunk. But drunk or sober, there was no telling what he might do, finding strangers in his barn.

Dodging the droppings she hadn't had time to rake up before dark, she hurried across the yard, her thoughts disjointed, chaotic. Drunk, her husband was meaner than a nest of cottonmouths. Sober, he wasn't much better. Either way, she had to get to those two babies before he did something awful.

At least she'd had the foresight to grab the rifle as she'd raced out the door. Gun in one hand, lantern in the other, she was almost to the barn when a shrill scream sliced through the night.

"Don't you dare lay a finger on those children," she whispered fiercely, running the rest of the way. If he was sober enough to think, Darther would know the rifle wasn't loaded because he refused to show her where he kept his ammunition, but the damned thing was heavy enough to do considerable damage before he could snatch it away from her. "Darther Adams, don't you dare hurt my boys!" she screeched, her voice jarring with every footfall.

Light showed between the cracks of the barn. He had lit a lantern. "Don't you lay a hand on—" She skidded to a halt just outside the doorway, her mouth falling open. The gun barrel hit the dirt floor. Rage and relief clashed inside her as she recognized the man wearing jean cloth trousers and a clean white shirt. He was holding the boys by the scruff of the neck while two pairs of dangling bare feet and two pairs of scrawny arms flailed uselessly.

Her prisoner.

Never in her life had Carrie heard such profanity as

came from the mouths of those babes, and over the past few years she had heard just about every cuss word ever invented—even invented a few of her own. But when she caught sight of the horses at the far end of the barn, she was tempted to join the chorus. Even in the dim glow of two smoky lanterns, it was obvious that they were quality. And just as obvious they didn't belong here. No wonder he'd been missing when she got back, damn his thieving hide, he'd been off stealing horses!

As angry as she was with her prisoner, she was even angrier with herself for being so disappointed. It wasn't as if she hadn't known what he was—the sheriff had told her that the man was a hardened thief. He'd hardly have been jailed for picking flowers from someone else's petunia bed. But knowing and seeing the evidence were two different things.

A horse thief. A common horse thief.

Both boys were staring at her as if she were their only hope of salvation. Which she was. Forcing back her anger and disappointment, she said reassuringly, "Don't worry, I understand why you don't want to sleep in the barn with a horse thief."

Shirt's knotted fists, still swinging uselessly, looked like galls on a pair of skinny oak twigs. "We don't care 'bout no hoss thief, but we ain't sleeping with no Injun," he growled.

"I'm pleased to hear you won't be sharing my quarters, for I find your stench extremely offensive." In language as precise and proper as her own, the horse thief addressed the pair dangling from his fist.

It took a full minute for the impact to register. Carrie shook her head. If one of the horses had spoken, she couldn't have been more stunned. "You can *talk?*"

He lifted one eyebrow in a way that made her want

to throw something at him. Here she'd been patiently trying to teach him words like *plow,* and *tree* and *rain,* and all along he could talk as well as she could. Better, in fact. She'd been taught well by her parents and later by the missionaries, although she'd be the first to admit she might've backslid a bit after a few years of living with trash like her Uncle Henry and Darther.

But that damned two-dollar Indian didn't—he couldn't have—

Utterly confused, she stared at the man she had considered an uneducated heathen, an acknowledged thief, and probably worse.

She pointed to the two horses, quietly helping themselves to Peck's high quality oats. "Who—where—what?" Even she knew enough about horseflesh to recognize that these were no plow horses. "I won't have stolen animals in my barn. When the sheriff comes after you and finds them on my land, he might try to blame me. So you can just take your horses and get off my property." She was mad enough to spit nails, and didn't try to hide it. And if part of that anger was disappointment, she would deal with that after he was gone.

He was still holding the boys with one hand, but they'd quit trying to escape. Now they looked from one to the other as if trying to gauge the winning side so as to know which way to jump. Shirt was sniffling. He wiped his face with a filthy hand, smearing a pale streak through the grime. His eyes were blue, rimmed with red. One of them was swollen shut.

"You turn those children loose this very minute," she ordered.

He released them so quickly they stumbled and nearly fell. Carrie couldn't bring herself to look at him, so great was her disappointment, and so she turned to the pair of runaways. "I reckon you'll just have to spend the rest of the night in the house." They could sleep on the rug and she could burn it tomorrow. It wasn't much of a rug, anyway, only crocheted rags worn so thin you could count the knots in the floor without even lifting it up. The whole house would have to be scrubbed down to get rid of the vermin, but she could hardly leave them out here with a horse-stealing heathen.

At the door, she turned. He was still standing there, looking so smug she wanted to flatten that proud nose of his. Wanted to yank every strand of that thick, shining hair right off his head. What right did he have to take over her barn, to risk getting her hauled off to jail? Why had he bothered to make her like him?

Not that he'd tried all that hard. All the same, she hated him for it. Hated him so much she could cry, only she refused to give him the satisfaction of knowing she cared. Because she didn't. She was only...disappointed.

Damn and blast the man, he lacked even the common decency to look ashamed. "I assume you have a name?"

Echoes from the past. *I assume you have a name, little girl. If we're going to consider taking you home with us for a trial adoption, you must learn to respond politely to your betters.*

"I assume you have a name," she repeated, every inch as haughty as the woman who had run the mission orphanage with an iron hand. "I need to know what to tell the sheriff."

Jonah could have told her his Kiowa name, but that would diminish his spirit. "Among your people, I am called Jonah Longshadow."

He watched her absorb the words. When she said nothing, he felt compelled to say more. It was an odd compulsion, as he had once gone more than three months without speaking. "I am called Longshadow because I am taller than any of my mother's people. I am called Jonah because three ships have sunk beneath my feet."

He waited. She looked at him as if he were some strange new form of life she had discovered crawling up from a hole in the ground. He had thought himself shamed by walking behind a white man's plow. It was nothing compared to the shame he felt for caring what this woman thought of him.

By that time the boys had slipped outside and were noisily drinking from the hollow cypress log that served as a horse trough. The woman moved to the door and lingered there, looking from him to the boys, to his horses and back again. He knew what she was thinking. He could easily have relieved her mind, but he chose not to. Let her sit in her dark, airless cabin holding her unloaded weapon for protection against being murdered in her sleep. Let her wait to hear him gallop off with the horses she obviously thought he'd stolen—or for the posse to ride in to recapture him and drag him off to be hanged.

He refused to tell her that the horses were his own. That he had worked and saved for four grueling years in order to purchase land and stock. That when one of the men he had sailed with, after losing everything he had won gambling with his shipmates, had accused Jonah of stealing his wages, his word had been accepted over that of an Indian. Jonah had been given no chance to produce proof of ownership. When he'd tried to explain, one of the sheriff's men had said only that papers didn't prove innocence, that anything could be bought with stolen money.

He had no argument for that. He had written a letter

to Lieutenant Pratt, but he had no way of knowing if it had been posted. Without the word of an honorable white man to stand up for him, everything he had accomplished would be used against him as proof of his guilt. At least he stood a better chance now that he had the deed for the land and the bill of sale for his horses in his possession, if the judge turned out to be a reasonably honest man. And if he could stay alive long enough to be heard.

That was a problem. The sheriff was not particularly vicious, but one of his two deputies was a slow-witted boy, the other a drinking man. Sober, he was merely mean and ignorant. Drunk, he might prove dangerous.

Carrie was up before daylight, half expecting her cabin to be cleaned out and her two small guests long gone. Instead, they were sleeping like dirty angels. Shirt slept on his belly with a thumb in his mouth. Hat slept on his back, the hat pulled down over his face so that only his chin was visible. The poor child was as black as if he'd been eating mud. She was obviously going to have to scrub them with her strongest soap to rid them of countless layers of dirt.

For long moments Carrie stood over them, fighting the urge to weep. The smallest one couldn't be more than six years old, certainly no older than she'd been when she'd been found by the missionaries, huddled in a root cellar with the few other survivors of the massacre.

Who were these children running away from? Why were they so terrified?

Carrie knew what it was to be a frightened child, totally dependent on strangers. While the other children who'd survived the massacre had been adopted, or family members had been found to take them in, she'd been left behind. A thin, silent child, she'd been passed over time after time as not strong enough, not bright enough or not pretty enough. Eventually she'd been taken to Ohio to live with Mrs. Robinson, an elderly missionary schoolteacher who hadn't really wanted a child, but who'd been too kind to leave her behind.

This was her chance to repay that kindness.

Perhaps the boys' family would come for them. Surely they would once they knew where to find them. Almost seven years had passed before Carrie's family had found her. She'd been thirteen when a journalist had interviewed her as a survivor of the infamous massacre and published her picture in the newspaper. A few months later, a letter had arrived from a man in Virginia claiming that his name, like Carrie's, was Vander. That he'd heard his brother and sister-in-law had been killed in that same massacre, that Carrie was the spitting image of his brother. He'd explained that he, like his brother, was a respectable merchant.

Carrie had quickly been packed off to Virginia so that Mrs. Robinson could finally retire and move in with her son and his family. Expecting a kindly old uncle who looked like her beautiful mother, even though he was supposed to be her father's brother—at that age, Carrie's dreams had been based more on fairy tales than on reality—she had been severely disappointed in her Uncle Henry. He was nothing at all like either of her parents. Stingy and profane, he had given her a pallet in a storage room, showed her where the privy was, and from that day on he had assigned her the job of doing the cooking, keeping the store clean, helping unload the freight wagons and putting away the stock.

Carrie had wanted to hear about her family, wanted

to talk about them, but her uncle had never once mentioned them. After a while she'd begun to wonder if he truly was her uncle, but as she had no place else to go, she'd kept her doubts to herself. She remembered wishing more than once that Mrs. Robinson had given her a book instead of a new dress. At least she could have taken refuge in fairy tales when real life turned out to be so unrelentingly grim.

Pulling her back from the past, one of the boys cried out sharply in his sleep. Carrie knelt and touched his shoulder. Skin and bones. First they would need to be fed. After that they would need to be scrubbed. And after that she would have to find out where they belonged.

Jonah was still here. Now that she knew he had a name—well, of course he had a name, only now that she knew what it was, she was even angrier with him than when she'd thought he had run away. He had made a fool of her. Probably been laughing up his sleeve all the time, damn his lying gray eyes.

No wonder he'd struck her as arrogant, even when he'd been wearing irons.

Once the boys showed signs of waking up, she dumped cornmeal and a pinch of salt into water, put it on to boil and got out a pitcher of wild honey that had cost her many a bee sting. If she'd still had a cow, they could have had fresh milk on their mush, but as it was, they'd have to make do with tinned. The next time Darther came home she would demand money to buy another cow. That is, if she didn't get hauled off to jail for harboring stolen horses. Or runaway children. Or a horse thief.

Or if Darther didn't come home and find his barn and his cabin full of strangers, which might be even worse.

Hat refused to take off his hat even long enough to

eat, and Carrie didn't insist. The more clothes they shed, the more vermin they would scatter. As it was, she was going to have to drag her mattress outside and smoke it with burnt feathers. "Now, soon as you're done here, we're going down to the creek, and you're both going to scrub real good, and then I'll see if I can find you some clean clothes."

Darther had shirts to spare. He liked fancy clothes, and he never threw away anything, even when the buttons would no longer fasten over his belly. His racetrack clothes, he called them, even though she knew by now that he was what Emma called a track rat. A shady gambler who made the rounds of every two-bit nag race in the region, scheming to win a big enough pot to move into more respectable racing circles. Emma might not get out much any more, but she knew all about what went on.

She would have to ask her about the boys.

Meanwhile, anyone who could afford to wear a fancy gold watch fob could easily afford to help clothe a pair of unfortunate boys.

"Come along now, time's a-wasting. 'Course, if you're ready to move on, I won't keep you." She half hoped they would, half hoped they wouldn't. She didn't like sending them away without knowing where they'd end up.

They followed her as far as the barn, bobbling along as if they were joined at the hip. Carrie carried a chunk of soap, two towels made from feed sacks, and two of the smallest, oldest shirts she could find. When Jonah stepped out of the barn, the boys hung back and stared at him.

Carrie couldn't much blame them. He looked...different. Beautiful was the word that came to mind, but men weren't supposed to be beautiful, not unless they were angels, and he was hardly that. His hair might gleam bright as polished mahogany in the early morning sunlight, but she saw no sign of a halo.

She reminded herself that he was still a horse thief. Just because he could speak English—just because he was wearing clean clothes that were in far better repair than her own, that didn't mean he'd suddenly turned into someone else. No amount of pride, stubbornness or arrogance could change the fact that he was a two-dollar prisoner, out on work parole until the circuit judge made his rounds.

He held out a packet of papers. When she continued to stare at him, he reached for her hand and closed her fingers around the flat bundle. He could have touched her with a red-hot poker and it wouldn't have affected her any more. "The deed to my land and the bill of sale for four horses. Those in the barn are T'a-Kon and Sa-bodle-te. I left behind two other mares. Know that I could have stayed away had I wished to escape," he said, as if that alone should prove his trustworthiness.

She looked at the packet in her hand, then met his steady gray eyes. "Well, deeds and bills of sale or not, you're still going to have to hitch up that mule and finish the work we started," she told him, not knowing what else to say and ashamed of where her thoughts had been straying. "I paid my two dollars. As for your papers, you can save them to give to the sheriff. Soon as I get back from bathing these boys, you be ready to go to work, d'you hear me?"

"Ain't gonna take no bath," one of her charges mumbled.

"Oh, yes you are, too."

"Not, neither." It was Hat, this time. She was beginning to be able to tell their voices apart. Hat's was deeper, softer. Shirt's was more like a whiny kitten. She'd asked them their names last night, but they'd refused to answer, refused to speak another word, and then first thing she knew, they'd been sound asleep.

Poor babies... "As long as you're here, you're either going to have to sleep in the barn or bathe."

Jonah stepped forward then and without a word, took the towels from her shoulder, the soap right out of her pocket, and collared a boy in each hand. "Come," he said, leaving no room for argument.

Carrie stared after them, wondering if she should follow. The boys were squawking and flapping like a pair of banty hens trying to fight off a chicken hawk. Jonah ignored them. As she led Sorry around from the makeshift paddock behind the barn, Carrie told herself he didn't need any help from her. He might scare the devil out of them, but without knowing how she knew, she was certain he would never hurt them.

Nor did it occur to her that a week ago she'd have been following with the Springfield to see that he didn't try to escape. Two weeks ago, and he'd still have been wearing those cruel leg irons that chafed his bare skin until it was raw and bleeding.

"Sorry, you know him better than I do—what in the world is he doing to us?"

Chapter Five

Carrie tied cold biscuits, a wedge of hard cheese and some dried peaches in a napkin, then filled two jars with water. She was determined to get started on the plowing. After that, if they were still here, she could figure out what to do with the boys. Emma would know who had sons between the ages of six and eight, or thereabouts. They couldn't have come from too far away.

But when Jonah brought them back some half hour later, clean, considerably subdued and relatively bug-free, one thing was clear. They were not brothers. One—the one she'd called Shirt—was white. Straw-colored hair, sharp blue eyes and more freckles than a hawk's egg.

The other boy was brown as an acorn. The hat was missing, revealing a thick crop of tight curls that framed his small face like a black halo. He scowled at her as if daring her to comment, but Carrie couldn't have spoken even if she could have thought of an appropriate remark.

Jonah looked at each boy in turn, then released them both. Evidently they had come to some sort of understanding. Neither boy made a move to run, and after a moment, Jonah nodded. Turning to Carrie, he said, "I will lead the mule. You may have the boys."

And so they proceeded, with Jonah and Sorry heading the parade. For the first time in almost more years than she could remember, Carrie felt the urge to giggle.

"Whur we goin'?" Hat's voice, deeper, softer, held an accusing note.

"To my cornfield."

"Ain't no cornfield 'round hereabouts."

"There will be," she replied firmly. And then, "How did you know that?"

Shirt spoke up then. His legs were shorter. He took three steps, then a skip to keep up. "We looked. Ain't nobody round these parts but the old lady that lives in the woods. We should'a gone there, she wouldn'a made us take no bath, I bet."

"Her name is Miss Emma, and she would've scrubbed the hide right off your skinny bones. Here, you can carry this. If you drop it, you'll have to do without drinking water." She handed him one of the jars from the burlap sack, remembering from when she was that age how important it was for a child to feel useful. First with Mrs. Robinson and later, with her uncle, she'd been made to feel so useful it was all she could do not to fall asleep on her feet before the day was done.

They fought over who was to carry the Mason jar, muttering and tussling, but careful not to drop it. Carrie handed the other jar to Hat, with a similar warning. Several paces ahead, Jonah turned to glance over his shoulder. After a warning look at the boys, he lifted his eyes to Carrie. Didn't smile, but she fancied she could see amusement in the clear, gray depths.

By the middle of the morning the boys were following Jonah around like a pair of playful pups, crying, "Watch this, Jonah," and "Look at me, Jonah, betcha you never seen nobody jump this far!" With no more than a few minor scuffles, they played as if they hadn't a care in the world. They were filthy again, of course, but that could easily be remedied.

With only a minimum amount of kicking and balking, Sorry pitted his considerable weight against the dry, root-clogged clay soil. Weeds and scrub alike fell to the newly sharpened plow. When they stopped at midday, Jonah led the creature into the woods to a shallow stream, allowing him to drink and then to linger and graze on the tender grass along the banks. The boys chased along behind, and came back wet and muddy, but laughing as children were supposed to laugh. Not once could Carrie recall hearing Jonah issue an order, either to Sorry or to the boys, yet they seemed to anticipate his wishes without a word being spoken. It must be a Kie-oh-way thing, she told herself as she plodded tiredly back to the cabin a few hours later.

So far today she had learned only that the boys were named Zac and Nate. Zac was Shirt—Nate was Hat. Not until several days later did she learn their story, and then not from the boys themselves, but from Jonah. After the second night spent on a pallet on her cabin floor, the boys had decided to share the barn, after all. Red Injuns weren't so bad, Zac informed her with a careless shrug, although both boys seemed disappointed to learn that Jonah was not a horse thief.

"Zachariah's father was a sharecropper," Jonah told her as they worked together repairing worn harness. "He does not remember his mother."

Carrie sighed. Some days she had trouble remembering her own mother. What few memories she had were all mixed up with the smell of cinnamon and fresh-baked bread and the sound of bloodcurdling screams. "What about Nate?"

"He lived with his grandmother, who worked in the kitchen of a man named Litkin."

"That would be the Litkin Plantation, over near Snowden. Emma told me about all the families in the area—I believe she said old man Litkin died last month, but as I never knew him, I didn't pay much attention."

"The boy's grandmother died before that. When her people came for her body, the boy hid. After they left, he returned to her cabin and lived there alone."

"How could he do that? He's only a baby."

Jonah shrugged. It was such an un-Indian gesture that Carrie could only stare at him. But if he noticed, he didn't let on. Tightly braiding two strips of new leather into the old, he said, "There was no one left but the old man. His mind had grown weak with age."

Carrie held the strap while he tested the mend. When it held, he laid it aside and picked up another frayed leather strap. "What about Zac? You said his father was a 'cropper?"

"From what the boy said, they lived in a tenant house across the creek from the Litkin farm. The two boys fished from the same pond, but on opposite banks. When Nate heard Zac's screams and woke to see the tenant house in flames, he crossed to the other side."

"Oh, my blessed Jesus," Carrie whispered. Her hands fell still as she heard Jonah describe the pitiful tale of a drunken sharecropper perishing in the fire he had accidentally set; the grandson of a slave who rushed into the burning cabin to rescue a terrified white child. "Poor babies, no wonder they ran away."

There was little emotion in his voice as he related his interpretation of the few facts that had been forthcoming.

It was if he were reading from the page of a storybook, yet Carrie found the words mesmerizing. He spoke quietly, with the merest hint of an accent, his eyes unfocused as he gazed into the deepening shadows, as if seeing the tale unfold with the telling. Even with her limited experience, she recognized a gifted storyteller.

How had he learned to use the language so fluently? His manner of speaking reminded her of some of the older settlers back in Minnesota who bent the English language around their own native tongue.

"No telling how long they've been hiding, poor babies." Even though he'd allowed no hint of pity to color his words, Carrie knew he was deeply touched. "Is there anyone else for either of them?"

"Family? I believe not."

"Then I guess they're ours," she said with a sigh, and then quickly corrected herself. "Mine, that is." She felt her face grow warm and hoped he hadn't noticed her slip. Being alone so much of the time, she'd fallen into the habit of uttering whatever half-formed thought popped into her mind.

"I will finish here," Jonah said quietly. "The boys have been told to feed your chickens and fill all the troughs."

The daily watering usually required half a dozen trips to the creek, even when she'd been able to carry two buckets. Now able to carry only one at a time, it took forever. She usually let the horse trough go a few days, with only Sorry here to drink from it. "I suppose now, with two more horses…"

She let her voice trail off, leaving him an opening to tell her about the horses. Were they truly his? The bill of sale had his name on it, but why had he brought them here? How long did he intend to stay? Had he forgotten that no matter how many horses he claimed to own, he was still a prisoner out only on parole?

Arms crossed over his chest, he spoke solemnly. "As you say, now there are two more."

Irritated at the way he avoided answering her unasked questions, she waved away a swarm of gnats and said, "All the same, they're just babies." Back to the boys. At least he didn't mind talking about them. "You shouldn't have asked them to tote heavy pails of water, you should've done it yourself."

Jonah smiled—the merest whisper of a smile, but it was enough to splinter her defenses. "Give a boy more than he can do and he will grow to the task. Give him too little to do and he will find trouble."

"Boys need to play."

"They will play. They will return from the creek wet and muddy. To a boy, that is play." This time he gave her a true smile, one that started in his eyes and creased his lean cheeks, revealing an unexpected dimple. Staring at it, she forgot to breathe.

Muttering something about supper, she turned and hurried toward the house, shaken right down to her toenails. The soft sound of his laughter followed her, making her wonder if her monthly miseries had taken a new turn. Either that or too many clouts on the head had stolen what little common sense she possessed. Obviously, something had addled her wits, for she found herself humming a few minutes later as she set out the wooden bread bowl and poked another length of pine into the stove for quick heat.

But the moment she caught sight of the rifle propped beside the door, where it had remained for the past two days, the humming ceased.

Darther. Sooner or later he would come home. He

always did, no matter how long he stayed away. This time it had been nearly a month, during which time she had rented herself a prisoner and done a prodigious amount of work on her cornfield, and taken in two homeless boys.

Darther didn't like changes. If Jonah and the boys were still here when he returned, she was going to have some fancy explaining to do. She could say the boys were locals, and had wandered away from home and gotten lost.

Yes, and she'd given them the shirts off her husband's back.

And Jonah? She could hardly explain him away.

She would have to think about all that—about what she would say, how she would explain everything in case they were all still here when Darther came home.

But oh, she thought wistfully, if only things could go on this way a little while longer, with Jonah to help with the heavy work and the boys to look after the chickens, and all of them together at mealtime, laughing and talking like a real family... With the boys showing off in the evenings after the day's work was done, trying to out-brag each other about how fast they could run and how high they could jump. And her gaze meeting Jonah's to smile over their antics.

At supper, Jonah would cut up their meat and she would mop up the watered-down tinned milk that would get knocked over and spilled when Zac's hands reached out to show how big a fish he'd caught in the creek.

Her floury hands growing still, she gazed out the window and sighed. After having no one to talk to but Sorry and the chickens for so long, unless she cut through the woods to visit Emma, it was a lovely dream, but that's all it was...a dream. She'd do well to remember that.

By the time Carrie had met the man who was to be her husband, she had almost forgotten how to dream. She'd been barely sixteen when Darther Adams, on his way home from a nag race up in Princess Ann, Virginia, had stopped by her uncle's store in Hickory on his way south. Hearing the sound of voices, Carrie had glanced through the door to see a stout young gentleman wearing a bright blue frock coat, a silk vest and checkered trousers, with a fancy watch fob shaped like a flying horse dangling from the gold chain. She had noticed him before, thinking he must be rich to wear such beautiful clothes. Afraid of being caught staring, she'd quickly backed away from the doorway. Her uncle never introduced her to any of his gambling friends, not that she would have known what to say to them if he had.

She'd gone on working, overhearing snatches of conversation while she struggled to drag sacks of grain into the storeroom from the supply wagon outside the back door.

"Damned horse come in drag-ass last! Lost damn near ever' dollar—"

"All the same, you owe me—" That had been the stranger's voice, deeper, not as whiny as her uncle's.

"You'll get the rest of your damn money, soon's I—"

"Been three months, Hen. Now, I'm a patient man, but—"

When her uncle had shouted for her, Carrie wiped a hand across her forehead, smearing dirt and sweat. She stood in the door, ashamed of her filthy dress and her uncombed hair. It had still been long then, worn in a single braid. She'd avoided looking directly at the stranger, who at close range, didn't look quite so young. "What do you need, Uncle Henry?"

"There, what'd I tell ye? Hard worker, knows her place. Come on out here, girl, let a man look you over."

Look her over? If her wits hadn't been dulled by drudgery, disappointment and too little food, she might have sailed out that back door and kept on running, but they had, and so she hadn't.

Both men had looked her over, as if she were a horse they were thinking of buying. Dusty from head to toe, her belly growling because she was never allowed to eat until she had finished her assigned tasks, at which time she was usually too tired to eat, she'd stood there like a knot on a tree.

Then the newcomer had nodded, and her uncle had nodded, and before she'd quite known what was happening, they had summoned a preacher and Carrie had become Mrs. Darther Adams, all in less than an hour's time.

Carrie remembered thinking, dazed, that life with a smiling, well-dressed stranger couldn't be any worse than life with her uncle. Half in shock, she'd heard the words spoken, choked on the swallow of whiskey she'd been handed by her uncle to celebrate the deal, and allowed herself to be boosted up into the saddle of a livery stable mare who tried to bite her on the knee.

She'd grabbed hold of the saddle to keep from slipping off, her head reeling from the swallow of hard liquor on an empty stomach. At least her bridegroom, mounted on the ugliest horse she'd ever laid eyes on, appeared to be well fed. He probably had a cook at home—maybe even a housekeeper—he could hardly look after a big house alone.

His coat was too tight. She remembered thinking that as she plodded along behind him. In a desperate attempt to make the best of the latest twist of fate, she'd told herself that her new life could hardly be worse than her old, and might even be better, even though her hasty wedding had been a crushing disappointment. The preacher had never even climbed down off his horse. They'd stood on the store porch, repeated a few words, a paper had changed hands between her uncle and her new husband—her marriage lines, she supposed. And then her uncle had given the preacher a bottle of whiskey, and he'd ridden off.

Henry had said something about a celebration and shoved a smudged glass in her hand. "You done me real proud, girlie, that you did," he'd proclaimed, grinning like a possum.

She was glad someone was proud. She hadn't even been given time to change into her good dress. She'd managed to wash her hands and face and bundle up her few belongings, before the preacher had arrived. By then her last fragile dream had been wavering like a rain barrel reflection once the dipper broke the surface.

Not that she'd really expected a fairy godmother, but at least she had hoped to be married in a pretty gown, with her hair all brushed out and pinned up on top of her head, with a circlet of flowers like the picture in her favorite book.

On the long, miserable ride south, Carrie had deliberately dragged out a few more dreams and laid them to rest. Disappointment was hardly fatal. If it had been, she'd have died long before this. Each time she'd been passed over for adoption in favor of someone younger, prettier, smarter. Each time her uncle had avoided her questions about her father, and what he'd been like as a boy.

Dreams were all very well, she remembered thinking at the time, but if reality turned out to be a hasty wedding to a well-dressed gentleman who looked as if he'd never gone hungry a day in his life, she could settle for that.

Reality had turned out to be a drafty two-room cabin with a leaking roof and a smoking chimney. Reality turned out to be a man who wore silk vests and dirty underwear, a man who took her to bed and then laughed when she cried out in pain. A man who got rip-snorting drunk the next day and took potshots at a nest full of baby squirrels, and who struck her with the back of his beefy hand when she dared to protest.

Reality was a man who spilled his whiskey and spat tobacco juice on the floor, a man who was too lazy to patch the roof over his head, who made her clean up after him when he was sick all over the bed after drinking himself into a stupor.

Reality turned out to be a man who valued few things in life, among them his horse, his father's rifle and his gold watch fob. Not to mention his own comfort, which was where Carrie came in. Her job, as it turned out, was to cater to his every whim. If he wanted his boots removed, then it was Carrie's job to see to it. And while she was at it, to scrape off the mud and polish them to a high shine.

If he wanted a fresh jug brought down from the hayloft, then she'd better see to it as quickly as possible. Darther didn't like being made to wait. He didn't like backtalk, and was quick to show his disapproval. For a large, lazy man, he was remarkably fast with his fists.

She might have left after the first few days, but her bridegroom beat her to it. When a small man with mean eyes arrived shortly after the wedding, the two men rode off without a backward look. Liam, as she later learned, was the jockey her husband relied on to race his big, ugly gelding. The two were inseparable. It was a wonder, she marveled later, that the man hadn't joined them in their bed. It would hardly have made a difference. Darther hadn't even bothered to unpack his saddlebags; it had been left to Carrie to unpack them and wash the stinking garments wadded inside.

Watching them disappear down the dusty road, with Liam wearing a bright pink silk shirt, which she later learned he wore at every race, Carrie had sized up her situation and concluded that a roof over her head, even a leaky one, was better than no roof at all. Going back to her uncle would do no good. He would either return her to her husband or hand her off to someone else—or work her until she dropped.

After studying her few options, Carrie had buried the last of her dreams and set out to improve her lot. Now, nearly three years later, the roof no longer leaked. The chimney no longer smoked. She had a good friend who lived less than an hour's walk through the woods. She knew people in the farming communities all around, and although they were not particularly friendly, she had no doubt they would come to her aid in a true emergency.

And for the moment, at least, she had herself a family, never mind if she was starting to dream again.

A few miles north in Virginia, Darther Adams tipped his chair back, spat in the general direction of the coal scuttle that served as a cuspidor, and waited for his friend to fold. He always beat Henry at cards. Both men knew the outcome before the first card was dealt, but once the last race of the day was run, whether it be nags, sulkies or dogs, they needed an excuse to continue their social drinking. Henry had suggested going in search of a woman, but neither man felt like expending the necessary effort. Darther mentioned finding a cockfight, but as that, too, required a certain amount of effort, they settled for cards.

Besides, Henry owed him money again, and Darther wasn't about to let him forget it. "If I lose this hand, we'll take it off what you owe me." Darther reached for the jug of white liquor under the table. "If I win—well, I already got me a wife. One's more'n enough."

"Still got her, huh? How's she workin' out?"

"Carrie? Tol'able. Talks too much, but I know how to shut her up. I been countin' aces, Hen, so don't bother to pull that card out of your sleeve."

It had been three years since Henry Vander, heavily in debt to his friend and unable to pay, had bartered his niece, Carrie, claiming she was a hard worker, a good cook, and didn't natter a man to death with a flapping tongue, the way most women did. Hell, he didn't know if she was his niece or not, but Darther, who had been trying without success to find a woman willing to look after his needs without cramping his style, had accepted the deal.

"Got to admit, she's a worker and a right fair cook. Not much fun in bed, though. I'd rather have me a good whore than a skinny woman who don't know a good man when she sees one. Still, I take her to bed now 'n' again to remind her of whose property she is." That was, he did when he was home. And when he was sober enough, which was increasingly rare. "Reminds me, I better head south pretty soon. Leave a woman alone too long, she gets fancy notions. Made me wipe my feet before I could come in last time. Had herself a *rug* on the floor." He waggled his head and smirked. "Nex' thing, she'll be hangin' curtains."

"Minds me o' my old woman."

Darther made an effort to focus his bloodshot eyes on the withered old sot across the table. "Never knew you was married, Hen."

"Yep. She died."

"Oh, my, now thassa dam' shame," Darther drawled, and both men laughed uproariously.

Jonah knew three days before that the mare would soon go into labor. Because she was slow-witted, he had given her the name, Sa-bodle-te. Carrie and the boys called her Boodle, the boys snickering because she ate wood, preferring the tops of rotted fence posts above all. Jonah sensed that Sa-bodle-te's first foaling would not be easy, but she was strong, gentle and obedient. She would be a good mother, if only he could bring her foal safely into the world.

When the time came, Carrie and the boys insisted on helping. He would have preferred to be left alone with the mare, but he merely nodded, showing Carrie where to hang the lantern, and warning the boys to make no sudden noises, no sudden moves. And then he turned his attention to the mare, calming her with a look, a touch, a soft-voiced word.

The foal was born some three hours later. Hardly daring to breathe, Carrie and the boys watched as Jonah reached inside the mare and gently led the wet, shiny creature, hooves and long, knobby legs first, out into the world.

"It's all wet," whispered Carrie, who had never before witnessed a birth. She watched in fascination as Jonah dealt efficiently with the afterbirth.

"Hellfire, that ain't nothin'," Nate growled. "You ought to see a real, live baby get borned. My granny, she birthed a whole bunch o' babies. Sometimes she used to let me watch.''

''Didn't, neither, you just snuck in,'' Zac whispered fiercely.

''She didn't run me out,'' Nate said smugly.

''Shh,'' Carrie admonished. She was enchanted by the dark, gleaming creature. How could anything be so awkward and at the same time, so graceful? They were leaning back in Peck's stall that Darther had had built for his precious gelding. Carrie had rarely even set foot inside the hallowed walls, but she hadn't questioned Jonah's use of it. Boodles needed a quiet, clean and private place.

They were seated in the straw, backs leaning against the slatted wall. The boys, restless from being confined too long, crawled outside the open stall, and were soon engaged in a game of pick-up-straws.

Somehow, Carrie had come to be seated next to Jonah, her right side touching his left side, her faded calico skirt lying half over his denim-clad thighs. She could actually hear the quiet sound of his breathing as they watched the mare nuzzle her baby. In that quiet, oddly precise voice of his, he had explained when they had first joined him that the entire process should take no more than an hour.

It had taken much longer. Jonah was obviously exhausted. He had washed his arms and hands, and forked out most of the soiled straw, but his clothes were badly stained. Light from the lantern emphasized lines of weariness in his face, cast shadows into the hollows beneath his high cheekbones.

What was it, Carrie wondered, that made this man, with his dark skin and his black hair, look more magnificent than all the yellow-haired heroes in all the story-books in Mrs. Robinson's library?

Unconsciously, she moved her hand closer to his. And then suddenly, she leaned forward. "Oh, look—Jonah, it's trying to get up! Don't let it—it might hurt itself—"

"Watch." Jonah didn't move a muscle. His voice remained unemotional, as if he had not just participated in a miracle.

So Carrie watched. Outside, the boys finally surrendered to the late hour and fell asleep on Liam's cot. Inside the stall, Carrie watched the long-legged creature stand shakily and begin nudging his mother's belly. "Oh, my," she whispered. Jonah's hand closed over hers, and it seemed the most natural thing in the world. "I've seen newborn kittens and puppies—once I saw a litter of brand-new pigs, but this is different."

Jonah pressed her hand. She laced her fingers through his, palms clasped together. Lantern-light, the smell of horse and blood and straw—the two boys, curled up just outside the stall, sound asleep—and Jonah. Could anything be more perfect?

Jonah studied the foal, seeing his strength, searching for weaknesses, finding none. He examined the legs, the chest, flanks and withers. For one long moment he looked into the large, dark eyes.

And then he nodded. This one would be a swift and tireless runner, like his sire. He glanced at Carrie, seeing the tender look on her tired face now, thinking of the wide-eyed wonder he'd seen there earlier. It would be so easy to lie with her here in the straw, to hold her while she slept. Nothing more than that. For now...

Using it as an excuse to free his hand, he leaned forward and touched the mare's flank. A ripple raced over her flesh, and she swung her muzzle around to butt his shoulder. Beside him, Carrie shifted, drew up her knees and tucked her skirt under her bare feet, and as quickly as it had come over them, the odd spell was broken.

But Jonah was worried about his shifting feelings. He had always made it a policy not to think about women any more than a young man could naturally help. Women—especially white women—had no place in his world.

"Is Con the baby's father?" Carrie's voice sounded oddly strained.

Con. His stallion was named T'a-Kon, for his black-rimmed ears. Both Carrie and the boys had shortened the name to Con. "Yes."

"I think he looks like his father, don't you? What will you name him?"

Jonah had not considered a name. With all he'd had to think of these past few weeks, there had not been time. Now he said, "You may give him a name if you wish."

He watched her eyes grow round, saw the flush of pleasure warm her cheeks, and almost regretted the impulse. This was a part of his life that would soon end, and the fewer reminders he had, the more quickly he could forget the past and move forward.

In the yellowish light of the lantern, her eyes glittered like the dark opal that came from the mountains of New Mexico. "Oh—could I think about it? I don't want to give him a name he'll hate—it has to be just right."

Solemnly, Jonah nodded. To an animal, the name would be only a sound. The goodness or badness of it depended on how it was spoken. But he liked seeing the look of joy and excitement on her face. It was far better than the fear and anger that he had seen there too often. Or the sadness, when her thoughts took her far away.

Chapter Six

The foal was named Howard after Carrie's father. She had thought about it all night long, wondering if her father would have considered it disrespectful, and decided that he would have considered it a great honor. "If we have a baby mare next, could I name her after my mother?" she asked, only half teasing. The teasing was something new that had entered into their relationship.

"That depends on your mother's name." Jonah spoke gravely, but Carrie had come to recognize the spark of humor lurking behind his somber mien.

"It was Achsah. It came from the Bible."

"From your Jesus Book."

Concerned, Carrie said, "We don't have to name her for my mother, we could name her for yours."

She had hurried out to the barn first thing the following morning, afraid something would have changed—afraid she might have dreamed it all. Liam's cot was neatly spread, the stall empty, with a layer of fresh straw replacing the soiled. Jonah had led the mare and her foal to the small area he had prepared behind the barn. For the past several days he had worked on repairing fences that had fallen into disuse, replacing rotted posts, pulling trumpet vine off the rusted wire.

Seeing them there—the docile mare and her new baby, Carrie felt a lump form in her throat. Con, or whatever his unpronounceable name was, stood just outside the fence, as if guarding his family. She wandered over to stand beside Jonah. "Do you think he knows Howard is his?"

"He knows."

"How do you know he knows?"

Jonah only looked at her. "He knows," he repeated, and she had to accept his word. The stallion was testy—Jonah had warned the boys not to approach him—but with Jonah, he was meek as a lamb. Carrie had seen them run, Jonah up on his bare back, his hair flying out behind him. She'd seen them sailing over fences, flying across the clearing and out onto the road. And she'd thought about the way Jonah had come here, tied behind her mule cart, his legs hobbled by those cruel leg irons.

Cutting him a sidelong glance, she wondered what it was about him that made her feel like crying sometimes, laughing at other times. Lately, all she had to do was think about him, and she would find herself wanting all kinds of impossible things. Dream things. Things she dared not wish for. Things she hardly even understood.

It had something to do with the man and woman relationship that Emma had tried so hard to explain without going into actual detail. Things that happened in the dark of night, under the covers, that felt so good you wanted to laugh and cry and shout, only you lacked the breath to do anything more than just lie there smiling.

Emma had actually said that. About the smiling. Carrie had waited for something like that to happen with Darther, only it never had. Just the reverse. Whenever he was home and sober, and happened to take a notion to lift her skirt, she felt sick in her stomach.

But with Jonah...

Well, that was something she could always wonder about, but she would never know. Which was probably for the best, considering how powerful it felt, even here in the shallow edges.

When the stallion whickered, the mare glanced up at him, then went on nuzzling her new baby. Carrie felt a warm thickness clog her throat. It was all mixed up with the way she was coming to feel about Jonah, and she knew better than to explore it any further.

Nate came to stand beside her, and she reached out to stroke his warm, wiry curls. "Did you find those raisin cakes I baked this morning?"

"Yes'm, I sure did." The boy favored her with a smile so bright she felt herself tearing up all over again. Fortunately, he broke the spell by turning to Jonah. "You gonna run 'im today, Jonah?"

"Yes."

Zac wormed his way between Nate and Jonah to put in his penny's worth. "I never seen a horse run that fast."

"I seen one run faster."

"Have not."

"Have so!"

"Boys, don't upset Howard. I think we should all take a day off, don't you?"

"You mean we don't got to work today?" Nate began prancing around, lifting his knees waist high with each step. Zac pointed his grimy forefinger at the trees and yelled, "Bang-bang! I'm gon' go huntin', git me a goose an' a rabbit for supper!"

Carrie met Jonah's eyes and smiled as the earth qui-

etly settled back into place. The Springfield was still
propped beside the front door, where it had remained for
the past two weeks. It would be many a year before
either boy would be able to lift the thing, much less load,
aim and actually fire it. "Why not catch some fish for
supper, instead? There's a cane pole around here somewhere, and you can dig worms out behind the chicken
house." She doubted if they'd have much luck—she
never had—but it would keep them out of mischief for
a spell.

Once the boys had gone whooping off to the creek,
Jonah whistled softly. Giving Carrie a wary look, the
stallion approached. "I will exercise him now, and then
I will work on the shed."

Another of his projects. There had once been a lean-
to behind the barn, but two of the supports had rotted
away and the roof had collapsed. Carrie, reluctant to
leave, said, "I reckon I'd better get the washing done,
long as we're having us a holiday."

They both smiled at the illogic of her reasoning, and
then Jonah eased a bridle over Con's head. The stallion
stood patiently, ears twitching, flanks quivering, whether
from anticipation or from flies, Carrie couldn't have said.
She wished she knew more about animals, but her father
had been a storekeeper, her mother a schoolteacher.
They'd had chickens—everyone had chickens—and a
mouser, but that had been the extent of her personal
experience with animals until she'd been sent to Virginia.

Since then she had personally dealt with one elderly
milk cow, any number of chickens—she'd had a brief
acquaintance with a milk goat, another with a wild
puppy, and an extended relationship with the stupidest,
stubbornest mule in the entire state of North Carolina.

Right from the first, the mule her husband called Sorry had gone out of its way to confound her. He moved when he wanted to move, stopped when he felt like stopping, and turned in whichever direction he decided to go, regardless of her commands. Sawing on the reins didn't do a speck of good, for the miserable creature had a cast iron mouth and a head harder than a cannonball.

Of course, Darther was no help at all. He'd either laugh or curse, depending on how drunk he was at the time. Eventually she'd learned that it took a river of profanity to make the beast pull either a cart or a plow, much less drag stumps from the ground.

And then along came Jonah. A few soft words, a soulful look or two, and the blasted mule turned sweet as molasses pie. It never ceased to amaze her, the gift that man had with animals and small boys.

The boys were at the creek fishing—or more than likely swimming. Now and then she could hear a shout of laughter. Jonah had set out at an easy walk, then picked up the pace to sail over the tumbledown gate at the edge of the back yard. Last she'd seen of him and that horse of his they'd been flying around the edges of the newly cleared cornfield. If Con was jealous of all the time Jonah had spent with Boodles and her baby, this should make up for it.

Carrie was gathering the eggs, her mind on getting the wash out so she could work on the pants she was making for the boys, when she heard the sound of someone galloping up the lane from the main road. A smile broke over her face, and she lifted her hand to her hair in an unconscious gesture. Holding four eggs, still warm from the nest, in her skirt, she hurried outside the chicken house, shading her eyes against the sun as a rider mounted on a familiar-looking buckskin slid to the ground, hanging onto the stirrup as if to steady himself.

Oh, dear Lord, it was Darther.

He turned and saw her, and her heart sank. She knew the signs all too well. He was not only drunk, he was mad as a hornet. Hooking the gate behind her, she carefully set her eggs down on the edge of the horse trough and fixed a smile on her face. It didn't take much to set him off when he was in this condition. "Where's Liam? Where's Peck?"

He glared at her as if she were a snake he'd found in his bed. "Dam' bastard sonovabitch lamed 'im!"

"Someone lamed Liam?"

The look he sent her made her step back. "No, you dumb bitch, the stupid bastard got drunk an' run my horse into a fence, broke his dam' leg!"

"Liam's leg is broken?"

Just as Darther lunged at her, catching her across the side of the face with a backhanded blow, Nate and Zac raced into the clearing, sloshing water from a rusted pail. Through watering eyes, Carrie saw them hesitate, then ease back into the woods. It was all she could do not to shout out a warning, but then Darther would only go after them. *Stay away,* she willed desperately, wishing she had Jonah's gift of wordless communication.

She'd known he would come home eventually. Why hadn't she planned what she would say? How could she explain Jonah and the boys? With no more gumption than a knot on a log, she'd let the days drift past, as if tomorrow would never come.

Tomorrow had come. While her left ear was still ringing from the blow, Darther spat and loosed another barrage of profanity. "Damn hoss's leg got broke. Busted clean to hell. Throwed th' race, lost m' money, me'n

Henry both, but I showed 'im. Yessir, I showed 'im real good.'' Yellowed teeth flashed in an evil smile, and Carrie shuddered.

Showed Henry or the horse? She didn't know and didn't care. She forced herself to say, "That's too bad. Darther, why don't you come inside and lie down a spell. I reckon you're tired from—'' From taking out his rotten temper on that poor winded horse, she wanted to say, recognizing the buckskin as one from her uncle's livery. "From the ride down from Virginia,'' she finished lamely.

Without even removing the saddle, he staggered toward the house. Carrie followed, after retrieving her eggs. One was crushed. She tossed it back into the pound.

"Fetch me my jug, woman,'' Darther ordered without even turning around.

Well, she thought—why not? The sooner he drank himself into a stupor, the sooner she could concentrate on what she was going to do about Jonah and the boys.

And then a new thought struck her. What if Darther saw the mare and foal out behind the barn? How could she explain those? Even if she sent Jonah and the boys to Emma, they could hardly take all the horses along. The only fence Emma had left was her chicken yard, and that wouldn't even keep the raccoons out. As for the barn, it was hardly safe to set foot inside.

She held the door open while her sot of a husband stumbled up the three wooden steps, lurched across her freshly scrubbed floor and fell heavily onto the bench beside the fireplace. Wordlessly, Carrie retrieved his house jug from the pie safe and set it beside him, praying he was too drunk to notice that she had helped herself to an ounce or two back when her monthlies had come on. He glared at it with narrowed eyes, and she held her breath. For reasons she had never understood, he sometimes pretended to be drunker than he actually was.

This time he wasn't pretending. Without even glancing at the mark on the side, he pulled the cork, tipped back the jug and drank noisily. Liquor trickled from each side of his mouth, soaking into his stained shirt to join the visible evidence of his last few meals. His jowls glistened from sweat and liquor, and Carrie could see dirt in the creases of his neck. For all his love of fancy clothes, her husband could never have been called fastidious.

Edging toward the door, she said, "I'll just—um, feed the chickens if you don't need me for a few minutes?" The chickens could wait. She had to find Jonah and the boys and warn them to stay away, at least until she could think of some way to explain their presence.

Once outside, she shaded her eyes and looked around. She was afraid to call, afraid to go off searching. *Where are you? What am I going to do about you? Oh, lordy, why couldn't he have broken his own leg instead of crippling that poor horse of his?*

Carrie stayed outside as long as she dared, trying to come up with a reasonable explanation for Nate and Zac and Jonah. Could she pass them off as Emma's relatives? Possibly Zac, but hardly Jonah or Nate.

She had hired them to help with the chores?

Using what for money? He knew to the penny how much she had, and made her account for every cent.

All right then, she had borrowed them. They had turned up one day and offered to work for food. If anyone appreciated cheap labor, it was Darther. That, after all, was the only reason he had taken a wife.

Hmm. That might work with the boys, but not Jonah.

There was no way she could explain the presence of a healthy, full-grown man, owner of three fine horses, without arousing suspicion. Even though Darther knew all about her dreams of growing a cash crop, he would know she could never afford to pay a man's wages. If she explained that Jonah was a prisoner out on parole, he would have a fit, accusing her of bringing home someone who would stab them in the back and steal everything in sight.

Picturing the sparsely furnished two-room cabin, she didn't know whether to laugh or cry. She'd do better to hope he would pass out and sleep until she could find Jonah and the boys and warn them to stay away until he left home again.

Let him drink and gamble away his money on nag races. Dog races—chicken races, for all she cared. If there was no race to bet on, Darther and that weasel-faced jockey of his would find the nearest card game or cockfight. She had even known them to bet on how many flies would land on a lump of sugar before one flew away.

But oh, God, why did he have to come home now?

In spite of the heat, she shivered as she tiptoed back inside without having caught sight of either Jonah or the boys. She didn't dare call out, much less stand in the back door and bang on the dishpan, the signal she and Emma had set between them in case of trouble.

He was still awake, his piggy little eyes fixed on the rifle beside the door, which she should have put up long ago. It was no longer useful even as a threat.

"Would you like some dinner?" she asked hesitantly.

"Poppa's rifle fall off the wall?" She knew by the nasty tone of his voice that he didn't believe that, not for a minute.

"I, um—thought I heard a fox in the henhouse the other night."

"Gonna scare 'im off with a' empty gun?" His words were slurred. By now she should be able to gauge more accurately just how drunk he was, but she'd seen him falling-down drunk one minute, and then the next he would be carrying on a conversation with Liam, sounding sober as a judge. With Darther, you never knew.

Taking a deep breath, she smiled brightly. "Did I tell you how much I got done on the cornfield? All the stumps are gone from the northeast part, and we've— that is, Sorry and I—we've even got most of it turned. Come spring, all we'll have to do is bust up the clods, hill it up and plant." The smile hurt her face, which was probably already swelling where he'd whacked her with the back of his hand. For a man who never did a lick of work, he was surprisingly strong.

The truth shall set ye free. She had done those words in cross-stitch when she was eleven years old, and a sorry botch she'd made of it. Telling the truth now couldn't be any more difficult than embroidering the words on a grimy scrap of linen all those years ago. "Darther, I, um—I hired—that is, I rented a prisoner with some money I borrowed from Emma. She said when the first crop comes in, I can pay her back in corn." Holding her breath, she waited, trying to interpret his mood. His eyes hadn't looked so muddy three years ago. Now they were bloodshot, buried in pouches of yellow fat. "So—anyway, he's a good worker. He's never tried to escape, and—"

Darther looked from Carrie to the rifle beside the door. His face grew a shade redder as he lurched up from the bench, swearing and panting and snorting. When he reached for the Springfield, she darted out through the door. The gun wasn't loaded. In his present condition, she didn't think he could even find his ammunition—she'd certainly never been able to locate it. And even if he did, she doubted if he could load up, take aim and fire, but she wasn't about to take a chance, not with all she had to protect.

She was halfway to the barn when he lunged at her, catching her on the arm with the rifle barrel. "Come back here, bitch," he roared. "Show you—show you—"

Suddenly, he seemed to forget what he was going to show her, but Carrie knew better than to get her hopes up. Unless he was passed out cold, she couldn't afford to let down her guard.

Jonah saw them coming, racing through the woods like a pair of startled white-tails. He knew before he ever heard their breathless shouts that the woman was in trouble.

"Jonah, you gotta come quick, he's a-gonna kill her!"

"You gotta make him stop hittin' her, Jonah!"

The breath froze in his lungs. At a silent command, the stallion wheeled and raced toward the clearing. Even with the wind in his ears and the sound of pounding hooves, Jonah could hear Nate screaming that a crazy man was hitting Miss Carrie, threatening to shoot the first thing that moved.

For a single instant, Jonah felt his blood freeze. Rage colored his vision as he flew along the edge of the woods to cut across the field. Trusting the surefooted mount on the newly turned earth, he sailed over the pile of half-burned stumps, up the back lane and into the clearing behind the cabin.

Carrie. Carrie Adams. Carrie needed him, she was in danger.

Weaving on his feet, Darther stared at the apparition. A flying horse?

He touched the charm that dangled from his heavy gold chain. If there was one thing he knew, drunk or sober, it was horses and riders. Peck's value had been that he was both fast and ugly as sin. One look and nobody believed he could outrun a cockroach, but with Liam up on his back, he'd placed in damn near every race he ever ran. Oh, my, yes, they'd had themselves a sweet little deal going until that damned jockey had got greedy and thrown in with a couple of sportsters from up north.

Much as it had pained him to do it, Darther had sobered up enough to borrow Henry's Colt and put the horse down with a single shot. And then he'd gone after Liam. It would be a long time before that cheating, ferret-faced runt would ride again.

Darther watched as the big bay stallion came to a stop, not even breathing hard. The rider—he'd lay odds the man was a breed—slid off and stood there with a go-to-hell look that made Darther want to take a swing at him. Dam' breed. Dam' Injun—couldn't trust 'em as far as you could throw 'em.

But he could ride, oh, yessir, he could do that, all right. And that damned horse of his was a gold mine. Look at those legs. Look at that chest. There was A-rab in that bloodline, or Darther Adams didn't know a horse from a rat's ass.

And right now, Darther badly needed another gold mine. Peck's reputation had been getting around, anyway. Word had spread—Liam might even have helped spread it, come to think of it—not to bet against the old boy. And hell, the whole game was in stretching the odds. The purse in these nag races was hardly worth spit. They'd had to go farther and farther afield to find a track where the ugly gelding's reputation wasn't known.

Whoever the breed was, up on that horse of his, he could easily win back everything Darther had lost, and more. Inhaling deeply, Adams fixed a smile on his face and managed to appear, if not entirely sober, at least not quite so drunk. "Carrie, why'nt you inter-duce me."

Reaching behind him, he caught her arm in a powerful grip and dragged her to stand beside him. "This here's m'wife. You a friend of hers?"

Without a word, the half-breed walked over to the lathered buckskin Darther had borrowed off Henry, looked him over and lifted off the saddle. Then he led the limping animal toward the barn.

Darther yelled, "You come back here, don't you walk off on me, you damned—"

His fingers bit into Carrie's arm, and she must have made a sound, because Jonah turned and walked back, his gliding movement a threat in itself. Wordlessly, Carrie pleaded with him not to make trouble, not to risk getting shot. *Run away,* she wanted to cry. Her eyes begged him to go and find the boys and keep them out of sight until it was safe to return, but she couldn't say any of that, not with Darther at this unpredictable stage. He was like a poisonous snake. One time he might allow you to walk past unharmed, and the next time, he'd strike without warning.

"Woman? I'm waiting."

"This is—this is—um, Jonah Longshadow. I told you I'd hired him to help with the plowing and clearing and all?" She waited for the explosion that never came.

Still gripping her arm, Darther nodded toward the stallion standing quietly behind Jonah. "Not a bad-lookin' animal. Don't look too smart, but as it happens, I'm in the market for a good, steady mount. I might see my way clear to offer—"

"Darther, I need to tell you about—"

His fingers bit into her arm painfully. "Shut up, woman."

Now that he knew about Jonah, Carrie felt compelled to get it all out into the open. "About the boys," she began.

"Dammit, woman, I told you to—" He scowled. "What boys?"

"The um—the two boys I've taken in?"

Darther drew back a fist and Carrie flinched, but the blow never came. Cautiously, she opened her eyes to see Jonah holding Darther's upraised arm.

Oh, God, her arm hurt. Soon there would be bruises there to match the ones on her face. But what hurt most of all was her pride. For Jonah to see her this way, knowing she had not only married this miserable piece of human trash, but stayed with him for three years—it was almost more than she could bear.

"You will not strike the woman." Jonah spoke calmly, his voice scarcely more than a whisper. Staring at the drunken bastard, he fought down the urge to kill. His own father, he reminded himself, must have been just such a man—quick to take what he wanted, to prey on those weaker than himself.

For one long moment no one moved. No one spoke. Carrie tore her gaze away to search the nearby woods. *Stay away, don't come back. Stay away until it's safe to return!* If that hateful sot laid a single finger on one of her boys, she would take a hoe to him—a pitchfork!

She stood slack-jawed as Darther brushed his pudgy

hands together and forced a laugh. As if the three of them were taking Sunday afternoon tea in Mrs. Robinson's parlor. When he went so far as to slap Jonah on the back, she waited for the world to come to an end. Was Jonah afraid of striking back? Why didn't he *do* something—or at least say something?

She looked from one to the other. Neither man was giving an inch. It was as if they were engaged in a silent battle of wills. Carrie knew very well who the best man was, but the best man didn't always win out over a drunken, brutal bully.

Darther broke first. Without turning his gaze away from Jonah, he said, "Woman, go cook us some dinner."

Carrie hesitated, afraid to stay, equally afraid to leave them alone together. Darther reached back and struck her on the hip, making her stumble. Her wide eyes fixed on Jonah, she watched as his muscles actually seemed to swell, but he said nothing, did nothing, and she felt her heart shrink to the size of a walnut, hard and brittle inside her chest.

A few minutes later, rubbing lard between her thumb and fingers in a bowlful of flour, Carrie told herself that Jonah was only being smart. He was a prisoner, after all. Sooner or later he would have to go on trial for whatever it was he was accused of having done. No wonder he wasn't willing to risk being hanged for attacking a white man. All the same, she thought…

All the same.

A single tear streaked down her swollen cheek and dropped silently into the wooden bread bowl.

Chapter Seven

His wife? Carrie, of the yellow hair and laughing eyes, was married to this vicious, slovenly animal? How could such a thing be?

The moment she disappeared inside the house, Jonah crossed his arms over his chest and waited. The pig-eyed man wanted T'a-Kon. Did he want him enough to kill for him? Did he want him enough to send Jonah back to jail and then claim what was his? Did he want him enough to treat his woman with respect and to provide for two homeless boys in exchange?

Such a man was without honor. His word could not be trusted, but as Jonah's only advantage was owning a horse the other man wanted, he had no choice but to hear him out. He knew, too, that Adams would be quick to pounce on any show of weakness once he learned that Jonah was a prisoner on parole, a half-breed far from his own homeland, his own people. Those factors alone put him at a disadvantage, but Jonah knew his greatest weakness was Carrie and the boys.

"Happens I'm in the market for a fresh horse. Racing's my game. A man can do real well for himself around these parts with the right horse.'' The older man hiccuped and hitched up his sagging trousers.

"T'a-Kon is not for sale."

"Well now, we could haggle over the price, or we could reach us a—what you might call an understanding."

Jonah's arms remained crossed over his chest. He schooled his face against revealing the disdain he felt for this wretched excuse for a man. "My horse is not for sale," he repeated softly.

The older man shuffled his feet in the dirt and spat. His wet lips stretched in an unconvincing smile, and he said, "I'll tell you straight out, boy, I don't hold nothing against Injuns. Ask me, you folks got a raw deal. Just so happens I'm in a position to make it up to you, though. See, there's this race coming up next week. Nothing reg'lar—off-season meet, you might say. What it is, is sort of a trial race. Bunch o' owners coming down from the north, looking over what we got down here. Be some buying, some betting, some trading. Play it right, and a smart man stands to make himself some money."

Jonah remained silent, his thoughts divided among the woman, the children, and this pig-eyed man who treated them no better than he treated his horse.

"Happens I'll be needing me a new horse an' rider. Liam—feller that used to ride for me, that is—he went and had himself what you might call an accident." Darther's face turned lugubrious. It was no more convincing than his smile. "Yessiree, it's a saddened man you see before you, boy."

Boy. Did it take lily-pale skin to become a man? Did it take drinking and mistreating those who were weaker to be called a man?

"I come home a broken man, and that's the truth."
Rolling his eyes, the man staggered and nearly fell.
Righting himself, he said, "Lost my horse and my
jockey, all in one day, so lemme tell you what I'm gonna
do." He hawked and spat and hitched up his britches
again.

Jonah read the signs easily. The man was as trust-
worthy as a croppy with a gut full of loco weed. He
waited for the trap to open.

"You lemme put that horse of yours in three races.
I'll make the arrangements, and we'll split the take."

It was all Jonah could do not to laugh, and he was
not a man given to laughter. He caught a glimpse of the
boys slipping past what Carrie called her kitchen garden,
heading toward the back door. Zac tripped over a trailing
vine, and Nate caught him by the arm and whispered
fiercely. Jonah spoke then, to cover the sound.

"The horse is mine. Why should I pay you anything?"

"Well now, I'd be what you call a handler. See, a
stranger can't just walk in cold and run with the pack in
these here nag races, he's gotta know the ropes. Gotta
know the right people. We got our own way of doing
things down here, just like I reckon you folks got
yours."

Jonah's back stiffened. Behind him, near the fence,
T'a-Kon whickered. "Indeed, we folks do have our
ways. It is our way to barter. If you want something from
me, you must give me something of equal value in return."

"Well now, didn't I just offer to split the take with
you, half an' half? After we take out the manager's cut,
naturally."

It was like trying to reason with a stump. "I have

work to do. Perhaps we will talk tomorrow.'' When Adams grabbed his arm, every muscle in Jonah's body tensed. It was all he could not to react.

"No need to work all day, boy. Come on inside, the woman'll have supper on the table by now. She's not much to look at, but she sets a right fair table.''

Jonah thought of the killdeer, who would feign a broken wing to lead a predator from her nest. He could not keep a man from his wife, but there were ways of protecting the young. ''As you say, my people have their own ways. The Kiowa do not tolerate cruelty to women and children.'' Which was not entirely true, but as a bargaining chip, it would serve well enough.

"Got my word, we'll treat that horse of yours like he was solid gold,'' the other man said piously.

Jonah had seen the lathered buckskin, left untended. He had seen Carrie's darkening bruises, her swollen jaw. ''I was speaking not only of horses. Your woman has treated me fairly. In exchange I have worked in your field. I would not like to see her mistreated.''

"Oh, now, Carrie, she's a good 'nough girl. Gets these notions, though—women are like that, son, but long's you let 'em know—''

Jonah's fists curled at his side. Through clenched jaws, he repeated, ''I would not like to see her mistreated.''

"Who, Carrie?'' Slapping Jonah on the back hard enough to cause him to stagger, Darther gave a snort of laughter. ''Keep her in line, that's all I'm aimin' to do. A li'l tap now'n then is all it takes.'' He grinned, revealing one gold tooth and two blackened ones, then turned toward the house.

Jonah stood his ground for a moment, willing his blood to cool. ''If I agree to race for you, there will be no more tapping. The children will be treated kindly and allowed to sleep in the barn.'' Would he, a paroled prisoner, be allowed to race? For Carrie and the boys, he must take the risk. A man could only hang once.

Darther bent over to collect the Springfield from where he had dropped it earlier. He staggered, nearly fell, and then righted himself. ''Children! Now, that's one thing you don't have to worry 'bout, there won't be no children litterin' up the place.''

''Before we go inside, I would have your word of honor,'' Jonah insisted. It was the best he could do for the moment.

This time the man's smile looked almost genuine. ''You got it, son, yessiree! We got us a gold mine, we have. We'll get us a good jockey—I know a few runts that hang around the shedrows, hoping to pick up a ride. With a good rider up on that big bay horse of yours and me managing the business end, come racing season proper, we'll be high-stepping it into ever' winner's circle between South C'lina and Princess Ann, up in Virginia, I'll lay you odds on it.''

''I will ride T'a-Kon.'' Jonah spoke softly, his voice hard as steel.

''Well, hell, boy, you're a—that is, the rules don't 'low outsiders.''

''If my horse races, I will be on his back.''

''Now, damn it all to hell and back, boy, you're making a big mistake here.''

Not by so much as a lifted brow did Jonah's expression change. ''A mistake?'' he repeated quietly.

''Well, y'see, a man your size, he'll slow a horse down, shave off considerable seconds. Might mean the difference between winning and losing.''

''If my horse races, I will ride him.'' Jonah merely

stared into the other man's red-veined eyes, his own eyes as cool as a January fog.

Darther cursed, his booming voice carrying clearly on the still, hot air. Inside the tiny cabin, Carrie dropped a spoon. Deliberately listening, she heard her husband say, "Done," and wondered what was done. What had been agreed on. Determined not to reveal how betrayed she felt—how bereft—she shaped the last biscuit, tested the heat by opening the oven door and holding her hand just inside until she felt her fingernails draw, then shoved the pan onto the shelf.

Kneeling in the narrow space behind the bed, the two boys were quiet, their eyes large and fearful. Carrie braced her shoulders and moved to stand between them and the door. When the two men appeared in the doorway, Darther glared at the empty table. "Dammit all, woman, I told you—!"

Swinging around, he caught sight of the two boys cowering behind the bed. "What in tarnation is that? What kind of swamp rats have you drug into my house, woman?"

Behind him, Jonah reminded him of their agreement. He looked first at the boys, then at Carrie, his cool regard calming in its effect.

"Who the bloody hell—" Darther roared, and then broke off, swallowed, and mumbled, "What did you do with my jug, woman?"

For a moment, no one moved. The scene reminded Jonah of one of those paper pictures he had seen down at Fort Marion in the Lieutenant's quarters. And then Carrie said tartly, "I reckon it's right where you dropped it in the yard."

"Well, dammit, go—" And then he seemed to collect himself. "You, boy—set my gun back up over the door.'' He handed the Springfield to Jonah, collapsed on the bench and glared at the two wide-eyed children kneeling behind the bed. ''What the hell are you two starin' at? You—burrhead! Go fetch me another jug!''

Carrie made a move to go, but Jonah laid a hand on her arm. Neither of them made a sound, but for once Carrie read his thoughts as if he had spoken them aloud. *Stay inside, I will go. As long as I have something he wants, you're in no danger here.*

Once the biscuits were done, the boys took their plates outside, leaving the three adults to eat at the scarred wooden table. The iron cookstove Darther had bought when Carrie ruined meal after meal in the drafty fireplace made the cramped room uncomfortably warm, but Darther insisted on dining in style.

''Give th' boy another biscuit, girl.'' He flashed a possum-like grin at Jonah, as if to say, see how well I treat my woman?

''Thank you,'' Jonah said solemnly, wishing he could explain to Carrie. Wishing he could reassure the boys. Wishing he could remove them to his own land and keep them safe.

Neatly drizzling molasses onto the split biscuit, Jonah helped himself to another slab of thick bacon while he listened to Adams boasting of the races he had won in the past, the races he would win in the future with T'a-Kon. He gestured expansively, spewing crumbs as he talked, washing his food down with whiskey.

Carrie had not uttered a word since instructing the boys to take their supper outside and wash up afterward in the horse trough. Jonah averted his eyes from her accusing face. He knew what she was thinking—that he had deserted her and gone over to the enemy. How could he explain in Adams's hearing that he had agreed to his part of the bargain only in order to achieve her protection?

"Come next week, we'll set out, you'n me and that horse o' yours. That'll give us a day or two to get 'im used to the ring. Horse don't always do his best in a new place, with a lotta strangers nosin' round." The effects of the whiskey were increasingly evident in the man's slurred speech.

"There is much still to be settled between us."

"Fifty-fifty, can't ask for fairer'n that, boy. With my handlin', we got us a gold mine."

Carrie spoke then, hesitantly. "Darther, you're not thinking of taking Jonah up to Virginia, are you?"

"Hush, woman, this is nothin' to do with you."

"Yes, but didn't Jonah tell you he can't leave the state? It says so right in the parole papers. He has to stay here until the sheriff sends for him."

Darther looked from one to the other, his red-rimmed eyes narrowing with suspicion. "You on workin' parole, boy? Hell, why'nt you say so?"

"How do you think I could afford to hire him? With all the money you left me?" Carrie let her bitterness show for one brief moment. "I thought I'd explained that Emma lent me the money, and I'm to pay her back next summer with my corn money."

"Corn money! Yer *corn money!* Haw, thassa laugh, woman." Darther turned to Jonah, knocking over the molasses pitcher in the process. Carrie righted it before it spilled. Ignoring her, Darther went on to say, "'Lusions o' grandoor, you ever heard of those, boy? Tha's what my woman's got herself a bad case of, don't you, girl? Ee-lusions o' grandoor."

Jonah heard the blood rush through his body like a hundred horses thundering across the plains. "My name," he said very carefully, "is Jonah Longshadow, not boy. Your woman's name is Carrie, not girl."

Darther waggled his head, a mannerism he had picked up recently from one of the "ladies" who frequented the tracks at Southside, in Virginia. "Well, lah-de-dah, whatever you say, b—*Mister* Longshadow. Mrs. Adams, fetch me a fresh jug, this'n's gone empty."

Somehow Jonah managed to get through the meal without strangling the man. While Darther described every racetrack, sanctioned and otherwise, in northeastern North Carolina and southeastern Virginia, Carrie quietly put away the remains of the meal, murmured something about feeding the chickens and slipped out the door. A few minutes later, Jonah saw her and the boys heading for the paddock behind the barn where Boodles and her foal were kept. Con whickered softly from just outside the fence.

"Henry, now, he's got a weakness for a good rear end and a nice set o' legs. Trouble is, he's running on dead broke. Don't matter how good a horse looks, ol' Hen can't win back his losings without a stake. Might be we could work something out there, so I could get paid back what he owes me. Hen's a right fair tout. We might want to cut him in, dependin' on how much action he can stir up."

Jonah's attention had strayed. Boodles and Con, he mused. When had he come to accept Carrie's names for his horses? What would she make of Zebat, named for the arrow mark on her face? And Saynday, a trickster who had led him a merry chase more than once. The horses had been bred in the East. They had had eastern names when he had bought them, but once they became his, they had taken on his heritage, in all but one way. Instead of mounting them on the offside, which was the way of his people and their horses, he mounted them from the left. T'a-Kon had taught him that lesson the first day.

"—so we want to go up a few days early to get the feel o' the place, but not too early. We can stay at Hen's place. He's got 'im this store a few miles over the border. Me an' Hen go way back. Got Carrie off'n him, did I tell you that? Yessiree, sweetest little deal I made in a long time."

Jonah felt his gullet tighten and burn. Henry and Carrie? Carrie and another man? By the great Taime, this Henry must have been a devil if Carrie considered Adams the better bargain.

Or perhaps she had had no say in the matter.

"M'wife says you're out on parole. Tell you what, boy, I'll make you 'nother deal. You promise me five races, my choice, and when the time comes, I'll stand up for you in court. Word of a white man goes a long way. Once you get clear o' whatever trouble you're in, we'll renego-nego-shate." For a drunk, the man had remarkable control of his tongue, but the word defeated him. He set down his half-empty jug with a thump. His eyes narrowed to slits and Jonah waited to see if he would topple off the bench.

When instead he slid into the corner and began to snore, Jonah considered dragging him across the room and tossing him onto the bed.

And then he thought of Carrie sharing the bed with such a man.

The image followed him as he stalked outside and whistled softly for T'a-Kon to come forward. The sun was a ball of fire hovering atop a distant wall of trees. Purple shadows spread across the gold-tipped sedge. So peaceful. So deceptively peaceful…

Using only a bridle, Jonah mounted up and gave the stallion his head, knowing even as he touched the responsive flanks that a man could never outrun his private demons. They rode his back, driving him until he dropped. Lifting his face to the hot summer air, he breathed in the fragrance of drying grasses, dusty hardwoods and resinous pines. The East did not smell like the West. The Red River did not smell like the nearby Currituck Sound. And while he might still dream of all he had left behind, his future was here and now. It was his to make.

Once before, he had overcome the loss of his freedom, a man's most precious possession. Through hard work, frugal living and careful planning, he'd been well on his way to building a new life in this new land when that, too had been taken from him.

Once he'd had hopes of proving his innocence and reclaiming what was rightfully his. Now even that was in doubt. He had been warned that if he left the state for any reason, his parole would be revoked. Deemed guilty of trying to escape, he could be shot on sight, or captured and hanged without a trial. In such a situation, the hottest heads often prevailed, and bullets were swifter than reason.

Yet, if he refused to go, Carrie and the boys would suffer.

She was married! The woman he had come to think of as his by some unwritten law, had a husband. When, he wondered, had she come to mean more to him than his own freedom? Was it when she had removed his irons and tended his bleeding wounds? Or the first time they had shared a water jug and a sense of satisfaction after a hard day's work? Or was it when she had looked at him on the bank of the creek that first day and seen him as a man?

Even now his flesh hardened at the thought and ruthlessly, he put it from his mind. *His Carrie was married!*

The man was a fool, his word not to be trusted, but Carrie belonged to him, not to Jonah.

What about the boys? They belonged to no one. Who would protect them?

With a touch of his heel, Jonah turned the stallion toward the newly cleared field, taking care to skirt the edges of the uneven ground. Truly, he had no choice. He would risk his freedom—perhaps even his life—and race for the man, keeping him away from this place for as long as possible. If eventually he won his freedom, he would take the boys with him, giving them a home for as long as they needed one.

As for Carrie…

In his mind, he saw her eyes, as blue as the flowers that grew along the banks of the Red River, wide with wonder at the birth of the foal. He had felt her warmth so close beside him, touched her small, capable hand, breathed in her spicy woman scent. At such a moment there had been no barriers between them.

He pictured her bending over to measure Zac's small waist for the flowered trousers she was stitching for both boys, her own thin skirt clearly revealing her woman's shape. He heard her cheerful voice singing out, ''Rise 'n' shine, everybody, come on, time's a-wasting!''

She was not Jonah's woman, but this much he could do for her. He would leave Boodles and Howard in her care, along with a paper stating that if anything happened to him, the horses belonged to her, not to Adams. Not that he put much faith in paper documents, but it was the best he could do for now. And then he would see to it that her husband stayed away as long as possible, if he had to run a hundred races.

As for the boys, he would tell them how to find his land and how to care for the other two mares. Nate was resourceful. He had rescued Zac from a burning house and managed to lead him to safety. If danger threatened, he would tell them to go with Carrie to her friend's house.

There was no lamplight showing from the windows of the cabin when he rode into the yard an hour later. Closing his mind to the two people sleeping inside, he rubbed down his stallion, watered him and gave him a measure of oats. After a brief visit with the mare and her foal, he drew a bucket of water from the horse trough, stripped off his clothes and poured it over his head. He dried himself, using his shirt, then spread the damp garment over the sweet-smelling branches of a fig tree. Taking time only to step into his denim trousers and button them up, he entered the barn, felt his way through the darkness and settled down for the night.

In the loft overhead, Zac whimpered in his sleep.

Nate stirred and muttered a few quiet words. Soon both boys were sound asleep again, while Jonah lay staring up into the darkness, thinking about the future. Trying not to think about Carrie.

The days were growing shorter as September waned. There was no question of working in the field. All but the last section had been turned, and before the ground grew hard with frost, Carrie's hand would be healed. She could manage without him. Amused and somewhat amazed, Jonah realized that he did not want her to finish alone what they had started together. He was willing to walk the white man's Plow Road, something every

Kiowa brave shunned, believing it would lead to a loss of his manhood.

Jonah was no longer quite so certain about that. He had walked the Plow Road, and his manhood was still powerful. Uncomfortably so, at times. Which was why, for the next few days, he led Adams on his borrowed buckskin as far away from Carrie as possible on the pretext of exercising T'a-Kon, putting him through his paces.

Adams would palm the stopwatch he carried on the end of a chain and time the laps. The stallion needed no practice, for running was in his blood. According to the man who had sold him to Jonah, his Arabian sire had a well-earned reputation in local racing circles. His dam had a less illustrious history, but Jonah had looked over the two-year-old and found in him a kindred spirit. He had bought the stallion and three mares from the same breeder, as the old man was ill and wanted only to see his stock in good hands before he died.

For the next few days the two men left early and stayed out late. The first day Darther had brought along a jug, but whiskey and hot sunshine didn't mix well. When he complained of an aching head and a sour belly, Jonah had handed him a jar of water and reminded him of the business ahead.

"You must tell me about these tracks. I saw horses racing in Florida, but that was some time ago."

"That a fact? Never been down to Florida, m'self, but you'n me, we might just give it a try once the reg'lar season gets underway."

"Florida is hot and wet. My horses would not thrive there."

"Horses, huh? You got more hid out besides that little mare and her colt out behind the barn?"

"Two mares. They are being kept by a friend." Being kept by the great earth spirit, Daw-k'hee.

"That mare you got at my place, she's nothing special, but I wouldn't mind buying that colt off you when he's weaned. Looks like he takes after his pappy." Darther cast an admiring glance at the big black-eared bay.

Jonah had had many horses as a youth. His main value to his people had been not as a warrior, but in his uncanny ability to track down and capture the best horses, to train them quickly and well. Some he had refused to capture, knowing they would not thrive. He would like to believe that those few still roamed free, but held out little hope. The white tide moved ever westward, trampling down all in its path. Better to remain in the East, where the trampling had been done long ago and life was no longer quite so turbulent.

The boys had snared a rabbit and skinned it. Carrie had stewed it with turnips, onions and beans, making a meal for five from one scrawny carcass, and saving a small bowlful to take to Emma.

"That crazy old woman still alive and kickin'?" Darther spat through the door, then took an ivory toothpick from his pocket.

"I assume so," Carrie replied, her lips tight.

Darther waggled his head and winked at Jonah. "She *assumes* so," he said in a mincing parody. "Word of advice, boy—don't ever take up with a woman that was raised by missionaries. No end to the fancy notions them folks crams into their empty little skulls."

Carrie's face flushed. Her eyes flew to Jonah, then fell again, and she went on scraping the dishes into the scrap pail while water heated for washing. Everything had changed the day Darther had come home.

Not that it was any wonder, for even a miserable excuse of a man like her husband had far more to offer than she did. The two of them shared an interest in horses. Darther offered him a chance to make money, and what had she done? Only brought him here in chains, treated him as if he were no more intelligent than that da—that blessed mule, and worked him from morning till night for no more than meals and a place in the barn.

In a few more days they'd be gone, which was just as well. She'd been starting to think of him as more than a hired hand, almost as a friend.

Well, not as a friend exactly—not like Emma. But certainly she no longer thought of him as a prisoner, which was what he was.

So let him go. Let him leave with Darther and turn into another drunken gambler, chasing from one nag race to the next, from cockfights to card games to dog races, wherever he could gamble away his money. Let him consort with the likes of her Uncle Henry and the men who came to his store. Let him cavort with the kind of loose women who hung around racetracks.

Oh, yes, she knew all about those. Darther had bragged to her about how sweet they smelled, and how pretty they looked in their tight corsets and their painted faces. She knew he took them to bed, and she didn't care. If it would keep him out of her bed, he could have a dozen women—a hundred women.

She could look pretty, too, if she wanted to. Which she didn't. Not for Darther. She could have painted her face and tied her hair up in rags every night. She could have begged and pleaded for a silk dress and a ruffled petticoat and even a pair of striped stockings. She knew all about fancy clothes and painted faces from the parties her uncle had held in the store whenever he'd won a race. To his credit, he had always sent her to bed in the storeroom before things got too wild, but how was a body supposed to sleep with all the whooping and hollering and carrying on?

Besides, Jonah would never think of her that way, even if she were free. So let him go, she'd had the use of him when it mattered most. And she still had Nate and Zac. Her hand was finally healing, and with Darther gone, she could easily get the rest of the field turned before the first frost. The boys could help.

Meanwhile she could take them to Emma's and introduce them, so that if they ever needed it, they would have a place to go and someone to look after them.

The next morning while Darther snored on the rumpled bed in the corner, Carrie folded up the pallet she'd made for herself on the floor, set a pan of cornmeal mush, a kettle of water and a flat iron on the hot stove. There would be no more working in the field until Darther left for the track again. She didn't even want to think about the fact that Jonah would be leaving with him.

Didn't want to think about how much he had come to mean to her in a few short weeks. She was a married woman. No married woman, no matter how miserable her marriage turned out to be, had any business thinking about another man the way she had come to think of Jonah. He was a stranger, a prisoner—half Indian, at that. Her parents had been killed by Indians.

Her hands grew still for a moment, and she gazed out through the open front door. Wearing the familiar snug jeans-cloth trousers that showed off his manhood in a way that would have been shameless in any other man, he was out beside the barn instructing the boys on how to care for Boodle and Howard. Telling them what to watch for, what to do in case of colic or scours. Between Darther's sodden snores, she could hear the voices quite clearly. Zac's high-pitched, little-boy excitement. Nate's slower, deeper voice. Nate always sounded slightly worried.

And Jonah. Carrie bit her lip, remembering the early days, when she'd addressed him as if he had no more understanding than a fence post, applauding when he'd managed to repeat a simple word like *plow,* or *rain.* It was a wonder he hadn't drowned her in the horse trough. For a man who was far more intelligent than he cared to let on, she'd have thought he would know better than to go off with a drunken gambler.

But there he was, fixing to run off to Virginia and risk his freedom, maybe even his very life, leaving behind two little boys who thought the sun rose from his shoulders.

Damn and blast the man.

She shook out a carefully mended sheet, folded it and crammed it any-old-way into the box she kept under the bed. Damn and blast him all to hell and back, if he fell off that damned black-eared horse and broke his neck, he needn't think he could come crying to her to patch him up with turpentine and sugar! She'd got along just fine without him before she'd hurt her blasted hand— she would get along fine after he left. She still had Emma, and now she had the boys. What more could any woman possibly need?

As heat from the small woodstove reached across the room, Darther muttered in his sleep and flopped over onto his belly. His hair was standing on end, making him look like a disgruntled hedgehog. A stubble of beard darkened his sweating cheeks, and Carrie held her hand over the spout to see if the water was hot enough for shaving. The wretched man never failed to come home reeling and reeking of whiskey and cheap cologne. And only too glad to be rid of him, she never failed to send him off freshly bathed and shaved, wearing clean linens and smelling of her best bayberry soap. It was another of those "do unto others" things that helped ease her conscience for despising the man she had married.

Thank goodness he had something to do and somewhere to go, else she'd be toting and fetching and dodging fists until one or the other of them went too far. "Darther, are you awake? I'll have the last of your shirts done up by the time you're ready to leave." If she could perform a miracle and scrub out a month's worth of stains.

She had heard him telling Jonah that the next race meet was scheduled for the end of the following week. Race meet, she thought in disgust. As if a flock of moth-eaten nags chasing one another around a makeshift track bore any resemblance to the fancy races she'd seen pictured in the newspapers her uncle saved as if they were holy writ.

Her uncle had been every bit as bad as Darther. Store-keeping took second place to his gambling interests. Carrie had known him to bet on the sum total of the bets that would be placed on a certain day. As usual, he'd lost his shirt.

"Darther, wake up, someone's coming," she said, glancing up from her task.

Her husband stirred, rolled over and mumbled into the pillow.

"Maybe it's Liam," she said, not wanting to have to deal with the weasel-faced rider who disliked her as much as she disliked him.

Worse, it might be a stranger, someone her husband owed money to. It wouldn't be the first time one of his debtors had come here, nosing around for anything they could claim to settle the debt. She didn't dare take the rifle down, not with Darther home, but surely with Jonah and the boys out by the barn, she'd be safe. A woman living alone in an isolated place couldn't afford to take chances.

Warily, she stepped outside and shaded her eyes. The rider, a half-grown boy who didn't look particularly dangerous, rode right up to the front steps. Without removing his battered felt hat, he said, "Pardon me, ma'am, you got a prisoner in your keepin'?"

Chapter Eight

The three men set out together, the sheriff's young deputy, Noah, Darther on the poor, overburdened buckskin, and Jonah, more beautiful than any man had a right to be, up on that handsome stallion of his. She hadn't had time to finish ironing Darther's shirts and packing his saddlebags, for the boy had said the judge was waiting for Jonah back at the courthouse. The best she'd been able to do was pack enough food and water for the journey, which Darther insisted on making to protect his newfound gold mine.

Carrie couldn't decide if the young deputy was more impressed or concerned when Jonah, unhampered by either leg irons or a lead rope, mounted the powerful bay stallion. He touched the holstered gun at his side uncertainly, glanced from one man to the other, and said, "I reckon we'd better get moving. Judge Powers, he don't like to wait."

Jonah looked at Noah. Noah looked back. Neither man spoke, but Carrie had a feeling they knew each other.

"We'll be back for supper," Darther called back confidently as they rode off. "Kill one o' them hens o' yours."

With only five dependable layers left, she wasn't about to kill one of them just to fill her husband's belly. As long as Darther insisted on spending every penny he won on whiskey and fancy clothes instead of bringing it home to his wife, he could eat beans and bacon and grits and greens along with everyone else.

"When's Jonah comin' back?" Zac whined. The two boys sidled up to watch the three men ride off. Carrie wrapped an arm around the sturdy little body and drew him close, more for her own comfort than for his.

"Hush up, he ain't comin' back," Nate whispered fiercely.

"Is, too! He said so."

"Ain't, neither. Don't nobody never come back once they's gone."

"Boys, today we're going to hitch up Sorry and go for a visit, what do you say to that?" It was all Carrie could do to keep from crying her heart out. Jonah had left without telling her goodbye. Without so much as a word, a smile or a single look, he had ridden off with that damned—that dad-blasted deputy, a boy who didn't look smart enough to lace his own boots.

She needed Emma. Needed a woman who could understand how she was feeling without her having to explain. And without making her feel guilty. Carrie knew in her heart that what she felt was not only wrong, it was sinful. What she needed to know was how long she would go on hurting. How long would her sleep be disturbed by dreams that made her blush with shame come morning?

Nate backed Sorry up to the cart and fastened the traces. He was remarkably good with animals. Zac shooed the chickens back in the pen and shut the gate in case a fox came sniffing around. Less than an hour after the three men had ridden off, Carrie and the boys were bumping along the narrow, rutted road. Carrie hummed a few bars of "Oh! Susanna!" But her heart wasn't in it.

"You mad at sumpin', Miss Carrie?" Zac asked after a while.

"No, honey, I'm not mad, I'm just—"

"She sad," Nate said with the insight of his superior age. "Her old man done left, so hush up and take your thumb out o' your mouf, baby."

Zac's grimy thumb popped out with an audible sound. "I'm not no baby."

"Are, too."

"Am not, am I Miss Carrie?"

Carrie sighed and tried to think of a way to take the boys' minds off Jonah's absence. He'd given them every reason to believe in him—he'd even brought his horses there and let them help Howard get born. Then, at the very first promise of something more exciting, he'd ridden off without so much as a backward glance.

Darther had said, "Come race for me, boy, and I'll put in a word with the judge. Come race for me, and we'll both be rolling in riches."

Damned blasted horse racing. Even Darther might once have been a decent man before gambling had eaten into his very soul. And now he'd gone and infected Jonah with the same fever. Not once since he had agreed to go along with Darther's plans had he teased her with that twinkling, gray-eyed smile. He hadn't said a word about the section of cornfield yet to be turned, nor the shed roof he'd been repairing so that Boodles and Howard would have shelter in case it ever rained again.

Let him go. Good riddance. She would mend the damned shed herself, with the boys to help her hold the posts steady while she nailed the rafters in place. She could steer a plow as well as any man once she had the full use of her hand, which would be most any day now.

But he hadn't gone off to the race, she reminded herself, sick with worry. He'd been summoned by the judge. She would almost rather he'd gone off to the races instead of back to face a judge and jury.

"Today's a holiday," she said brightly. "Everyone needs a day off now and then, but come tomorrow, we'll have to get on with the work. Nate—Zac, I'm counting on you." She managed a smile, but it was a bit damp. Her blasted nose was stopping up—damned goldenrod always made her eyes water!

"Las' time we had us a holiday, you done the washin' and Jonah carped. Didn't nobody do no playin' 'ceptin' Zac and me."

Snapping the reins over Sorry's backside, Carrie said brightly, "Emma used to have children. I wouldn't be at all surprised if they'd left behind a toy. Maybe a jumping rope, or a storybook." She tried to infuse her voice with enthusiasm, but it was a doleful trio that pulled up into the widow's front yard later that morning.

The first thing Carrie noticed was that Emma moved slower than ever, as if she ached in every bone. The old woman admitted to having good days and better days— never bad days. Carrie would like to think it meant rain was finally coming, but she'd do without rain if it meant her friend could do without pain.

Even living alone in the cabin that was hardly bigger than her old parlor had been in the house where she and her husband had raised a family, Emma dressed each day in one of her faded silk gowns, a lace-edged collar pinned on with a small gold bar. Her thin white hair, as always, was neatly braided and pinned up on top of her head with half a dozen tortoiseshell pins. On her misshapen feet were a pair of crocheted slippers, as she was no longer able to fit into her shoes.

Carrie felt a rush of guilt for having borrowed money that might have been better spent. One of these days, she vowed silently, she would make it up to her. Repay her for all the times she had come crying through the woods, a young bride totally unprepared for the role.

Emma found a sack of marbles, and after they all exclaimed over each one as if it were a precious gem, the two boys raced outside to draw a circle in the neatly raked dirt, leaving the women to drag two rockers onto the tiny front porch.

As they shelled speckled beans and dried field peas from a basket on the floor between them, Carrie told her about the boys, and how good Jonah was with them. About the way she had come to trust him; how he did all the small tasks she had never managed to get around to doing, and how he had delivered Boodle's foal.

The older woman watched her face as she talked, seeing the way her eyes glowed, the way her hands would fall idle as she described the young man's way with animals and small boys.

And with young women, too, she thought, seeing more heartache ahead for her young friend.

"Oh, Emma, you should see the way he makes the boys laugh. I don't think they'd done much laughing before they came to us, but you ought to hear them now. Not that they don't still squabble, but Jonah says all little boys do that."

Jonah says, Emma thought sadly. Before they came

to us? Did the poor child have any notion what was happening to her?

"And now he's gone, and he probably won't come back. I mean, even if the sheriff doesn't lock him up again, he'll likely get in with those racetrack men and that'll be the end of that. He never really liked farming anyway, you know." Carrie's rocker thumped over the uneven porch floor as if she were trying to outrun her thoughts. "But don't you worry, I'll still be able to get my crop in come spring," she declared. "I'm over the hump now. I can turn the last few rows myself." She flexed her hand, demonstrating how much better it was. "Once the frost kills all the bad seeds and grubs, I'll be all ready to hill and plant my corn. I remember everything you told me about how to do it."

But Emma knew what was worrying her young friend, and it wasn't her cornfield. "I'm sorry the way things turned out for you, honey. I reckon he touched your heart same as he did those young'uns out there, but hearts mend. Scars last a while, just like memories, but after awhile they don't hurt more than a body can bear."

Carrie had never actually stated her feelings toward Jonah, but no matter what was said, Emma always seemed to understand what was left unsaid. Which was why Carrie had needed to visit today. She was so full of feelings she couldn't understand and didn't know how to deal with, that she had to let it out or, with all the misery trapped inside her, she would burst right wide open.

They had first met when Carrie had gone to the market at Shingle Landing to buy seeds for her first kitchen garden. In a generous mood, Darther had given her three dollars before he and Liam had left for the Warrenton racetrack. It was Emma who had told her which vegetables would thrive and which took more care than they were worth. She'd warned her about the deer and rabbits just waiting to devour every sprout as soon as it popped from the ground.

Since then, the two women had come to be great friends, despite the half-century difference in their ages. Both had lost their entire families. Both had managed to survive. Hardship, Emma had told her once without a speck of self-pity, was a way of life for a woman. The only way to get through it was to make the most of each small victory and look forward to the next. If the cake didn't fall, it was a victory. If a hen laid a double-yolk egg, that was a victory. Once a body reached a certain age, each new day was a victory, rain or shine.

And Emma, in her small, drafty cabin, with a few pieces of beautiful furniture mixed in with the crudely built benches and tables; with a few exquisite china cups to go with the thick ugly white plates, had chosen to look forward. Carrie could do no less.

While the children played outside under an ancient cedar tree, Emma and Carrie sat on the front porch, rocking, shelling dried field peas and talking now and then. "Emma, what if Darther can't get him off? D'you think they'll just—" She couldn't say it, couldn't bring herself to think about it, yet she could hardly think of anything else. "He left his mare and foal and told the boys how to look after them. Does that mean—?"

"No sense in borrowing trouble, honey." The old woman set the slat-back rocker into motion again as her knotted fingers deftly worked over the dried peas in her lap. Sun glinted on the tiny gold pin at her throat. "That's what my Luther always said whenever I went to fretting."

Carrie's fingers traced a neat mend on the skirt of her

visiting dress, which was only slightly better than her everyday dresses. Among the many sins she had been warned against as a child were covetousness and vanity. She could still remember coveting her best friend's new ruffled pinafore, and she'd been barely five years old at the time. She'd spent half a day alone in a pitch dark cellar for that, and another half day after being caught admiring her reflection in a pond a few days later. Evidently, she'd been slow in learning the lesson of humility, for she'd been sent to the cellar again hardly a week later when she'd had her head shaved to rid her scalp of lice, and refused to go to church until it had all grown back.

And then, of course, she'd been lectured on the evils of disobedience.

Another life, she thought, watching as Nate and Zac put away the marbles and went to poking for doodle bugs. How many lives did that make? How many had she already used up? One life before the raid—another one after the raid, waiting in vain to be adopted. After that had come her life with old Mrs. Robinson, where she had learned her times tables and memorized hundreds of Bible verses, and been punished for reading secular stories on the Sabbath. Her next life had taken a drastic turn when she'd been sent east to live with Uncle Henry.

And now there was life with Darther Adams. How many lives was one woman allowed? As many as a cat?

Oh, Lord, now she'd be punished for the sin of heresy. She was already in trouble for lusting after a man not her husband, and she didn't even rightly know what constituted lusting.

She had a pretty good idea, though, that it had to do with the way he made her feel with the touch of his hand. Or the way she felt watching him walk behind the plow, so surefooted on the uneven ground, the sunlight glinting off the sweat on his bronzed forearms. Or the way he would sometimes catch her staring at him and smile at her, slowly—not even really a smile, but a sort of…warming of the eyes.

She cleared her throat and applied herself to the crisp, dried bean pods. "Leaving his horses behind like that— I reckon that means he plans to come back for them, but what if he can't? Emma, what if they decide to hang him? I know in my heart he didn't steal anything, but even if he did, it was a mistake."

Emma chuckled. The unexpected sound of her laughter made the boys glance up from the tiny holes they were probing with spittle on the end of a straw. Somewhere nearby, a mockingbird tuned up. Grasshoppers rasped, and a dog barked in the distance. As the late afternoon sun slanted down through the trees, Carrie felt a sudden urge to gather it all—Emma and the two boys, the laughter and the quiet sounds of Indian summer—to hold it all and absorb the sweetness, the security of this one single moment.

Make the most of each small victory and go forward from there.

The moment passed when the familiar chorus of "Did not,", "Did, too," tuned up again.

"I reckon we'd better head back," Carrie said reluctantly, standing and gathering up her share of the dried peas, dumping them into a graniteware basin. "Come on, boys, time to go home."

"Do we hafta go? I nearly 'bout got me a doodle bug," Zac whined.

"Git up, baby, them hosses needs us," Nate growled, and dusted off his pink-palmed hands.

"Come back next week and I'll see if I can't find some more play-pretties," Emma promised. To Carrie she said, "Luther was always making the boys whistles and slingshots—might still be one or two around here somewhere."

Carrie watched as the old woman made her way slowly down the two wooden steps, a cane gripped in one twisted hand. Once Emma had been as young as Carrie, full of hopes and dreams. She'd been known from the Pasquotank River to Currituck Sound for her beauty and her temper, she'd confided one day after sharing a few glasses of blackberry wine.

But that was before her house had been burned by marauding Yankees. Before she had lost her husband to the war. Before the fever of '78 had taken her last living child. Now she lived here alone on a few acres, selling cures to those who could afford them, giving to those who couldn't.

Last summer her mule had died, and several men whose families had benefited from her skills had showed up to bury the animal. They brought her meat occasionally, and Carrie herself shared whatever she could trap or grow. Somehow or another, the old woman managed to survive with grace and humor, looking forward to each change of season as if it were a splendid show just for her benefit.

Carrie only hoped she could manage to live her own life with half as much dignity.

Nate brought Sorry in from the broom sedge field and hitched him to the cart. In many ways, the boy was a lot like Jonah. He would miss him almost as much as Carrie would. Zac was young—he would eventually forget, but Carrie had a feeling Nate forgot very little.

"Is she a ol' witch?" Zac asked after they'd ridden some distance in silence.

"Miss Emma? No, you dum' baby, she a wise woman. My granny was a wise woman, she knowed everything they was to know 'bout bringin' babies and drivin' out devils. Didn't you see all them bushes hangin' down from the rafters? Same bushes my granny done hung up to dry. Some you burn and breathe in the smoke, some you b'ile and drink, some you mix up with bear grease and rub on you head or belly, 'pendin' on where the devils be at. I know all 'bout that kind of stuff."

"You don't, neither."

"Do, too."

"Do not."

Carrie sighed. Sorry plodded along, coming to a dead halt now and then to clear away the flies with a sweep of his tail or to sample a patch of weeds before moving on again. Poor beast couldn't seem to manage two things at once. Carrie didn't bother to curse or threaten him with the whip. The house would be waiting when they got there…empty. Suddenly it seemed as if even the sun had grown dimmer.

Darther and Jonah found themselves herded into a cramped and airless room with half a dozen men, none of whom seemed eager to dismiss the charges against a half-breed who came from a reservation out in the Western Territory by way of a prison in St. Augustine, Florida.

After an initial discussion, one of the men addressed the prisoner. "You wanna tell us again how you come to settle here, boy?"

Jonah felt the tension gathering at the base of his neck.

Darther had yet to say a word on his behalf, but at least the man was reasonably sober. Schooling himself not to react to the open contempt in the stranger's voice, he repeated the story he had told countless times, while the sheriff stood silently by, hoping, no doubt, to catch him in a lie.

"My ship went aground near a place called Pea Island. I was rescued, fed and given dry clothes. Later I was taken by boat to a place called Manteo, where I heard of land further inland that could be bought. I bought it."

"You bought it," repeated the judge, who had spoken little so far in the hearing. "Just like that, you decided to buy land in a place you'd never even seen and put down roots. Using what? The money you were accused of stealing from your shipmates?"

"A man tires quickly of swallowing saltwater. I have no family. The land here is good, better than much I have seen. The money I earned from four years of sailing had been collected by Lieutenant Pratt of Fort Marion directly from the shipping line, and deposited in my name in a bank. I used that money to buy land and stock." It was all he could do to force the words out. The process had not been so simple, nor had it happened quickly. But it had happened. The land had still been available when Pratt's letter containing his good wishes and a bank draft had arrived, and Jonah had bought it. Why did these men find that so hard to believe?

The hearing had been going on for hours. Jonah had produced his papers, which had been passed around to everyone in the room, whether or not they could read. Some, he suspected, could not.

"An' them papers, you say they're supposed to prove you're not lying through your heathen teeth?" put in an armed man with a sagging belly, earning himself a look of disapproval from the judge.

His heathen teeth? The man was even more ignorant than he appeared.

In the end, it was Darther who tipped the scales in his favor. Somewhat flushed, but steady on his feet, he stepped forward. "Well now, speaking as a landowner, I can tell you that this feller, Longshadow, is a hard worker who never once, to my knowledge, lied, stole, or mistreated livestock, women or children," he pronounced pompously. "The boy works for me 'n' my wife. Done a right fair job of it, too, clearing my fields, gen'lly looking after the place while I was away on other business."

There was a guffaw or two, obviously from men who knew Adams either personally or by reputation. Then, in a deft exchange, folding money changed hands among a few of the men. The armed man grinned, patted his pocket and spat on the floor. The youthful deputy, Noah, blushed and pocketed a few coins. The circuit judge, a quiet man, well-dressed man, sighed and glanced out the window, as if he preferred not to witness what was happening. Jonah had no way of knowing if the man was convinced of his innocence or not. It wasn't the first time he had seen bribery. The captains who sailed for Royalty Freight hauled tonnage that was never listed on the manifests, much of the excess cargo hastily and improperly secured. That and the fact that certain inspectors were paid off, certain repairs left undone, was responsible in large part for the loss of three ships. Pratt had later learned that the ships had all been heavily insured.

Outside the courtroom, Jonah thought only of leaving as quickly as possible. He had no fond memories of this place. Darther had other ideas. "Thought long's we're this close, we might as well head on up to the track and look around. Maybe have us a drink or two, pick up a game of cards. How're you with the pasteboards, boy? Ever played poker?"

"I will ride for you in three races when the time comes. You have my word."

"Well now, it seems to me, seein's how I just paid for your freedom, so t' speak, I got a right to expect better'n that. What if I was to get me another rider?"

"Three races. If T'a-Kon runs, I ride."

"Six."

"Three."

"Five, and that's my final offer," Darther pronounced, grinning as if the outcome had never been in doubt. "Five races, my choice, with you up, wearing my colors."

"Four, wearing no man's colors. Those are my terms." Breathing deeply of the air of freedom, Jonah told himself he should be more grateful, but the thought of racing for this man—of having anything more to do with him, made his flesh crawl. He was finally free to collect Sa-bodle-te and her foal and return with them to his own land, not because his story had been believed, but because this man had literally bought his freedom.

But he had given his word, and he was an honorable man. "Those are my terms," he repeated, crossing his arms over his chest as they stood under a late afternoon sun outside the courthouse.

"We'll settle it later. I can see you're wantin' to get back. I noticed the way you were looking my wife over. Carrie, she's a good girl, I'll say that for her. Aggravating as flies in 'shine, with all her highfalutin notions, but she's not too bad to look at. Now, if you two was to want to get together, I reckon I could take a jug up to the hayloft.'' He shrugged his plump shoulders, and it was all Jonah could do not to wrap his hands around that fat throat until the man sagged under his own weight. '''Course, we might have to re-negotiate our deal if that's the case. Say, a full season's racing, then we might see how that foal o' yours shapes up.''

Taime, lend me strength. Big Bow, Fast Bear, Stumbling Bear, lend me your courage and wisdom so that I may not gut this man and leave his entrails for the buzzards to pick over.

By the time the moon rose over the treetops, Nate and Zac, exhausted from toting water up from the creek and helping with the evening chores, had gobbled down plates full of beans, greens and cornbread and gone to sleep in the loft. Carrie had invited them to sleep inside the house, but they had insisted on returning to the barn.

Missing Jonah.

Carrie refused to admit that all the warmth and brightness had gone out of her own heart. Darther had said they'd be back by suppertime, but suppertime had come and gone. Even if he'd managed to get Jonah off, the two of them might be celebrating. Either that or Jonah had returned to his own land. Sooner or later he would come for Boodles and Howard, but if he was a free man, there would no longer be a reason for him to stay.

Which was good. She rejoiced for him, truly she did. She would do as Emma said and make the most of each small victory. She still had Zac and Nate. And a cornfield all cleared and layed off.

And a husband. A husband she would tolerate because she had no choice if she wanted to make a home for her boys. Once after he'd beaten her badly, she had considered asking Emma to take her in, but Darther would just come after her there and make a mess of Emma's life as well as her own.

Standing on the front steps, Carrie wrapped her arms around her for warmth. September was almost over. Summer's end. Somehow, it seemed as if far more than summer had come to an end. In the distance, a dog barked. For a moment she thought she heard riders turning in off the road, but as the sound was followed almost immediately by a rumble of distant thunder, she forgot about everything but the possibility of rain.

Chapter Nine

The rain came just as Darther and Jonah rode into the yard. Darther slid off his horse—he was still riding Henry's buckskin—and hurried inside, leaving Jonah to see to both mounts. "Get me a dry shirt, woman."

They're here! Jonah's back!

Unable to hide her jubilation, Carrie turned away and took a clean shirt from the basket in the corner. "Did Jonah came back for his horses?" He wouldn't stay long, at any rate. No more sharing suppers out by the barn, watching the stars come out one by one while the boys jumped and skipped and threw acorns at a line scratched in the dirt.

Rain pounded down on the shake roof and blew in through the open windows. She wanted to run outside, lift her arms to the skies and shout in pure joy. And not entirely because of the rain.

Struggling out of his wet clothing, Darther scowled at her. "You get rid of those young'uns yet?"

"I can't just send them away." She was all prepared to defend her stand when surprisingly, he allowed the matter to drop.

"Got a jug in the house?"

"Only the one you left behind."

"Well, fetch it, woman, don't just stand there with your mouth hanging open!" Lurching toward the door, he shouted into the darkness. "Jonah! C'mon inside where it's dry, boy, we got us some celebrating to do!"

The evening went downhill from there. Jonah appeared in the doorway, but Carrie could tell by the way he hesitated that he was reluctant to enter. He looked from one of them to the other like a buck deer sampling the air, ready to flee at the first sign of danger.

"Come inside and shut the door, boy. For God's sake, girl, shut the windows! Come on, boy, set and have yourself a drink. You Injuns don't have no problem with whiskey, do you?" He laughed uproariously, and Carrie, closing the windows against the blowing rain, cringed in embarrassment.

Jonah shut the door and moved inside, and Carrie was reminded of the wild pup she had tried to adopt, the one that had lapped up her milk and eggs, messed on her floor and then nearly knocked her off her feet making his escape. Some creatures were never meant for captivity.

While the two men talked horses, with Darther doing most of the talking, Carrie threw a shawl over her head and dashed outside to check on the boys and fetch Darther another jug. The sooner he drank himself insensible, the better off they would all be.

Jonah had watered both horses and led Con into Peck's old stall. She hoped he had Darther's permission, because both the buckskin and the big bay were nose-deep in Peck's fancy oats. Trust Jonah to see to their welfare. She had no doubt he had checked on Boodles and her foal, as well.

From the loft, she could hear excited whispers. "He's faster 'n any racehorse in the whole wide world."

"You ain't never even seen a real racehorse."

"Have, too!"

"Have not!"

Carrie lit a lantern and carried it up to the loft. "Boys, settle down. You've had your supper, now you'd best get to sleep. Jonah's counting on you to help him with the horses tomorrow." She didn't know what Jonah was counting on, but it seemed the most likely inducement.

"Is he gonna stay?" Zac asked as she headed for the corner where her husband stored his supply of Buffalo City moonshine.

"'Course he ain't gonna stay, dummy! Him an' Con's gonna win ever' race 'tween here an' South'ard Downs, and then they's gonna come back an' build a great big house, bigger'n ol' man Litkin's, and we kin all go live there and look after Howard an' Boodles and Con an' all them other hosses he gonna buy when he gits rich."

Carrie's jaw dropped in amazement. "Is that what Jonah told you, Nate?"

"No'm, he ain't tol' me nothin' but to rub the buckskin down real good an' give 'im some oats when he settles. I done it. He ain't much of a runner, is he?"

"Uncle Henry's buckskin? I wouldn't know about that. Pull that spread over you, boys, and watch out for leaks in the roof." The words were punctuated by a big fat drop landing on her left cheek, which made the boys flop back and howl with laughter. Carrie escaped, her rump easing past the rungs one by one as she lowered herself carefully down the sloping ladder face out, carrying the lantern in one hand, the heavy jug in the other.

Darther and his damned whiskey. She was tempted to pour the stuff down his gullet herself, else he was apt to take a notion, with it raining cats and dogs, to have himself a chicken dinner. It wouldn't be the first time she'd had to go out and kill one of her precious layers in the middle of the night, and then had the fool pass out before she could get the poor bird plucked, singed and drawn.

Once inside the house, Carrie dried off as best she could. There was no privacy in a cabin no bigger than twelve feet square. She couldn't even pull the curtain across one corner, for Darther claimed it shut off all the air.

What it shut off was the sight of the man she had married so hopefully three years earlier, his face now bloated, his mouth slack, his little pig eyes glittering with malice. At least, where she was concerned, it was malice. But when he went to rambling on and on about all the races Jonah and Con were going to win for him, it was pure greed.

She fried bacon and set out cold beans and cornbread in case Jonah was hungry, then tried to ignore both men as she sat on a stool and threaded her needle. It was too dark to do any mending, but she still had the last of her green beans to string together. Leather britches, they were called, and leathery they were, hung up to dry in their shells, but she couldn't afford to waste food. Between the rabbits and the deer, she had to fight for everything in her garden, and a body craved something green in the dead of winter.

"C'mon, boy, a man don't like to drink alone. We got us some celebratin' to do! Hellfire, I saved you from doin' the rope dance, least you could do is drink to your good luck."

Arms crossed over his chest, Jonah quietly declined. He had made his bargain. He would uphold it, but nothing in those terms required him to drink with the man.

''You got somethin' against whiskey, boy?''

Jonah was tempted to tell him that he had seen at first hand what whiskey could do to turn men into animals, to rob them of their wits, their ambition, their judgment. It would do no good, and so he said only that he was more hungry than thirsty.

Carrie hurried to refill the molasses pitcher and set it on the table. When her arm brushed against his shoulder, he heard her gasp. The look she sent him could only be described as stricken.

Sprawled on the low-backed bench, his feet propped on the hearth, Darther smirked and waggled his head. ''Well now, tha's another thing, boy. When yer candle's lit, too much to drink can put out the fire. If you won't drink a man's whiskey, maybe you'll settle for beddin' his woman. Tha's real hoppis—hospi—'' He made several attempts at the word *hospitality* then gave it up. ''Carrie, you be nice to this ol' boy, y'hear? He's gonna make us all rich, ain't you, boy?''

Furious on Carrie's behalf, Jonah barely restrained himself from knocking the miserable excuse for a man right through the cabin wall. Instead, he turned away and applied himself to the cold supper. He ate slowly, methodically, careful not to look at either Carrie or her husband.

Unfortunately, the man was right. From the first time he had laid eyes on her outside the jailhouse, the woman had set his blood to boiling. With her pale hair and her pale skin, and the inbred arrogance of her race, she had paid two dollars for his release, and then tied him to her cart as if he were no better than a mangy dog, leaving him to follow as best he could with his shackled legs. Being jailed on false charges had been bad enough. Being sold to the woman for less than the price of a gallon of whiskey had been the final insult. He had seethed with anger and resentment, wanting to strike out at the injustice of it all. When had that begun to change?

When she had drawn a line in the dirt around her house and forbade him to cross it? When she had wrinkled her nose at the stench of his body? After twelve days in a cramped jailhouse with few amenities and barely enough water to drink, much less to wash in, he had offended his own senses. Had it been when she had knelt at his feet and gazed with horror at his raw and bleeding flesh? Or that first night, when she had brought him a blanket and a plate of food?

Or the next morning when he had stood before her in the creek and shed his clothing?

Even then he had tried to picture her without that shapeless gown she wore, her small body even more pale than her face. Was her woman's hair golden, too, like the thick, cropped hair on her head? He had lain with a golden-haired whore in Barbados once, and been disappointed to discover that the thicket between her thighs had been as dark as his own.

As for Carrie Adams, he would never know. The woman still warmed his blood, but not with anger. Not always even with lust. Anger would have been safer and far easier to bear than lust, but over some matters, a man had no choice. Perhaps when he was an old, old man, no longer led around by his man-part, he would forget her.

Perhaps…

Darther continued to drink. Behind him, Jonah could hear the repeated gurgle, followed by the thump of the jug hitting the floor. He was determined not to leave until the man had drunk himself unconscious, knowing that short of that condition, the least thing might set him off, and he would strike out at the nearest target. And that target would be Carrie.

Sometime after midnight, the rain ended as quickly as it had begun. The sky cleared rapidly, leaving the air cool and redolent with the spicy fragrance of wood smoke and autumn leaves. Moonlight reflected from the overflowing horse trough, from dozens of small puddles in the yard. Each time Jonah tried to leave, Darther would rouse and command him to sit down, to have a drink, to help himself to some supper...or anything else he might want.

And each time, Jonah burned with rage, and with shame for the woman who shared his vigil. He was tempted to knock the man out and be done with it, to take his own horses and leave, but he knew very well who would bear the blame.

Together they waited. Neither of them spoke for a long while. Darther, staring morosely at the rifle over the door, steadily drained his jug. He had an incredible tolerance. A normal man would be dead to the world long before now.

"I put Con in the good stall," he said quietly, and Carrie nodded.

Just as quietly, she said, "I hope you know that the boys expect you to win every race from now on, and build a castle with your winnings and take them to live with you like little princes." She smiled tiredly, the marks of strain showing clearly on her face.

Ignoring the remark, ignoring the temptation to smooth away the lines of worry on her brow, he asked softly, "Why do you stay?"

They were seated at the table. Her gaze shifted past him to the man on the bench in the corner. He wasn't out yet, but he was probably past hearing. Past understanding what was said, at least. "Because I have nowhere else to go."

"What about your friend?"

"Emma? Her house is hardly bigger than mine. Besides, it's too close. He'd come after me, and Emma would suffer, too." She smiled again, as if it was of no import. Jonah told himself she was either the bravest or the most stupid woman he had ever encountered.

"There's the boys, too, don't forget—unless you really are going to build them a castle so they can live like princes?"

He shook his head, smiling gently. "You know how I feel about living inside four walls."

"I know you'd rather sleep outside."

"A roof is good. Walls are too much like a prison." His hand was on the table, one finger toying with the handle of his three-tined fork.

Her hand lay close by. She had removed the bandage, and daringly, he reached out and traced the jagged red scar that twisted across the base of her thumb. Unlike the hands of the women of his tribe, whose skin remained supple from the fat of the hides they scraped, Carrie's hands were dry and callused. Still touching her fingers, he met her gaze and wondered what she had thought when her husband had suggested she sleep with him. Had she been insulted by his seeming lack of interest?

He wanted to tell her that he had refused because he had wanted it too much, but never under those circumstances. He wanted to tell her how many times she had invaded his dreams, how many times he'd been tempted to ignore every grain of intelligence he possessed and take her in his arms. If she ever came to him, it must be her own choice. If she ever came to him freely—if ever he touched her, held her and kissed her—the decisions that affected his future would no longer be his own. And together they had no future. She must know that as well as he did.

Or perhaps she had been insulted at the thought of lying with a half-breed, a man not her husband.

Abruptly, he dropped her hand, and she buried it in her lap. "I'd better open up the house now that the rain's stopped," she said too quickly, and he rose, too, and began opening the four windows. Suddenly, he needed action, needed to race the wind, to outrun the demons that had invaded his mind, seeding it with notions that had no part in his future.

With a cool, fresh breeze blowing through the cabin, they turned and faced each other across the drunken man sprawled across the bench, his head tipped back at an awkward angle. His mouth gaped open. A loud snore broke the stillness. Carrie sighed with relief. With any luck, he should sleep for at least twelve hours.

The distance between the bench where he lay and the bed was no more than a few feet, but Darther was heavy, a dead weight. Stepping in front of her, Jonah leaned down and pulled the man's arm across his shoulder. Then he stood, turned, and in a deft maneuver, dropped his burden onto the feather mattress.

Bracing herself to touch him, Carrie unfastened his suspenders while Jonah tugged off his boots. Carrie unbuttoned his collar and cuffs, and carefully removed his watch and chain and laid them on the shelf beside the bed. Then, after covering him with a spread, she drew the curtain and turned to Jonah.

"Thank you," she whispered. "I know why you stayed, because you were afraid he'd turn ugly, but I can handle him when he's this way. If I'm watchful, I can usually move faster than he can, even when he's sober.''

Her eyes were shadowed, her smile slow in coming, but the warmth of it made him want to sweep her up before him and ride with her somewhere far away, where they could forget such men existed. *Fool,* he thought. *Taime has traded you your life for your wits.*

"Tell your man when he awakens that I will return in time for the race. I gave my word.''

"You're leaving?'' She looked so stricken he had to fight against the urge to hold her, to offer her what small comfort he could provide, which was far too little.

"Send Nate and Zac to your friend. Surely she can find room for them for a few days. When I return for your man, you can bring them back.''

Carrie nodded, knowing the wisdom of his advice. Darther would be in no mood to put up with a pair of noisy little boys when he woke up tomorrow. A whisper could set him off. Only after he was gone would she dare bring them back. Meanwhile, Emma could use their help with the chores.

Helpless to hide the feelings that swelled inside her head and her heart, Carrie told him she would do as he suggested. In a silence broken only by the dripping eaves, they stared at each other, their eyes speaking words neither of them dared to voice. Then Jonah turned away and Carrie closed the door behind him and leaned back against it, fighting tears and a growing sense of hopelessness.

Forcing herself to make plans for tomorrow and the next day, and the day after that, she unrolled a worn quilt that she had made into a pallet and spread it on the floor. Darther would sleep until noon, at the very least. The mattress would be soaked with his sweat and worse, which meant she would have to drag it outside and scrub the ticking, then raid her feather barrel to replace the ruined stuffing. He would wake up growling and grumbling like a bear fresh out of hibernation, but as long as she kept her distance she would be safe enough. He wouldn't actually shoot her, for then who would look after him while he recovered from one of his binges?

She was up the next morning at daybreak, through force of habit, even though she had hardly slept at all. After building a fire and setting a pan of coffee on to boil, she went outside to let the chickens out to scratch.

The boys stood outside the barn, staring off down the road, looking as if they were about to cry. When she saw Jonah riding off in the distance, leading Boodles and Howard, she felt like crying, herself.

But she didn't. Forcing a cheerfulness she didn't feel, she said, "Boys, I've just had the most wonderful idea. How would you like to go stay with Miss Emma for a few days?"

Zac immediately protested, but Nate turned those dark liquid eyes on her, eyes that had seen far more than any child should ever have to see. "Jonah say to mind Miss Carrie and do what she say. You gonna come with us?"

"I'll go with you, but then I'll have to come back and take care of Sorry and the chickens."

"Mmm-hmm," the boy said, his tone openly skeptical.

Together they stared out at the road that ran arrow-straight between gum trees and loblolly pines for a quarter of a mile or so before it curved westward. After the rains, there was not so much as a cloud of dust to mark Jonah's passage.

"He be back directly, Miss Carrie," Nate said, nodding his wise, wooly head, and Carrie had to believe him because she couldn't bear to think of never seeing him again.

By midmorning, Jonah had found the trail he sought, marked by a huge, lightning-shattered pine tree. Paralleling the main road, he cut through the woods, skirting the planted fields along the way, stopping now and then to check on Boodles and her foal. More than once he considered turning back. Darther Adams was cruel and completely without honor. He could not be trusted, drunk or sober. How, he wondered not for the first time, could a woman like Carrie have chosen such a man? She had said she'd had no choice, but a woman always had a choice.

Didn't she?

And then, riding slowly toward the south, to the acres, a few cleared and fenced, most still wooded, that he now called his own, he thought about the choices a woman was free to make. His mother had not chosen to be raped. She had not chosen to have a son by that assault, yet through no fault of her own, those things had set her apart from those women who had once been her friends. Not openly, perhaps, but in her heart where such things were felt.

The Kiowa people were known for their kindness to all children of any race, yet Jonah had felt set apart by his white blood, perhaps because he sensed his mother's shame. Because young men were so few in his village, he had earned the right to wear the red sash of a warrior.

He had not chosen to be captured and thrown into prison. He had not chosen to be transported to Florida. Since then he had taken advantage of every opportunity, yet among whites, he was set apart by his Kiowa blood.

Both Taime and the white man's Jesus must be laughing, their combined breath sending smaller creatures tumbling across the face of the earth like dried leaves in a winter wind.

Touching his heels to the stallion's flanks, he sat up straighter, his keen gaze picking out landmarks as he neared his own property. Another difference—if he had stayed on the reservation, he would not have had his own property. There, all the land belonged to Daw-k'hee and the Federal government.

Here in the East, he had become a landowner. A wealthy man who could afford many wives. Yet here, a man was allowed only one wife at a time. As a young man, Jonah had enjoyed the favors of many women despite his mixed blood, yet he had never considered taking a wife. Among the Kiowa, a man could take as many wives as he could support, for with so many young men killed in the war, there were far more women than men. If a Kiowa man tired of one of his wives, he could throw her away and thus end the marriage. If the match was not to the woman's liking, she could end it by simply returning to her parents' lodge.

But Carrie had no parents. According to Adams, her uncle had offered her to him to settle a gambling debt. Even if she left her husband, she could never go back to such a man.

As he neared the land he now called home, a land so different from the hills, the plains, the river valleys where he spent his youth, Jonah marveled at the route his journey had taken. He had traveled through towns and cities by rail and wagon—he had sailed to islands he could never have imagined, and finally ended up here among people he neither trusted nor particularly liked, who neither liked nor trusted him. Perhaps it was his white blood coming out that had given him the urge to possess land, for it was not a Kiowa trait.

If he were an eagle soaring high overhead, perhaps he could see the patterns of his life more clearly, but he was no eagle, only a man with a dream. And now even his dream was threatened because of the one weakness he had not counted on. Lust for another man's wife.

Chapter Ten

After checking to see that her husband was still sleeping heavily, Carrie slid the pot of coffee to the back of the stove to stay warm, turned down the damper and hurried outside to join the boys, who were just finishing their breakfast. Nate had lured several pullets to the chicken yard fence and was feeding them biscuit crumbs, letting them peck the palm of his hand through the wire fence.

He grinned up at her. Zac giggled. Waving them toward the shortcut, Carrie said, "Come along now, we'll have to hurry." She tried not to pass on her own sense of urgency, but there was never any knowing what Darther would do when he woke up after one of his binges. He would be furious when he learned that Jonah had left, and he'd likely take out his wrath on the first poor creature to cross his path. She'd once seen him stomp a cottonmouth that had been sunning itself by the horse trough, and not even get bitten. She had pitied the snake.

"Now, I can't stay, but if you need me, you'll know how to find your way back on the shortcut," she told them. ''Cross the creek twice, and turn off on the deer path by the broken cedar.''

''We already knowed that,'' panted Zac, his short legs pumping to keep up. ''Me'n Nate, we know these woods real good, don't we, Nate?''

In spite of her worry, Carrie had to ask, ''Why didn't you stay at Emma's in the first place? Why did you hide in my barn?''

''You got a better barn. Hers 'bout to fall down.''

''But—well, there are other farms you could have chosen.''

Nate shrugged. It was a curiously adult action, but then in some ways the boy was far older than his years. She suspected he had chosen her place because it was several miles away from Shingle Landing, the closest settlement. Short of breath from trying to keep up with Nate, who seemed to sense the urgency of their mission, she let the matter drop. Not until they neared the clearing and smelled the smoke from Emma's breakfast fire did she speak again. ''Now, listen, I'll stay long enough to explain everything, and Miss Emma will be glad to have you, but promise me you won't make a mess or eat too much, or—''

''Yes'm.''

''And you either bang on the dishpan or come for me if there's the least trouble, you hear?''

''Yes'm.''

''And don't eat more than one biscuit at a time, because Emma has to go all the way to Shingle Landing to buy flour, and now that she doesn't have a horse, she has to rely on other folks to take her.''

''Yes'm,'' both boys repeated obediently, and then, Zac, bless his heart, tugged at her hand. ''Miss Carrie, is he a-gonna hurt you bad? Me and Nate, we could come hit him and make him back off, and—and I could put ants in his boots that'd crawl up an' bite his pecker off, an'—''

Right there beside Emma's front gate, Carrie fell to her knees and gathered both boys to her. She managed to laugh, but she felt more like crying. "Listen to you, you're a regular warrior, aren't you? Now, hush up and pay attention, I'm going to be just fine. Mr. Adams is— that is, he might have a real bad headache when he wakes up, but I'm used to that. Don't you worry about me, you just take care of each other—and take care of Miss Emma, too, because she needs someone young and strong to help with the chores.''

Emma was waiting on the front porch. The explanations took no more than a few minutes. Emma knew the situation. At the best of times, Darther was difficult. Sick with the whiskey poison, he couldn't be trusted not to turn violent for no reason but that he wanted everyone around to be as miserable as he was.

"You take care, child," Emma called after her. "If you need help, step outside and beat hard on the dishpan, and I'll send the boys for Walter.''

Walter Gilbert, the nearest neighbor, lived a good three miles away. He was almost as crippled with rheumatism as she was, but he'd been a good friend to her late husband, and he did his best for Emma.

Carrie smiled and promised to bang for help if help was needed, and to come back in a day or so to collect the boys. Her smile faded as soon as she turned away, hurrying past the woodpile, the chicken pen and Emma's "yarb" patch, to enter the low, swampy forest again.

All morning she tiptoed around the cabin, collecting Darther's clothes to be washed, his boots to be waxed.

Dirty boots and soiled shirts were among the many things that set him off at times like this. She'd known him to snatch up an iron skillet and hurl it at a carpenter bee droning around the door frame.

There would be no cheerful "Rise 'n' shine!" today, she thought as she scattered corn for the chickens to scratch and peck. She missed her boys, and they hadn't been gone but a few hours.

As for missing Jonah, she didn't dare even think about him. Trouble was, she couldn't help it. The minute she let down her guard, thoughts came piling into her head like snowflakes in one of those howling blizzards she remembered from her childhood in Minnesota. As if he were standing right there before her, she could see his glossy hair neatly bound with a strip of leather, his shirt damp with sweat, stretched tightly across his broad shoulders. Those pale gray eyes in a face the color of a chinquapin, and the proud nose, the square jaw, the mouth....

Her hands grew still, and she stared off into space. And then, "Blessed sakes, woman, you're as bad as that stupid, ornery old mule!" she muttered.

And that was another thing. She had to lay out five yards of cussing and reach for the whip before the miserable creature would even move, but just let Jonah look at him and he'd fall all over himself trying to please.

And Lord help her, she was no better.

With the wash still to be done, she stacked firewood in the small circle of rocks in the back yard, poked in a few sticks of kindling and a handful of dry grass and set it alight, then lugged out her tub. By the time she toted enough water up from the creek and got it to boiling, Darther would have rolled out of bed—on his hands and knees, most likely—and she'd be able to collect his sheets and whatever clothes he had managed to shed. She'd have to set another pot to heat for his silk shirt. The first time she had ever washed one of his store-bought silk shirts, she had thrown it in with his cotton drawers and undershirts and boiled it with a chunk of lye soap, poking it down with her wash stick. The thing had fallen apart when she'd tried to lift it out with the stick, and Darther had near about skinned her alive.

Later, when she'd told Emma about it, the older woman had told her how to wash silk. After that she'd been careful, but it still galled her to think that he wore silk when he begrudged her the money to buy a single dress length of calico.

While water simmered in the big metal washtub, she gathered the eggs and rinsed and refilled the chicken's trough. From behind the barn, Sorry let out an ear-splitting greeting, and she veered toward the barn to cut open a new bale of hay. Waking up after one of his drinking spells, Darther had been known to take a shot at a pair of robins squabbling over a big fat worm. If he shot the mule, her corn wouldn't get planted, and without her corn, he might have to part with a few more of his precious gambling dollars to buy bacon and flour and meal and feed for the stock.

Best to stay on his sunny side. "And that means you, too, you noisy old windbag," she muttered as she broke off a sheaf of hay and tossed it into the manger.

By early afternoon, the wash was strung out on the lines to dry. Darther had waked up cussing, grumbling and moaning, but he hadn't taken down the rifle. Things could be a lot worse.

As the day wore on, Carrie managed to dodge his fists, as well as his wicked tongue. She laced his first mug of coffee with whiskey to settle his belly. Darther called it a hair of the dog, for reasons she had never understood. Next time she poured in a measure of Emma's concentrate of willowbark and disguised the taste with honey and a tad more whiskey.

"My lucky boots better be shining by the time the boy gets back," he growled.

If he came back at all, she thought, trying to ignore the pain of never seeing Jonah again. "I've got the wax all warmed and ready."

By the time she had polished his boots to his liking, Carrie was wringing wet, her fingers stained by Brown's French Boot Dressing. Taking time only to scrub her hands with a brush, she went calmly about her chores. It helped to have more to do than she could possibly get done in a day's time. At least it left less time for fretting. For missing people. For missing those two little rascals who were all the family she was ever apt to have…if they didn't run off and take up with someone else.

For missing Jonah.

She saw to the buckskin, leading him outside to the paddock Jonah had repaired, and that set her to thinking about him all over again. Even after a full day in the field, he would find things that needed doing and do them without asking. It was as if he wanted to be sure she got her money's worth.

Would he come back, or keep on going now that he was free? The first race was set for the weekend, and Darther always liked to get there well ahead of time. Sometimes she lost track of the days, with one day so near like another, but she always counted carefully when Darther was home, waiting for him to leave again.

The whippoorwills were just tuning up the next evening when Jonah rode into the yard. Carrie had not dared let herself hope. She had gone outside to latch the chicken yard gate, and seeing the familiar figure turning in off the road, she touched her hair, wishing she'd taken time to brush it. Taken the time to change into her best dress and put on her shoes, which she had waxed right along with Darther's boots, no matter that the soles were nothing but patches.

Jonah looked tired, his long limbs dangling free of the stirrups, his arms hanging loose. Con didn't need directions. Carrie could imagine Jonah telling the beast to take him back to the Adams place, and to wake him when they arrived.

As he came closer, his eyes seemed to move over her, searching, and Carrie nodded her head imperceptibly. Meaning yes, the boys are safe, and yes, Darther's still here, and yes, oh yes, I'm so very glad you're back!

Words she could never utter, but they were there in her eyes. Any man who could read the mind of a horse should easily be able to read a woman's thoughts.

Jonah nodded toward the cabin and lifted one eyebrow.

"He's inside," Carrie said quietly to the unasked question. "He was sick most of the day, but he managed to eat a good supper. I reckon he'll be glad to see you, he's been grumbling all day about you running off to God knows where."

That brought a quick smile. "So my land has a name now? God Knows Where."

"I'll paint a sign to hang on your gatepost." Carrie was amazed to hear herself teasing. As if every nerve in her body had suddenly come alive, she felt like laughing and singing and weeping all at once. She felt like dancing, and she'd never danced a step in her life. The missionaries didn't hold with such nonsense.

He's back! a voice sang inside her. *He's here! I could
walk right up and touch him if I wanted to.*

If she wanted to?

At least she could gaze her fill. She could feed him,
and bring freshly washed sheets for him to spread over
the straw in the hayloft or out under the shed. She was
never quite sure where he slept. She could prompt him
with questions and listen while he talked about his land
and his horses in that quiet voice that was at such great
odds with her first impression of the kind of man he was.

"The boys?" Jonah swung down off Con's back, and
the stallion nuzzled his shoulder affectionately.

"They're with Emma. I told them to see to her woodpile and take care of the chickens for her, and not to get
into any mischief."

"And Carrie?" he asked, his voice husky as he gazed
searchingly at her face in the deepening gloom.

She swallowed hard. His look was almost as physical
as a touch. "She—I'm just fine. I've been busy...."

Busy avoiding her husband. Busy missing Jonah.
Busy worrying about what the future held, now that her
eyes had been opened to all the things that might have
been.

*What if she hadn't married Darther? What if she had
still been working for her uncle, and Jonah had come
into the store one day to buy—oh, something or other.
A sack of corn. Leather strapping, or muskrat traps, or
coal oil for his lantern.*

*What if he had seen her and asked if he might pay
court?*

What if her uncle had said, Yes?

"Woman, git your lazy ass in here an quit lallygag-
gin'!"

Carrie jumped as if she'd been bee-stung. Jonah

turned and lifted the saddle off T'a-Kon's back. Both
man and horse would rather do without the contraption,
but in a race, even one of the nag races Adams had
described, a saddle was required. Little else was. The
horse's age and lineage mattered not at all, so far as
Jonah could tell, as long as the owner could put up the
entry fee. The more entries, the larger the purse, and
money, after all, was the point of these affairs, not sport.

Four times we will do this, the man whispered silently,
and the stallion flicked his ears. *Four times we will run
his race, and then we'll go home again to Sa-bodle-te,
to Zabat and Saynday and Howard.*

Back to God Knows Where.

They left early the following morning. The track was
in southeastern Virginia, a dirt affair with few amenities
other than a makeshift shedrow consisting of stalls and
tack rooms, and half a dozen taverns. The betting was
conducted informally. On the way, according to Adams,
they would spend a night in a place called Hickory,
where Carrie's Uncle Henry kept store. They would set
a leisurely pace so as not to tire the horses. At that rate,
the ride would take all day through the flat, coastal
plains, much of which had been laid waste during the
war and had yet to be rebuilt.

Darther had not touched the jug again once Jonah had
arrived. Watching them ride off together, Carrie thought
her husband looked better than she'd seen him look in
ages, even though his features were bloated, his face
now permanently flushed. He wore his favorite green
frock coat, freshly sponged, a yellow silk shirt and a
checkered vest. Across the front of his tight brown trousers was draped a gold chain bearing the lucky watch
fob in the shape of a flying horse that had never, to

Carrie's knowledge, brought him noticeably good luck. He had even allowed her to trim his hair and scrub it with her best soap.

Really, she told herself, he wasn't such an awful man when he was sober. Perhaps with Jonah's influence—without Liam forever leading him into wickedness…

Carrie wanted to believe her husband could change—that her life could change for the better. But she had held out such hopes too many times in the past, only to see them dashed each time he came home drunk, raging over having lost another race. Or worse, winning the race and then losing the money on a card game or a cockfight or some other such nonsense. Naturally, he lost only because everyone in the whole wide world cheated.

She watched the two men until they disappeared around the bend of the road, knowing very well why Darther had been on his best behavior. He was afraid of giving Jonah an excuse to back out of their deal. Carrie had no such fear, because whether or not her husband would admit it, the man he called Boy had more honor in his little finger than Darther did in his entire over-stuffed body.

Jonah, Carrie told herself, was no boy. What he was, was a strong man, a beautiful man—a man who filled her every waking moment with quivering awareness, even after he had apparently cast his lot with her husband.

To Darther he was only a means of winning money.

"First thing we'll do is get you'n that hoss o' yours signed up with the man that owns the track, man named Deane," Darther said as they pulled up before an un-painted storefront with a small livery stable on the side. "I'll get Henry to handle it, he owes me money."

Darther chortled. "Hen most always owes me money. Only man in the world that can bet on a sure thing and come out a loser."

Inside the cluttered store, which reeked of badly cured hides, salt fish and tobacco, Darther made the introductions. "This here's m' new rider, Hen, name of Jonah Longshadow. Got hisself a stallion that makes poor old Peck look like a freight train backing into the yards."

"Stallion, huh?"

"Wait'll you see him run."

"Last man entered a stallion in one o' Deane's races got his neck broke when the horse took off after a mare and ran damn near all the way to Deep Creek. I don't know, Dart."

"Good, good! Remind everybody of that, will you? This'n won't be a speck o' trouble, you just do whatever you have to do to get 'im entered, then spread the word he's a flash in the pan. We're both gonna make a bundle on this ol' boy." Adams slapped Jonah on the back. The man called Hen, or Henry, looked him over, spat on the floor, and nodded.

This was Carrie's uncle? How could her bright spirit have survived these two men, each one worse than the other?

Fists curled at his side, Jonah thought fleetingly of how it had felt to find himself unexpectedly clinging to a broken spar, miles from the nearest shore, surrounded by mountainous seas. He had survived the cold of Oklahoma's Fort Sill, the damp dungeons of Fort Marion. He had survived three shipwrecks. He had survived being jailed for a crime he had not committed. For Carrie's sake he could survive four horse races. Once his debt was fully paid, he would be free to go home to his own land.

To *God Knows Where,* he thought with an inward smile.

The longer he kept Adams away, the better it would be for Carrie and the boys. That much he could do for her.

It was arranged that Jonah would not be seen in the company of either Henry or Darther once they neared the racetrack. The storekeeper would ride ahead and spread a few rumors, drop a hint among the rabble that hung around the track hoping to get lucky, that for all he was a promising looking prospect, the bay with the black ears was reputed to be all show and no go. Never placed in a single race, and that was a matter of record.

It was a fair bet that few would even bother to ask how many previous races the last-minute entry had run. Well lubricated with the free-flowing spirits, most of the regulars would be eagerly looking to put their money on better prospects, thus lengthening the odds. By the time anyone discovered the truth, the first few races would be over, the side bets collected, and after paying Jonah a share of the purse, he and Henry would have divided the rest of the day's take between them, Darther thought smugly.

Which was more or less the way it went, up to a point. Jonah and Black Ears—they had decided to enter him under that name rather than the Kiowa translation—stayed well away from the shedrows and the paddock where owners worked out nervous entries. Both Jonah and the horse were uneasy. As a youth and as a young brave, Jonah had raced for the sheer joy of the sport. The feeling among those gathered for today's race—owners, breeders and gamblers—was different. He did not like the feel of this place, these people.

T'a-Kon danced and shook his head. Jonah spoke

softly, sharing his unease, as he walked him before the first race. Moments before the race was to begin, he led the high-strung stallion toward the gate and mounted the way the horse had been trained, from the left rather than the right.

From the start, they led the pack, horse and rider wanting only to see an end to the affair as quickly as possible. According to the breeder who had sold him, the big bay stallion had been bred for harness racing, but he'd spooked at being followed by anything more substantial than a cloud of dust.

Today he was followed by an entire field. He outran them easily. Afterward, walking away from the noisy mob, Jonah leaned over the horse's lathered neck and whispered, "You did well, my friend. One more stop to collect your winnings and then we'll go home. Three more such races and we will return to your ladies."

Jonah envied the stallion. The lady he himself would have chosen had already been taken, and the white man's laws would not allow her to cast off her marriage and walk away.

They met at the prearranged place, well away from the track. Grudgingly, Darther handed over Jonah's share of the purse. Deliberately, Jonah counted out the bills. He said nothing, merely looked at the man.

With an embarrassed laugh, Adams peeled another few bills from the roll in the inside pocket of his coat. "Musta miscounted," he muttered. "You sure you don't want to think it over? I'm fixin' to meet up with Hen at MacNeally's Livery. Once he pays me what he owes me, I'm going to put it all on a sure thing in the fourth race. Be glad to add your share to the pot, boy."

"I will meet you here in three days." Turning his

back on the man, Jonah proceeded to rub the stallion's flanks. They had agreed that it would be wiser to wait for T'a-Kon's spectacular win to be forgotten. Even so, word would spread. The odds would never again be so favorable. Several men had wanted to buy the big bay horse, for these races were held partly as an excuse to gamble, partly for the purpose of buying, selling and trading promising contenders before the regular season got underway.

Hearing the other man walk away, Jonah took time to examine the stallion's hooves, to feel his legs for heat or swelling. Then he offered him a treat before mounting up again. The ride back to God Knows Where would take the rest of the day and half the night at an easy pace. There was a creek with good water where they would stop and rest along the way. "Look at it this way, my friend," he said softly as they left the ragtag mob behind and headed out of town. "If you'd been born a mule, you might have had to pull a plow for five years to earn your oats and apples."

He had gone no more than a few miles when something made him pull up. It was as if a cold wind had blown over his naked skin. The sky was clear, the air warm and dry. There was no wind and little traffic on the narrow country road. A farmer passed by leading a cow. Two boys herding a flock of white geese glanced at him curiously. A half-grown boy plodding along on a cob nodded and offered a shy smile.

Jonah nodded in return. After a moment, he shrugged his shoulders and continued on his way, thinking of the acres he could afford to fence with his share of the winnings. A few more wins and he might even look for another good brood mare.

* * *

"Payoff time, Hen. Hand over what you owe me, and don't forget that dog race down in Shingle Landing."

The older man stretched an unconvincing smile. "Got a better idee. Way I see it, we can double our money if we put it all down on the last race. I been timing that buttermilk mare, and Dart, I'm telling you, she's a sure thing."

Darther, his speech slurred by having begun his celebration earlier that day, shook his head, staggered and steadied himself by leaning against the wall. "'Druther place m'own bets. Jus' gimme m'money, Hen."

"Aw now, Dart…ain't I your friend? Didn't I give you my own brother's girl for a wife? Don't that make us practic'ly kin?"

"Don't need kinfolk, I want cash money, before you lose it on some whey-bellied hammerhead."

The storekeeper heaved an exaggerated sigh and reached inside his tobacco-stained coat. Darther lurched away from the wall, a look of greedy anticipation in his bloated face.

The look quickly changed to one of disbelief when his best friend's hand emerged not with a wad of bills, but with a double-bladed knife.

Chapter Eleven

Jonah would never know what made him rein in when he did. There was not a house in sight, only a pair of tall chimneys standing amidst a heap of rubble, remnants of a war long since fought and lost. But it wasn't the desolate chimneys, much less the memories of a war that had ended while he was still a beardless youth, that made him stare off into the distance, listening for a sound just beyond the range of his keen hearing.

Something was wrong. He felt it in his bones. Jonah had always trusted his instincts, yet this time his inner voices were at odds. While one voice urged him to keep going, to remove himself from this place as quickly as possible, another voice whispered, *Go back.*

Something was terribly wrong. He could keep on riding south, but it would change nothing. A man could flee, but in the end, trouble outpaced the swiftest runner. Reluctantly, Jonah turned and headed back toward the racetrack and the half dozen or so taverns that had grown up around it. The road led past the livery stable where Darther had left the buckskin. Where he had gone to meet his friend.

There was no sign of either man. No sign of anyone,

only the soft stomping and whuffling of the few horses in the paddock. Another race was about to get underway, and everyone was either at the track or inside one of the nearby taverns. Jonah sat for a long moment, absorbing the unsettling stillness. Then slowly, he dismounted. "Easy, friend," he murmured, dropping the reins.

The stallion stood motionless. Jonah, his feeling of dread growing by the moment, approached the open door. From the paddock, several horses, including the buckskin Adams had been riding, watched his movement. One of the mares rolled her eyes and reared. Another one bridled. As his eyes adjusted to the gloomy interior of the stable, he called out, "Adams?"

There was no response. Behind him, the buckskin whickered nervously. Turning away, Jonah spoke quietly to the nervous horse, signaled to T'a-Kon to stay, and began circling the long wooden building, his uneasiness mounting with each step.

The body was half hidden by a blackberry thicket. It had obviously been dragged several yards through the muck and dumped there. Feeling as if he had swallowed a leaden weight, Jonah stared down at the figure sprawled on the ground, feet apart, hands over its head, a startled look still evident in the small, glazed eyes.

He was quite obviously dead, the blood already darkened on the front of the yellow silk shirt. Jonah had seen death before, many times. Even violent death. He had once been, after all, a warrior.

But there was nothing valorous about the scene before him. Bluebottle flies swarmed noisily. From somewhere in the distance, a dog yapped and then began to howl. Overhead, two buzzards sailed in for a closer look.

Every instinct he possessed urged him to mount up and ride out as quickly as he could. Experience had taught him that getting entangled in the affairs of a white man could lead to more trouble than he was prepared to handle. He had traveled that road too many times before.

Regardless of what he did now, Darther Adams was dead. Neither the white man's law nor *Satanta* himself could change that. He could ride away and leave the remains to the mercy of furred and feathered predators, or he could report the crime and more than likely, find himself thrown in jail for a murder he had not committed.

Or he could return the poor devil to his widow, dig his grave, help her to bury his mortal remains, and then leave her to weep and wail out her grief. Someone else could report the man's death.

From a mile away, he heard the roar of the crowd. Another race was underway. Soon men would be drinking their winnings inside the stinking taverns, and then pissing them away against the outer walls. If he thought there might be one sober man among them, Jonah might have considered reporting the crime, but a drunken mob could turn into a treacherous force with no warning. He had seen it happen too many times in the past.

The buckskin was not happy at having to carry the man's body. Even T'a-Kon snorted and stamped nervously when Jonah attached the lead to his saddle. They set off at a walk on the uneasy journey south. Before darkness fell they passed a number of travelers, receiving more than a few curious stares, but no questions were asked.

Henry hitched up his trousers and adjusted his expression before entering Barney's House of Beer. He had gone over his story again and again, until by now he was almost convinced of its veracity. Just inside the door, he paused. Not a head turned. He cleared his throat loudly, and when that failed to gain him the attention he needed, he wailed loudly, ''Lawd, he'p us!''

Two men glanced over their shoulders, then went back to their drinking. Furious at being ignored, Henry began waving his arms. The stupid fools were drunk, every last one of them. He had been well on the way himself, but the instant he'd felt the knife strike bone, and then sink to the hilt in something warm, wet and disgusting, he'd turned stone, cold sober.

A man lurched through the door behind him, sloshing beer down his backside. ''Whassa matter, ol' man, you 'fraid to go home to the li'l woman?''

Pushing the drunk away, Henry searched the crowd for someone who looked marginally sober. ''Shut up, you crazy bastards, I'm telling you, there's been a murder! Just shut up a minute and listen to me, will you?'' This was not the way it was supposed to go. ''My best friend's been stabbed to death out behind MacNeally's.''

A few heads turned, and then a few more. Henry waved his arms again. ''Go fetch the sheriff! If he ain't at the track, he'll be in one o' the taverns.'' The local sheriff could be counted on to attend these affairs. Fist-fights were considered a part of the day's entertainment, especially when, as occasionally happened, one got out of hand.

But this was no mere fistfight. As his words penetrated, the crowd fell silent. Henry took advantage of the lull to relate his carefully concocted tale, leaving out the part about vomiting up his breakfast and a pint or so of whiskey, huddling in an empty stall while he thought through what had happened, and the best way to deal with it. It had never once occurred to him to tell the truth and throw himself on the mercy of the court.

Both Darther and Henry had been so careful not to be seen with the half-breed before the race. Now it was up to him to plant the seeds of suspicion. According to Darther, the breed had been jailed down in Currituck County not long ago. That alone should be enough to get him strung up before any awkward questions could be asked.

"I'm telling you, I saw him with my own eyes. Found him laying there, deader 'n a doornail. He was robbed, too—I couldn't help but notice when I was feeling to see if his heart was still beating. Prob'ly by that drunk half-breed that was sneaking around the livery. I saw the two of 'em together after the first race—they looked to me to be arguin'. Poor Darther 'peared to be tryin' to calm 'im down, but the breed just kept on cursing and actin' like he was on the warpath or sump'in.''

The shocked silence held for a few more seconds, then all hell broke loose. "Robbed, you say? Why, tha's awful!''

"You jackass, he was kilt, too!''

"What breed? They was one in the first race today— gray-eyed Injun up on that black-eared bay, only one I seed around here.''

"Tha's him, tha's the one,'' Henry cried excitedly. "Somebody go fetch the sheriff!''

"Anybody seen the sheriff? He was here just before the second race.''

There was a chorus of "Fetch the sheriff!'' and "Go find DuValle,'' and several minutes later the crowd parted to allow the entry of the local lawman. Clearing his throat for dramatic emphasis, Henry repeated his story once more, elaborating on several points, such as his devotion to the deceased, and how much money poor Darther had been carrying before he was robbed and then tragically murdered by an unknown assailant who just might possibly be a man of mixed ancestry who had recently been released from a Carolina jail.

The sheriff, too, had been celebrating, having bet on the black-eared bay stallion, even though someone—he thought it might have been the same man who was yammering at him now—had told him the horse was a knothead who'd been known to stop dead in the middle of a race. At twenty-to-one odds, he'd made himself a nice little bundle.

"Awright now, s'pose you show me where you found this here body."

As one, the crowd surged outside. Leading the parade, Henry thrust out his chest until it almost equaled the girth of his belly. After today, he told himself proudly, wasn't nobody going to call him a loser, a skinflint, a stupid old man who'd shortchange his own mother, if he hadn't watched her choke on a raw oyster forty-odd years ago.

Things were going just the way he'd planned. The fools believed every word he'd said. Still, it wouldn't hurt to grease the skids a little more, so he waved toward the tavern they were passing and called out, "Drinks on me, friends. Happen, I won me a bundle today, too." He patted the roll of bills securely tucked in the inside pocket of his coat.

As one, the crowd veered toward the makeshift establishment. One man reckoned as how poor old Adams weren't going nowhere anyhow, 'ceptin' to hell. Another one observed that a man needed to settle his belly before he looked on a dead body. Perhaps two dozen men in all crowded into the rough-plank tavern that consisted of a crude bar, three galvanized buckets to serve as cuspidors, and an ornate, gilt-framed mirror.

Fumbling inside his coat, Henry managed to peel off a few bills without revealing the full extent of his riches. He dropped them on the bar and proudly repeated his order. Every man downed a full measure of his choice of bourbon, beer or shine, all except for Henry. He lifted a glass of white liquor, turned a sickly shade of green, and set it down again. Some kind soul—he never knew which one—finished it for him.

It wasn't that he regretted what he'd been forced to do. The damned ungrateful bastard had it coming to him, but all the same, he'd do well to keep a cool head. There was too much at stake to risk a careless slip.

Seeing that there would be no more free drinks forthcoming, the crowd flowed back outside and set off in the direction of MacNeally's, imbued with a fuzzy-minded sense of righteousness. Jugs, jars and flasks passed freely from hand to hand. At a time like this, a man needed all the courage he could muster.

Arriving at the livery, Sheriff DuValle came to a halt. Swaying only slightly, he held out his arms and muttered something about evidence. "Now, Henry, s'pose you show me where this here body's at?"

Any possible remaining evidence was quickly trampled into the mud and horse manure as a few dozen pairs of clumsy boots tromped around the barn without finding anything resembling a corpse. Halting the procession at the front of the building again, the sheriff removed his hat and scratched his head. "You sure he was dead, Vander? 'Pears to me he musta got up an' walked off."

"Damn right, he was dead. Bled like a stuck pig, didn't he?"

"I seen men bleed a tubful and live." Sheriff Omar Ernest DuValle spoke as the voice of experience. He had been in the law business for more than thirty years.

"He was dead, I tell you. I felt his body and he was cold as a mackerel, his eyes all rolled back in his head."

"Then where's he at?"

A half-grown boy, somewhat more sober than the rest of the crowd, shoved his way forward. "Sheriff," he panted, "I seen that Injun that rode that black-eared hoss—he was headed out o' town 'bout a hour ago, leadin' a buckskin that was carryin' a load o' som'pin on 'is back."

"A load o' what?" the sheriff inquired suspiciously. If there was one thing he could do without it was having a serious crime crop up on race day, especially a crime involving a mystery, which usually required a sober head.

The boy shrugged and looked as if he regretted having spoken up. "Dunno—could'a been a dead body, I reckon."

"A dead body. Well now, ain't that just dandy," the old lawman sneered. "You seen a murderer hauling off a dead body on a hoss, and you just let 'im go."

The boy looked as if he might burst into tears. Henry stepped forward and went into his act again. "Lord ha' mercy, the murderin' thief's done stole the evidence!"

Another shouting match ensued. It ended when the sheriff climbed up onto a fence rail and fired his Colt revolver into the air. "Sheddup! Jest sheddup an' lemme think!"

Only one thing was certain. The body was nowhere to be found. By the time every inch of the grounds had been thoroughly searched, the crowd was rip-snorting drunk, the sheriff to a somewhat lesser degree. Further confusion arose from the fact that while the murder had taken place in Virginia, the victim was from North Carolina, and as far as anyone could determine, the mur-

derer had escaped with the corpus delicti—a term the
sheriff had seen fit to use more than once—back to Carolina.

By that time, Henry was feeling sick as a dog. He
would just as soon have gone back to Hickory and forgotten the whole thing, but his role wasn't yet over. He
no longer felt like the hero of the hour, but at least he
was sober enough to know that he'd better stay that way,
no matter how much he might like to drown his troubles
in white liquor and forget the past few hours. No matter
how miserable he was at the moment, he reminded himself, there was one big consolation.

A jubilant voice whispered inside his head, *You're
rich, Henry. Gonna be even richer when you sell off
Darther's land. You could buy yourself a nice plantation, take on a few 'croppers to work your fields, hire
you a woman to cook and clean. Might even keep Carrie
round. Yessir, for once, you done dealt yourself a winning hand.*

It was decided to wait before riding south to confer
with the sheriff in Currituck County just over the line in
North Carolina. The last race of the day had yet to be
run, and the taverns had not yet run out of booze. It
would be several days before the next race meet was
scheduled, and then only if enough entries were rounded
up to make it worthwhile.

"Poor ol' Dart, he ain't gonna get no deader," as one
man piously expressed it.

"'Sides, there's a bangtail filly set to run in the last
race today, if she don't kick down the fence and take
off first. One o' them wild Chincoteaguers."

"Gen'lemen," said an elegantly clad, softspoken sot,
"I suggest we let Nawth C'lina take care of her own
problems."

And with that, the crowd turned and headed back toward the track.

Henry took one last look in the direction of the track and reluctantly turned away. He knew his own weakness. It was widely known that he was more often than not in debt. He could no more be around gamblers and not gamble than he could be around drinkers and not drink. By now, every ounce of his corpulent body was crying out for alcohol, but one drink would lead to another, and one slip of the tongue could lead to disaster. He'd played a few wild hunches in his time, like sending off for that orphan, claiming she was his niece just because they happened to share a last name. But this time he couldn't afford to make any mistakes.

In an unconscious gesture, he slipped his hand inside his coat pocket and fingered the small gold watch fob. He had long admired Darther's lucky charm.

Didn't bring you much luck in the end, did it, Dart?

Henry had stolen the thing in a fit of anger when he'd discovered that Darther had already paid off the breed. The way Henry saw it, greasing a few palms down in Currituck had been payment enough. There was no reason for Darther to give him half his share of the purse as well.

He was still five miles from home when the sun went down. His head hurt, his belly felt like he'd swallowed a bucket of nails, but he comforted himself with the thought that if he could just make it through the next few days—the next few weeks—he could walk away from this stinking damn store and live like a goddamn gentleman.

Carrie dragged the washtub inside the cabin and filled it with water from the kettle. She wanted to think, and she thought best sitting in water. In the summertime she would go down to the creek, peel down to her bloomers and her camisole and sit for hours, just thinking of what needed doing, and the best way to go about it.

But the early fall nights were too cool, and besides, snakes came out at night. And besides all that, the thoughts that insisted on filling her head weren't at all proper. If she was going to think them at all, she'd as soon think them inside the privacy of her own home.

Would they come home together? Or would Darther come home alone while Jonah went to his own place? Would Jonah even return at all?

She dared hope that he could come back alone to tell her that Darther had gone on to Warrenton or Suffolk or wherever he could find another race or a cockfight or a game of cards. Why would he come back home? There was nothing for him here but fields he couldn't be bothered to work and a wife he cared less for than he did his damn blasted rifle.

But neither was there a reason for Jonah to come back, now that he was free.

Carrie extended one leg and lazily scrubbed her knee with a coarse cloth. Soaking she loved. Scrubbing she cared less for, but she did it because she needed it—because farming was dirty work, and because the last thing Mrs. Robinson had said when she'd put her on the train was to remember always that she was a lady.

Sometimes it was hard to remember, but she tried. With Emma as an example, she could do no less.

Thinking of Emma reminded her of the boys, and she wondered when it would be safe to bring them back home. No way of knowing, she thought resignedly as she slipped down into the tub until only her head, shoulders and knees were above the water. One of these days, when she had enough corn money, she was going to buy herself a real bathing tub, big enough to wet her whole body and her hair and everything without bruising her neck on the rim in the process.

She happened to know that Jonah bathed in the creek, even now that the nights were growing chilly, instead of just using a bucket from the horse trough. She probably ought to warn him about the snakes, but then, a man who could get inside a mule's head probably knew all there was to know about snakes and raccoons and possums and black bears, and all the other critters that crawled in the night.

And then she daydreamt some more, thinking about the man and his soft voice, and his gentle way with the boys, and with horses...and with her.

Would he be as gentle with a wife?

Her heart lurched and went to thudding like a churn. Despite the cooling water, she felt her face grow warm. She already had a husband. She had done that awful thing in bed more than a dozen times. There was no pleasure in it for a woman, and not much for a man, if Darther's reaction was anything to go by. Sometimes he cursed, sometimes he rolled off and went to get himself a drink of whiskey. Emma said once that her Luther always thanked her when it was over, and held her hand until they fell asleep.

That would be nice. Holding hands with someone lying beside you, feeling all warm and...together.

Carrie could barely remember when she had felt "together" with anyone. She didn't even have pictures of her parents, for everything had been left behind in that wild dash eastward. None of them would have escaped alive if it hadn't been for a warning by a few friendly Indians. The missionary teachers had collected whatever

survivors they could—mostly it had been the children—
and fled.

Carrie sighed and eased herself from the tub. The water had grown cold, and there was no comfort in sitting
in a tub full of cold water, even if it did smell faintly of
bayberries. At least her thinking time hadn't been
wasted. She had made up her mind that first thing tomorrow she would go and bring the boys back home.
Darther might be gone a week, two weeks—even longer.
During the real racing season, he had been known to
travel all the way up to Maryland when he was on a
winning streak. Once he'd even brought her back a
dress—not that she'd ever worn it. It had been red, and
not very clean, reeking of sweat and strong perfume.
Fortunately, he had soon drunk himself senseless and
forgotten he'd ever given it to her. Part of it was still in
the ragbag, the rest she had cut into strips and used in
the rug she had crocheted.

Carrie slept well for the first part of the night. She
awoke when the moon broke through the clouds. She'd
always had trouble sleeping during a full moon. Lying
awake she listened to the whippoorwills and the tree
frogs and waited for the rooster to crow. And because
she was awake and listening, she happened to hear the
soft thud of hooves on the hard dirt road.

They were back, then. Both of them, from the sound
of it. And because in the hours just before daybreak, her
defenses were always at their lowest ebb, she allowed
herself to think again of what it would be like if there
had never been a Darther. If there was only Jonah and
the boys. The boys asleep in a room added onto the back
of the cabin and Jonah in her bed, holding her hand
throughout the night.

Reluctantly, she rose and crossed the room to stoke

up the cook fire. Darther always wanted coffee if there was none in the pot. If there was coffee on the stove, he would ignore it and send her to the barn for a fresh jug.

She hoped he had won. If Jonah and Con had won him a bundle, then he wouldn't be quite so hard to please. She might even be able to bring the boys back and ease them into the picture.

But if he'd lost…

Chapter Twelve

The yard lay in shadow, with bright patches of moonlight dappled between the few large trees and the outbuildings. Carrie had seen the same scene a hundred times before, but for some reason, everything looked strange tonight, as if she were seeing it all in a dream. She had a fleeting memory of putting her shoes on the wrong feet once a long time ago and staring at them with the same vague feeling that something wasn't quite right.

Then someone—her mother, she thought—had knelt and taken her shoes off and put them on the right feet, and the feeling was gone.

Now, even before Jonah rode up to the cabin and dismounted, she knew that whatever was wrong would not be so easily put right. Her gaze moved past him. The other horse appeared to be carrying a roll of blankets on his back. A feeling of coldness crept through her that had nothing to with the predawn chill.

Jonah mounted the bottom step and stopped. With his back to the moonlight, it was impossible to read his expression. He started to speak and then stopped, and that made her even more uneasy. The Jonah she had come to know might be a lot of things, but hesitant was not among them. Even in irons, he had known precisely who he was and where he was going, and be damned to anyone who got in his way.

Somebody had to break the silence. "Darther?" she whispered.

He nodded toward the other horse, standing head down at the end of a long lead. "I brought him home."

And then she knew.

It wasn't until some time later that she got the whole story, or at least as much of it as Jonah knew. Before they could carry her husband's body inside, certain things had to be done. More broken memories crowded in on her like torn photographs. *Because this is the way things are done, child, now go outside and play and stop asking questions.*

She didn't really want a dead man in her house, much less in her bed, but if the missionaries had taught her anything—and actually, they had taught her a great deal, only most of it had long since been forgotten—it was proper respect for the dead.

Knowing that this was the way things were done, Carrie silently set about stripping the bed and spreading it with clean linens. There was a single mirror on the wall, Darther's shaving mirror. She covered it with a handkerchief. Just why, she couldn't remember, but it was the way things were done.

Jonah watched silently as she removed the feather pillow from the bed. Actually, she couldn't recall if pillows were permitted or not, but it seemed proper to lay the deceased flat, with his arms crossed on his chest and his eyes closed. Then, if he looked too uncomfortable, she would cram his pillow under his head.

Jonah had to help her with the eyes, for she couldn't

bring herself to touch his face. "I need to wash him and get him into a clean shirt," she whispered.

"Give me the shirt and a wet cloth," he said, "Then you go outside and breathe deeply. Feed your chickens. Do the things you do each day, and then come back."

And like the coward she was, she obeyed. By the time she returned, he had covered the body from head to toe with her good spread. "I think we're supposed to light candles now," she whispered.

Jonah looked at her, then glanced outside. Less than an hour before daybreak, the eastern sky was already streaked with bands of yellow light, but he nodded. Throughout the whole procedure neither of them had spoken much. Somehow, it didn't seem proper to talk with Darther lying there dead in the same room. Her tub was still there on the kitchen side of the cabin, filled with cold, gray water, waiting until morning to be bailed out and turned upside down to dry.

Dear Lord, don't let me do this all wrong. You know how I felt about him—I can't help that now, it's too late, but at least let me do this one last thing right, please.

"Bring in the bench from outside the barn. Oh, and would you knock the dirt-dauber's nests off the bottom, first? We'll need more seating when folks start coming."

Thank goodness Jonah didn't ask who or why. She wasn't sure she could have answered, but someone would come. People always did at times like these. After he went outside, she drew the curtain across the bedroom portion, then opened it again. Either way seemed disrespectful.

As did her bath tub. She dipped it out until she could drag it to the back door and tip it outside. By that time Jonah had returned with the crudely built bench, now brushed clean, and she directed him to set it along the front wall. Then she shifted the two chairs, placing one near the head of the bed, one near the foot. The thought of sitting there beside the dead body of her husband made goose bumps race down her flanks, but she braced herself to do things properly.

First, though, she needed to know what had happened. There'd been dried blood—a good deal of it—on Darther's shirt. He had died a violent death. She'd often heard Liam and Darther talking about the fights that seemed to be taken for granted at horse races, dog races, cockfights and the like. Cockfights seemed to be the worst. She had just assumed they were fistfights, but obviously she had assumed wrong.

"Do you want me to stay?" Jonah asked quietly. While he was outside he had taken care of the horses.

Wordlessly, she nodded. Then, swallowing hard, she said, "I need to tell Emma. I need to put a pot of beans on to cook. People will come…"

But would they? So far as she knew, Darther didn't have a single friend. He never went to church, never visited anyone in the scattered farming community so far as she knew. Come to think of it, even Liam hadn't seemed to like him all that much.

Emma said it was because Darther was a carpetbagger, one of the hordes who had come South like a swarm of locusts during the Reconstruction years to claim anything of value that had been left standing. But even if not a single soul came to his wake, Carrie had to do what was right. "I'll go tell Emma. Will you stay until I get back?"

"Take the buckskin."

She sent him a stricken look, then hurried outside. Jonah waited a moment, snuffed out the candles, and went outside after her. Finding her leaning against the sagging wire enclosure, staring at the horse that had brought home the body of her husband, he placed a hand on her arm and said quietly, "You stay. I will go."

She shook her head. "Emma doesn't know you. I— she'll tell me what I need to do, I probably forgot something." She took a deep, shuddering breath, and then, as if it were the most natural thing in the world, she turned blindly into his arms and buried her face against his chest.

Tension locked Jonah's body for one long moment. Acutely aware of her strength, her fragility, her warmth, he breathed in the dry, sweet scent of her hair. Holding her to him with one arm, he lifted a hand and brushed away the short, unruly curls that tickled his jaw.

This was wrong. Not only wrong, but dangerous. He had faced many dangers in his lifetime, but never had he experienced anything like the feelings coursing through him at this moment. Bracing himself to set her away, he made the mistake of allowing his lips to touch her brow. *Softer than the softest doeskin. Sweeter than all the wild honey in the world…*

He forced himself to set her away. "Show me where, and I'll dig a grave." Even to his own ears his voice sounded harsh in the early morning stillness, so he cleared his throat and tried again. "I will also build a burial box."

"A—a coffin."

He nodded. "A coffin."

"I think there's some wood left over from—oh, and I need to tell Liam, only I don't know how to find him. Do you think anyone at Shingle Landing would know where he is?"

Jonah had heard Adams mention the man who had once ridden for him. He did not know where to find him.

From the little he had heard, the two men had parted on bad terms. "Go tell your friend. She will know what to do."

"I wish I could ask Mrs. Robinson." She sighed. He had heard her speak of the woman before. Her friend, the missionary, could not help her now.

"Drive the cart. Your friend will not want to walk. I'll hitch up the buckskin."

"Will he mind, do you think? I—I couldn't bear to ride him, not now."

Torn between amusement and understanding, Jonah told her that the buckskin would not enjoy drawing a cart, but he would do it more willingly than the mule.

"I won't have to cuss to make him go, will I? I don't particularly want the boys to pick up any more bad habits than they already have."

This time there was no denying the smile. Touching her on the arm, feeling the heat of her body along with the surprising strength, Jonah said, "I will personally instruct him to obey your every command."

Her own fleeting smile was quickly erased. Jonah saw guilt fill her eyes. She had neither liked nor respected the man lying cold on her bed, yet she must grieve, for her own sake. For the healing it brought. "Wear a hat. The sun will be warm soon."

She glanced at his hand on her bare arm, then lifted her eyes to his face, and for one unguarded moment, he saw the pain, the guilt and uncertainty there. Wanting only to gather her to him once more, he forced himself to speak evenly. "He's at rest, Carrie. First I will build a box, then I will dig a grave. Go to your friend now, tell her what has happened."

"I don't know what to tell her. Jonah, I still don't know what happened," she wailed softly. He thought she was going to cry, but though the tip of her nose grew red, she bit down hard on her lip and drew her arm away from his hand. "Well, I guess I do. He must've cheated someone. I think he did that a lot. Do you know who did it?"

"No. I found him behind a livery stable. He had been dead long enough for the blood to stop flowing."

"Did you—I mean, was there any—what I mean is, was anyone else there?"

"No one."

She gnawed on her lower lip again. "Do you think I should go tell the sheriff, or does he already know?"

"Adams was killed in Virginia." Jonah had no wish to see the Currituck lawman who had thrown him in jail and held him there for twelve days. The judge had seemed a fair man. Weak, perhaps, but not dishonest.

As for the others present at his mockery of a hearing, some had eagerly accepted Adams's money, others had not, but even those who had kept their hands in their pockets had not seemed surprised at the open bribery on his behalf.

Carrie shook her head. "Well, I reckon we can sort all that out later. The first thing to do is to get him buried before…"

All around them chickens clucked softly as they went about scratching for breakfast. A squabbling of crows settled noisily onto a nearby tree. Inside the house lay a man who had died a violent death, yet his passing seemed to have gone unnoticed.

"You can dig over there, I reckon." She pointed to a spot of shade under a massive water oak tree.

Jonah nodded. The roots would make digging difficult, but she was not likely to want to cultivate the section. It would do as well as anyplace else for a graveyard. He turned toward the barn. He would dig first, before the sun grew any hotter. Then, in the heat of the day, he would find enough pine boards for a box.

Reluctantly, Carrie returned to the cabin to put on her shoes and her best dress. The occasion seemed to call for a certain formality. She took one last look at the mound on the bed before hurrying outside again. He was dead. The man who had rescued her from a life of drudgery, only to subject her to drudgery of a different kind, was dead. Never again would he mock her and call her stupid, or ugly, or lazy. Never again would he hit her without warning, or kick her out of bed, or do that thing to her that was even more embarrassing than it was painful.

Darther was dead. And Heaven help her, she was relieved. Which brought on a whole new surge of guilt.

Jonah had the buckskin hitched to the cart when she went outside again. After one long look at her best dress, her ugly, but gleaming shoes, and the curls she had tamed with water and pulled ruthlessly behind her ears, anchoring them with a pair of plain tortoiseshell combs, he handed her up onto the seat.

Just as if she hadn't scrambled in and out of the thing a hundred times, she thought with a painful kind of amusement. She clucked her teeth and they set out at a trot. Carrie fixed her gaze on the shiny tan rump with its thick black tail and let her mind float free. She didn't know what she could tell Emma or the boys because she didn't really know what had happened, only that Darther had gone off to the races with Jonah and come home dead.

"Carrie, Carrie, we cooked cakes!"
"Carrie, I caught a snake, I got 'im in a snuff tin an'

and Miss Emma says I can keep him long's I don't let him loose in the house.''

The boys raced out to the edge of the woods to greet her. "You look funny with your hair all done up like that," said a wide-eyed Zac, and of all unseemly reactions, Carrie laughed aloud.

Was it possible they could have actually grown in only a few days? "Mercy, let me catch my breath," she cried as they leapt on her and dragged her toward the house. Words tumbled over words as they both tried to talk at once. Emma came outside and stood on the front stoop, drying her hands on her apron, and called out a greeting. "I guess you came to take away my boys. Nate, unhitch the horse, please, and lead him o'er to the shed.''

"I came to—well, the truth is, it's going to take some explaining.''

"Zac, why don't you fetch that plate of cakes out here. We'll sit outside for a spell.''

The minute both boys were out of hearing, Carrie said quietly. "Darther's dead. I think he was killed in a fight.''

"Oh, Lord ha' mercy.''

The older woman lowered herself carefully into one of the cane rockers and Carrie hitched forward its mate and sat down. In the few moments before the boys returned, Carrie quickly explained all she knew. "Jonah—I told you he promised to race for Darther after Darther went with him to the courthouse. Well, anyway, this morning before daylight Jonah brought his body home. He's digging a grave now.''

"Did he kill him?''

"Jonah? Of course not.''

Emma was silent for several moments. Inside the

house came the sound of a breaking dish and a childish, "Dammit, dammit, dammit, oh, hell!"

Then Nate came around the corner and said, "I done unharnessed 'im, Miss Carrie. He don't like to be strapped up thataway."

Zac emerged with a red face and a napkin filled with molasses cakes, and Carrie took a deep breath and launched into her explanation. "Boys, my husband— that is, Mr. Adams—he's been—well, he died. And I— that is, we—well, the family's expected to—"

Emma stood, one hand to her back as she slowly straightened herself to a proud four-feet-eight inches. "What Carrie's trying to say is that we have to go home with her."

Nate began backing up. "I ain't sittin' up wi' no dead man."

Zac, his eyes round as turtle eggs, said, "Me, neither."

"Nate, you ride over to the next farm and tell Mr. Gilbert to pass the word. While you're gone we'll get things ready to go. Zac, go and see if you can find me a few more eggs. Carrie, come inside and we'll start on the food."

Carrie thought later as she sat on a chair at the foot of the makeshift bier that, as senseless as it seemed, there was a reason for going through the motions. Whatever their feelings, there wasn't a soul in the entire country who would mourn her husband's passing, yet they all went through the motions. They came and brought food, at least a dozen of them. They murmured condolences, people Carrie had never even seen, much less passed the time of day with. And she took comfort in their presence.

They all knew Emma, of course, and they knew what

was expected under the circumstances. Nodding to both women, they walked past the open pine box Jonah had built and gazed down, their faces expressionless, at the stranger inside. And then they moved on to the kitchen table and helped themselves to the food they had brought. Fried chicken. Ham. Cabbage and plates of pone bread, cornbread and biscuits. Someone had even brought light rolls for the occasion.

"Gonna be a rainy fall," said one man.

"Cold winter, too. I never seen so many figs on a tree," a woman observed quietly.

"Thinking 'bout clearing that piece over near the river. It don't flood but ever' five, ten years or so."

Nothing was said about Darther Adams. He was generally known and generally disliked, and while that dislike hadn't touched Carrie personally, other than that no one could find time to help her work her husband's land, she felt the curious glances from time to time. After a minimal length of time inside, the men gathered outside to talk about the price of corn, the price of hogs and how much muskrat pelts were apt to bring this season.

The women began straightening up in the kitchen area. When the house was in order again, not a dirty dish in sight, Emma led Carrie outside. "It's time, I reckon," she said.

Jonah, who had stood apart from the other men, came forward then to meet them. Carrie had introduced them all earlier, then Jonah had taken the boys, who'd been overjoyed to see him again, down to the creek, leaving the others to observe the brief wake.

"The preacher's down with a sick head," Emma said. "I'll ask Walter to say what needs saying."

Walter was Emma's closest neighbor, and while he hadn't come right out and said so, it was plain that he, like the others, was here only for her sake. Some of the women had thawed to the point of including Carrie in their conversation about children and the fig crops and who had the best recipe for pickled walnuts.

Carrie laid a hand on her friend's arm and said, "No, don't do that. I knew him best. I'll say what needs saying." Knowing their sentiments, Carrie couldn't bring herself to ask one of the neighbors to pray over the departed.

Carefully not looking at Jonah, she waited while the men brought the pine coffin outside. Darther was a heavy man, and the box was large. When four of the older men struggled to carry the thing down the steps, Jonah eased into position and took most of the weight on his own shoulders.

"Thankee, son," one of the men murmured.

With measured steps, the women followed the procession, Emma and Carrie in the lead. When the coffin was lowered into the ground, Jonah stepped back. The men stood on one side of the grave, the women on the other. In all, there were fourteen people present.

Jonah's gaze met Carrie's, and he nodded imperceptibly. It was time.

Carrie felt as if her tongue was glued to the roof of her mouth, but she had a duty to do. She might have forgotten much of what she'd been taught as a child these past few years, but she did remember that much. Emma edged closer. Someone—a young woman whose belly was swollen with child—began to sing, and then several more picked it up. Only the women, not the men. The words were unfamiliar, the melody painfully slow, but Carrie joined in the best she could, grateful to be part of a group again.

When the hymn was over, she stepped forward, took

a deep breath, and said, "Darther wasn't from around here. I don't know if he has family somewhere up north. He had two good friends, a man named Liam, but I don't know where he is either—and my Uncle Henry up in Virginia. I'll write to Uncle Henry and tell him, but I guess right now, Darther would be real proud to know you were all here to, um—to see him on his final journey."

Oh, blast, she thought, shutting her eyes and trying desperately to think of what to say next. He's not going anywhere but into that hole in the ground. "That is— well, he's on his way somewhere, I guess. The Lord is his shepherd, too. So...I thank you all for coming. Amen."

There was a muttering of amens, and then Emma nodded at the mound of loose dirt. One more duty and then I'm done here, Carrie thought, and she picked up a handful of sandy clay and tossed it onto the yellow pine boards. "Come cool weather and I'll plant something pretty on his grave," she murmured to no one in particular.

Corn. She would like to plant corn, not that it would grow in the shade. A feeling of shame washed over her, because it had been a purely spiteful notion. All the same, it would serve him right, the old sot, for making fun of her cornfield.

As they turned back toward the house, a few women touched her arm, a few more nodded in a way that was almost friendly. With an air of relief, the men began hitching up and preparing to leave.

"You want to come home with me?" Emma asked.

"You could stay here for a few days," Carrie said quickly as it dawned on her that soon she would be all alone here, except for the two children. Jonah wouldn't stay. He was no longer her prisoner, no longer under any obligation to Darther. And besides, it wouldn't be seemly, an unmarried man staying on with a newly widowed woman.

"I sleep best in my own bed, child," the older woman replied with a look of concern.

One of the neighbors—Emma's friend, Walter Gilbert, she thought—offered Emma a ride home, and Carrie hurried inside and came out with a platter of fried chicken. "Here, you might as well take this, there's plenty left for Jonah and the boys."

After the last cart drove off, she turned to look out at the big old water oak, its leaves already turning yellow. The grave would have to be filled in later. They'd have to do it soon, before it rained. She probably ought to start on it now. It was enough that Jonah was looking after the boys, without expecting him to do anything more. She had done well enough alone before he came— she would do well enough after he was gone.

All the same, she was glad he was here now, to help distract the boys. It never occurred to her that he wouldn't know what to say to them. She knew from experience that when it came to unexpected death, children could harbor strange notions. In this case it wasn't like saying, "Grandpa's tired, he's gone to Heaven to rest now."

With one longing glance toward the woods that bordered the creek, Carrie sighed and went inside to change into her work clothes. She had work to do.

Chapter Thirteen

Jonah drew a map in the wet sand bordering the creek. "We are here. The creek grows wider here and flows this way until it joins the Currituck Sound."

"The same water? Then where do it go?" Nate devoured the lesson in geography with avid interest while Zac fell asleep watching two ants drag the corpse of another ant into a hole.

"Into the ocean."

"The 'Lantic Ocean." Nate nodded decisively. "I be a sailor when I grow up."

Jonah didn't know whether to encourage such an ambition or discourage it. Glancing at the lowering sun, he wisely did neither. "Shall we go help Miss Carrie with supper?"

"She don't need no help, they's all that fun'ral food. Lady from Greentown, she make a powerful choc'late cake. She brung one to old man Litkin's fun'ral."

In one fluid movement, Jonah stood and dusted off his hands. This boy whose age Jonah guessed to be no more than eight or nine years old, knew more about the customs in this area than Jonah did. He had wanted to shield them, but no one had shielded him when his old grandfather had been shot off his horse and then kicked in the head by the maddened animal. No one had shielded him when his mother had taken her own life, victim of a sickness of the mind.

Children were hardier than they appeared.

Still, he carried Zac rather than waking him, finding comfort in the warmth of the small, sleeping body. The goaty scent reminded him that he should have seen to their baths before they left the creek, but it would not hurt to go without washing for a few days. If that were the case, there would be far fewer boys and men in the world.

In the deep, late-afternoon shadows, Carrie was leaning against the trunk of the tree beside her husband's half-filled grave, shovel in her hand. She had changed into the shapeless dress she wore in the field. Damp with perspiration, it clung to her body. With her head tipped back and her eyes closed, she looked as if she had fallen asleep standing.

Jonah approached silently. "You should have waited. I would have done that." He indicated the grave, that had been partially filled with loose dirt.

Opening her eyes, she flexed her shoulders and then her fingers. Her hand had healed, but the skin was still tender from being protected for so long by a bandage. "Some of the men offered before they left. I told them I had someone else to do it."

"Then why didn't you wait?"

Conscious of a pair of round black eyes peering owlishly into the open grave, Carrie shrugged away from the tree. "Because I need to stay busy. I've been idle too long, as it is." It had been more an unconscious need for penance than a need to stay busy, she suspected. She could only do her best and pray forgiveness for her shortcomings. "Come inside, I'll set out the food again."

"Is they any choc'late cake?" Nate asked wistfully.

"Well now, I know there's raisin pie and fig cake—I'm not real sure about the chocolate, maybe you'd better go look."

Nate took off at a run. Zac rubbed his eyes, wiggled down from Jonah's arms and trotted after him. Jonah turned to Carrie and said quietly, "I will go home tomorrow. My horses need me. But first I will finish the grave and put up a wooden marker. Tell me what you want it to say."

Carrie shook her head. She didn't want to think of graves and markers now—most of all, she didn't want to think of Jonah's leaving. "You could bring your horses back here. There's room enough in the paddock."

She knew before he spoke that he was going to refuse. She was a newly widowed woman. He was a single man. It was not only unseemly, it was begging for trouble. "Yes, well...I didn't think you'd want to stay, but I thought it was only polite to ask."

She'd thought no such thing. What she thought was that if he left her—*when* he left her—she would probably cry until her eyes and nose were swollen shut, and then feel guilty because she hadn't shed a single tear for her murdered husband. There was nothing like a double dose of shame and guilt to make a woman miserable.

She set out cold ham and boiled potatoes, an assortment of pickles and relishes, and all the desserts that were left. Jonah cut the boys' meat when Zac would have picked up his slice of ham with both hands. Carrie, making fresh coffee, wondered where he had learned such patience with children.

And with women.

She let the boys share the feather bed, telling herself there was nothing wrong with it, only she didn't think she could sleep there again, not for a long, long while. They hadn't seen Darther lying there stone, cold dead, and so they piled in, too sleepy to question why she would give up her own bed in favor of a pallet on the floor.

More guilt, Carrie thought ruefully as she set about collecting their wet, muddy clothing for the wash pot tomorrow. She had some lengthy praying to do before she could live with her conscience again.

"Tonight I will sleep in the barn. Tomorrow I will finish what needs to be done, then I will leave." Jonah was standing in the open doorway. With the remains of the meal put away, the two boys sleeping soundly, Carrie joined him there. She tried to think of an inducement to lure him into staying a few more days...a few more years. "You don't have to—that is, you could always..."

Jonah gave her a steady look, reminding her that they both knew why he must go. The longer he remained here, the more a single idea became fixed in his mind. If she were his woman, they would lie together under the trees, under the moon, under the hot summer sun. They would make love in all the ways there were and it would still not be enough to quench his thirst. Far from robbing him of his manhood, following her Plow Road had made him burn until all he could think of was bedding her. Burying himself in her woman's body again and again, night after night, until they were both too old to do more than warm themselves by the coals of the fire that had once burned so brightly.

Adams had valued this woman with her warm heart and her quick laughter, her proud strength and shy beauty, less than he valued his rifle. He might have bedded her, but he had never loved her.

Jonah would have loved her more than his own life, this small, brave woman who was strong enough to harness a stubborn mule one-handed, determined enough to curse him into action, and tender enough to find room in her heart for two homeless boys.

Behind them, Zac whimpered in his sleep. A drowsy Nate muttered gruff words of comfort, then both boys lapsed into sleep again. Jonah touched Carrie's arm, and they stepped outside. And then, because the moon had just risen over the woods, lending an aura of cool mystic beauty to the old barn and the ramshackle chicken house, he led her out into the yard, where they stood side by side, neither quite able to break the growing silence.

Standing close enough to catch the bayberry scent of her hair, Jonah thought of the many women he had known in the past. None had ever aroused in him such powerful feelings of tenderness, lust, protectiveness and possessiveness. He had neither sought, nor did he welcome those feelings, yet he could no more deny them than he could deny the hard-earned lessons of a lifetime.

"Will you come back sometime? For a visit, I mean, not to stay." She tried to sound as if she didn't care, yet Jonah knew her better by now. She cared. She cared very much, and that caring frightened her, for she saw the problems ahead as well as he did.

It was that unspoken caring between them that made what he had to do all the more difficult. "I will come back again." He tried for a lighthearted tone. "We are neighbors, after all."

It wasn't enough, she wanted more. "And friends?"

"And friends," he agreed. They were more than friends, only he didn't know how to describe their relationship, much less how to deal with it. He only knew that this was not the proper time.

Her shoulders squared as if she were facing an entire regiment. "I'll—that is, the boys will miss you."

"I will say goodbye to them before I leave." Bathed in the illusive light of the moon, they were still standing between the horse trough and the barn, looking toward the big water oak and the half-finished grave.

Suddenly, Jonah had a sense of time flying past like cloud shadows on a windy day. Saw himself years from now, old, alone and filled with bitter regret. Yielding to impulse, he turned and caught her to him, burying his face in her hair. *Carrie, Carrie, heart of my heart, come away with me.*

And he kissed her.

The kiss would have ended as abruptly as it began, but Carrie refused to allow it. Both arms wrapped tightly around his sinewy body, she was like a stick of lighter wood tossed on a smoldering fire, all heat and energy. As her unskilled hands moved restlessly over his back from shoulders to hips, she met him more than halfway, learning as the kiss grew into something dangerously volatile. Eagerly, sometimes awkwardly exploring, wanting more and still more, hands fumbled, hearts pounded as one kiss grew into another and yet another until, breathing rapidly, they drew apart to stare at each other, stunned by the forces they had inadvertently unleashed.

"Carrie?" Jonah's voice was shaken, his hands on her face unsteady.

"Oh, please," she whispered. It was little more than a sigh, but it was enough.

Somehow they managed to reach the barn. The dark interior, redolent of horse and summer grasses, leather and ancient dust, was reassuring in its familiarity. Jonah led her to the single stall, where fresh straw had been spread after the foaling.

Again, an inner voice whispered that the time was wrong.

Again, he ignored the voice. The time might be wrong, but everything else was right. This woman in his arms was right. Carrie was his in ways he couldn't begin to understand. He only knew they belonged together.

The nagging voice whispered, *Someday, perhaps, but not now. Not yet. Not with the grave of her husband still unfinished.*

Valiantly he tried to break away, but her hands clung to his body. "Don't leave," she pleaded softly, and he didn't know if she meant, don't leave me alone here, don't go back to your own land, or don't leave off kissing me when every inch of my body is wet and aching with need.

He was swollen with need himself, fiercely aroused. And she was here, ready and eager for the comfort he could give her. There was no one to know or care. Not long ago he had thought that, like him, she was an outcast.

He had thought that at first, but after today, he was no longer sure. People had come to her house. They had done for her what they would have done for any other widow under the circumstances. They had accepted his presence, accepted his help…accepted him.

Perhaps they were no longer outcasts, but that didn't mean they could ignore the conventions. He had watched his mother suffer subtle slights until she had retreated somewhere inside her mind. He would not do to Carrie what a careless Union soldier had done to an innocent Kiowa maiden some twenty-nine years ago.

"We will do what is right," he said decisively, hoping his own conviction would be enough.

"This is right," she argued.

"It is right, the time is not. Your friend Emma would tell you that we must wait. When enough time has passed, I will come to you, and we will talk."

But Carrie didn't want to talk. For the first time in more years than she could remember, she felt as if she belonged to someone—truly belonged, in a way she had never belonged to her uncle or her husband, or even Mrs. Robinson, no matter how kind the elderly mission schoolteacher had been.

Jonah stood and held out his hands to her. She wanted to cry. Wanted to howl like a baby, wanted to throw something.

But she didn't. With as much dignity as she could muster, she rose, brushed the straw from her dress and straightened the bodice that had become twisted when he'd gone in search of her breasts.

Her breasts ached. The secret place between her thighs, that she had been warned by the missionaries she must never look at, or touch, or even think about, throbbed with almost painful intensity. Jonah had touched her breasts, and the more he touched her, the more she ached, in places not even close to her breasts. And the urges she felt—

Oh, my...

Darther had touched her breasts, but it had hurt. She'd wanted to smack his hands away, but she knew he'd only smack her back, so she'd lain there and let him do it to her. It had been nothing at all like this. She had actually wanted Jonah's hand on her breasts, and his mouth, and any other part of his body she could uncover.

She knew what he looked like without his clothes,

from that day at the creek. Now she wanted to do far more than look at him, she wanted to touch him everywhere, to join with him in what men and women did together. Never before in her whole life had she wanted *that*.

Sins of the Flesh. She'd been warned by the missionaries about Sins of the Flesh, along with coveting and bearing false witness and killing and all the other sins. At the time she'd thought Sins of the Flesh meant eating undercooked pork or certain other kinds of meat—perfectly sensible things Moses had warned against when he set out to lead a whole flock of people through the wilderness. But when she'd asked for specifics, she'd been told in horrified tones that decent people didn't speak of such things, so she'd simply put it away with all the other questions no adult seemed willing or able to answer for a curious child.

Well, she thought dolefully as she followed Jonah from the dark barn, if this was what a sin of the flesh felt like, it was hardly worth the trouble. This itchy, achy, unsettled feeling inside her that made her feel somehow…incomplete.

What she needed was to go to bed with a hot brick and a strong dose of whiskey-laced yaupon tea. That always got her through her woman's time. It might serve to cure what ailed her now.

Jonah was waiting outside, hands in the back pockets of his close-fitting denim trousers. His head was lowered as if he was searching for something on the ground, but it was too dark to see.

She hesitated, and then spoke. "Jonah, if I did anything wrong, I—"

He turned and glared at her, his pale eyes taking on light from the moon. "Hush, woman! You did nothing wrong. The wrong was mine, for taking you inside the barn. I meant to—''

"I guess we both know what you meant to do. I meant to, too, so don't go taking all the blame on your own shoulders. I know all about Sins of the Flesh. It wouldn't be a sin if it weren't so tempting, but we never actually got to the sinning part, so…''

"So?'' he prompted, sounding almost as if he were amused.

"So I reckon I'll get some sleep. The boys will be up early, and I've got washing to do, and—''

"Carrie.''

"—and then there's the marker.'' Pushing past, she fled to the only sanctuary she could claim. A two-room cabin, a pallet on the floor, two orphaned boys who might or might not decide to stay with her…and an un-loaded Springfield rifle, which she supposed was now hers.

Carrie slept soundly, a result of the exhausting past few days. The boys were already outside when she awoke, the remains of fig cake and a few crumbs of chocolate attesting to their self-sufficiency. Her first thought was that she would make sure they ate meat and greens for dinner. Her second thought was that Jonah would be leaving, if he hadn't already gone.

Jonah hadn't. T'a-Kon was saddled and ready, and even from the house she could see that the grave was completely filled, the earth neatly mounded, with a plain cypress cross marking the head. She would carve the thing herself, or maybe paint on the name and date. She honestly couldn't find it in her heart to do more.

Jonah was talking to the boys, his voice too soft to carry. If he was inviting them to go live with him instead of staying on here, she didn't know what she would do. Bribery might work, she thought as she hastily buttoned on her best dress and raked a comb through her flyaway hair. She had cake and pie. He didn't. She could bake more when those were gone. He probably made do with tasteless hoe cakes and canned beans. Her uncle had eaten from tins until she'd cleaned up his filthy kitchen and taught herself to cook.

On the verge of hurrying out the door, Carrie was suddenly overcome with an attack of shyness. She was still hovering there in the doorway when Jonah swung up into the saddle, saluted the boys and turned to look at her, standing there with her heart, she sadly feared, in her eyes.

"Well...goodbye," she called out, forcing a smile. "Come to see us when you have time. We'll look forward to it, won't we, boys?"

And then she choked up, unable to say another word, even if she could have thought of something sensible to say. She was still standing there when the big bay stallion settled into a trot that carried them around the bend, out of sight.

She would be safe now, Jonah told himself. He would see that she had ammunition for her rifle. Not that he expected her to need it, but it made her feel more secure. He had left her the buckskin. If her uncle objected, they could settle it between them, but she needed a horse to ride and the buckskin was calm and dependable. The boys had assured him they would look after Miss Carrie, and Miss Emma, too, if she needed it. Jonah thought these woman were a far hardier breed than their men gave them credit for being, but all the same, he had made

Nate promise to come for him if there was the least sign of trouble, and given him directions.

And then his thoughts turned back to the questions that had kept him awake all night. How long must a man wait before offering for a new widow? Was it the same in the East as it was among his people?

He told himself he was only thinking sensibly of his own future. A wife, he reasoned, was not a bad thing to have. With a wife, he could have sons of his own. That, too, would be a good thing, for he liked children, finding in them the same basic honesty that he did in horses.

Carrie cooked well. She worked hard. She was honorable, with none of the deviousness he had seen in many women, including those of his mother's people. Besides, she would need help raising two boys. Nate, he suspected, was of mixed blood. Whatever his bloodlines, he would need help in years to come, and who better to help him than another mixed breed?

How long, he wondered again as he turned off the road toward his own land, would he need to wait? If he waited too long, another man might take advantage of her. If he offered too soon—a week was probably too soon—he might offend her.

He might offend her by offering at all, he reminded himself, but quickly dismissed the thought. She had been willing and eager. She had come to care for him long before she recognized her own feelings. In many ways she was as innocent as a child.

In the ways of love she was almost completely untutored. He looked forward to teaching her, but first he must offer and she must accept. They were both too close to the edge of being outcasts to take risks.

His body reacting enthusiastically in anticipation, Jonah adjusted his trousers. Shifting his weight on the saddle as T'a-Kon settled into a smooth canter, he passed mile after unbroken mile of wine-red gum trees and tall green pines. They rode by a newly cleared field beside a log barn, where a man he recognized from yesterday's funeral lifted a hand in greeting. Jonah waved back, going so far as to smile.

Truly, he liked living here in the East. The past was behind him now—his days as a warrior, as a sailor—as a prisoner. He had much work to do, though, for a woman like Carrie would need boundaries. This very day he would begin cutting trees to build her a square cabin with a roof, four walls and a floor. The money he had earned in a single race would buy an iron stove and possibly even window glass. If he had to sleep in a house, he would prefer one with more windows than walls.

In time he might even build a second cabin nearby so that she would have her friend Emma to help her when the babies came. At such a time, women needed other women, that much he remembered from his youth.

For the first time in a long, long time, he began to sing, his voice a surprisingly pleasant baritone, the words a mixture of English, Kiowa and Spanish. Over the years to come, he told himself, generations of Longshadows would walk these fields, trap in these woods, fish in the nearby waters. Tall young men who would raise the finest horses. Yellow-haired girls who could charm the birds from the trees with their laughter.

One week, he decided. He would wait one week for the asking, three weeks more for the wedding and bedding. "We have much to do, my black-eared friend," he said softly, letting the words flow past him on the fragrant autumn-scented breeze.

Chapter Fourteen

By the time Jonah had satisfied himself as to the condition of his horses, the moon was high overhead. Boodles and her foal, Howard, were thriving. Zabat and Saynday would be dropping their foals soon. Seven days, he predicted. Both mares being experienced in such matters, they were placidly awaiting their time. He had planned to finish his barn by the Time of Agantsanha—the moon of Cold Warning. But that could wait. First he must build Carrie's house.

Carrie...

Lying on his back gazing up at the bright sky, he thought of the woman he would have as his wife. His only wife. With Carrie, he would have no need for other wives, even if the white man's law had permitted such things. The more he considered the matter, the more confident he was that she would accept his offer, despite his mixed blood. She had feared him at first, which was a wise thing to do. The jailer, after all, had handed him over in chains, calling him a thieving half-breed.

But she had come to know him as they worked together over the days and weeks, to accept him as a man like any other man. Perhaps not as good as some, but far better than others. Reading a woman's mind was not quite as easy as reading a horse's mind. With women there were layers upon layers. Women did not always understand their own thoughts, which made it doubly hard for a man to understand them, but it seemed to him that she had come to like him greatly—even to want him in the same way he wanted her, which was in all ways.

From nearby, T'a-Kon whickered softly. *You worry too much, man. Night is for resting.*

"You're right, my friend," Jonah replied, smiling at his own foolish conceit. Jonah had unsaddled the stallion, rubbed him down, fed and watered him, sensing T'a-Kon's contentment at being back in a familiar place, even as his own mind was busy with plans for the future. He had left his saddle, which he seldom used, on a rack just inside the barn. One day he would finish his barn, and add on a stable with large stalls and a tack room. He would plant grain and cultivate the kind of grasses that grew best here in the East. With Carrie at his side he would follow the Plow Road and eventually become a successful breeder of fine horses, a valued member of the community.

With Carrie at his side, he thought with amusement, he could follow the dread Plow Road without fearing at all for his manhood.

Closing his eyes, he pictured the woman who had led him away from the jail, her small face mutinous in its determination, shaded by a ragged straw hat pulled down over her sun-streaked hair—cursing her mule as she struggled to balance reins and a heavy rifle with one good hand.

He had seen her a few days later letting a rooster peck corn from her hand, touching his battered comb with a gentle finger. And later still, as she tried so hard to guard her heart against two homeless boys. But the best memory of all was seeing the stricken look on her face when she had knelt in the dust to remove his leg irons. Still wearing the same faded gown, the same ragged straw hat, with the gun lying forgotten in the road beside her.

He remembered the many times her eyes had met his in a look of shared amusement, or satisfaction in a job well done. One by one, the barriers between them had fallen. He'd tried not to think about that first day on the creek bank when sheer rage at injustice had led him to shed his clothes. Since that day, determination to put the incident from his mind had only focused his thoughts on what he was trying so desperately to forget. Following her damned plow, he would feel her eyes on him and he would wonder if she, too, remembered. If she was picturing him as she had seen him then—the way he had tried to visualize her so many times, standing bare on the creek bank, with sunlight dappling her pale skin. Lying on a mossy bed, her arms and her heart open to him as she waited for him to come to her.

Oh, yes, he had no fear of losing his manhood. It would survive the Plow Road well enough, so long as she shared his sleeping place each night…as well as each morning, and many times during the day.

Shifting restlessly, Jonah forced himself to think of more practical matters. The work he still had to complete on his barn. The fenced paddocks and green fields that would one day stretch as far as the distant woods, with a square house large enough for a man and a woman, two growing boys and as many babies as Carrie wanted. There would be a row of windows on each side. Three, perhaps four. And a brick chimney at each end.

An owl called softly from a nearby tree and he

reached out to the empty place beside him, smiling in his sleep.

A pale dawn was just beginning to push back the darkness when next he opened his eyes. Without moving, he took time to absorb the sound of awakening birds, the cool, damp feel of morning mist drifting just above the warm earth, the familiar scent of horses. One of the mares whickered softly. T'a-Kon answered, and Jonah smiled, a sense of well-being flowing through his veins. Rising, he stretched his arms over his head, yawned and then scratched his belly.

It was then that he heard the sound of approaching riders. A prickle of unease came over him, and he reached for his shirt. It was early for company. Since the funeral, he felt somewhat more comfortable with his neighbors, but they were hardly on visiting terms.

Nearby, the bay stamped nervously. Jonah murmured quiet words as he folded his sleeping blanket and reached for boots. He had bought his first pair of boots when his last pair of moccasins had worn out. In the summer months he often wore nothing at all on his feet, but when trouble threatened he preferred to be fully prepared.

And something warned him that trouble had arrived.

"Longshadow! You in there?"

With the rising sun in his eyes, he could not see the two men clearly, but he recognized the voice. It was not one he welcomed. As his sleeping quarters consisted only of a tarpaulin stretched across four posts and a single blanket spread over the ground, he was clearly visible. Nevertheless, he stepped away, his face giving away nothing of his thoughts at the sight of the sheriff and his deputy. At least the man had given him the courtesy of a warning. He could have crept up and taken him while he still slept.

The deputy, Noah, scowled in an effort to appear older. Both men dismounted. The paunchy, middle-aged sheriff bit off a chew of tobacco and glanced around, taking inventory of the unfinished barn, the big bay stallion, the three mares and colt in the far pasture, and the half-cleared section Jonah had been working on when he'd been hauled off to jail back in the early summer.

"This your place, huh?" The sheriff's tone was non-committal. If he was impressed, he declined to admit it.

"This is my land." He could have told him the name Carrie had given it—God Knows Where—but he was not sure the man would appreciate the subtle humor.

"Know anything about a knifing that took place up in Virginia a few days ago?"

Jonah's mind touched on the possibility of being jailed once more for a crime he had not committed, and quickly veered away. "Yes."

"You wanna tell us what you know about it?"

He did not, but saw no way out of it. "I know that a man named Adams was stabbed. I found his body, and as I had done work on his farm, I took him home to his widow." It was the truth as far as it went, but he had a feeling it wouldn't go far enough. He could have added that he had also raced for the man even though he despised him, but that would only lead to further explanations. Besides, it had nothing to do with the murder. The sheriff knew that it had been Adams's money even more than his word that had turned the tide at his hearing.

The deputy looked around the three-sided barn. He kicked aside a mound of straw and ran his hand over the tack hanging on the wall. Looking for a murder weapon?

His knife was not in the barn, it was still in the scabbard on the side of his saddle, in plain view.

"How come you was the one to find his body? Just happened to know where to look, that right?"

There was no way he could explain to this man why he had followed his instincts to the place where the murder had taken place. Powerful events engendered powerful emotions, disturbing the atmosphere so that those who were attuned to such things could feel them long afterward. So he said nothing.

"Did I mention the *dee*-ceased was robbed, too? According to the sheriff up Princess Ann way, he won a fat stake in one of the races and was on his way home with the money when he was attacked and killed. Word's going around that he was seen arguing with a breed. Now, I'm not saying it was you, Longshadow, all I'm saying is, you knew the victim, so you—"

"Sheriff?"

Both men turned at the sound of the excited voice. With a sinking heart, Jonah saw that the young deputy had made a damning discovery. Taking his time about it, the older man dismounted and sauntered over to where Jonah had left his saddle.

"Whatcha got there, Noah?"

"Money! Looks like you was right on target. This here feller was hidin' a roll o' money big enough to choke a hog."

The sheriff spat a stream of tobacco juice. Turning, he hooked his elbows over the fence and said in a deceptively mild tone, "You wanna try to explain where you got all that money, boy?"

If lying would have helped, Jonah might even have attempted it, but nothing would help him now. Once again he had been judged and found guilty without a hearing. He could explain, but who would believe him? He had walked that path before. "The money is mine. My horse won a race up in Virginia."

"You admit you was at the track that day, then?"

"I told you that. And the money was not hidden."

"Weren't exactly laying out in plain view, either. Reckon maybe you'd better saddle up and ride down to the courthouse with us."

Nate took care of Sorry and the buckskin. He had a way with horses. Zac had a way with nothing, so far as Carrie had been able to learn, but he shooed the last of the chickens inside the pen and fastened the gate, even though he had to stand on a box to reach the latch. Give a boy responsibility and he will live up to it, Jonah had said. Goodness knows, she had responsibility enough to share.

"Can we go see Miss Emma tomorrow?" Nate asked, after turning the feed bucket down over a fence post. "She say she be glad to see us mos' anytime."

"We'll see. If you eat enough supper, maybe we can bake raisin cakes before bedtime." She had stewed the last of the funeral ham with potatoes and onions, to make it go further.

"Miss Emma bake 'em better."

"Miss Emma can cook most things better than I can, she's had more years to learn, but we'll stay home for a few days, in case—" In case Jonah decided to come back. She didn't dare say it, hardly even dared think it, but just the same, she'd as soon be here in case anyone came visiting.

As it happened, someone did, within the hour, only it was not the someone Carrie had hoped to see. "Uncle Henry, why—how—?"

Carrie hadn't heard from her uncle once since he had married her off to Darther. Clapping a hand over her mouth, she said, "Oh, my—I guess you heard about Darther. I would've sent word, but there hasn't been time…"

"Don't tell me you went and had young'uns, Dart didn't say nothing about no babies." And then his eyes narrowed on the pair huddling together behind the horse trough. "Them ain't yours. 'Specially not that—"

"These are Nate and Zac. They're my—my wards. I'm their guardian."

A grin spread over the old man's face. "Well now, ain't that something. Just like I was to you, only these two ain't no kin, 'specially not that there one. What's your name, boy?"

For a minute Carrie thought Nate would refuse to answer. "Name's Litkin. Nathanial Litkin," he said with a defiant air.

"Litkin, huh? What about the other one? He ain't no spawn o' Darther's, is he?"

Carrie stiffened indignantly. "He is not."

"We're orphans," Zac said helpfully.

Nate elbowed him and then said, "No we ain't, we's leftovers."

Carrie felt like sweeping them up in her arms. Both boys had heard tales of wicked things happening to orphans, the least of which would be separation, which was why Nate insisted on denying the truth.

The storekeeper nodded, a thoughtful look on his face. He turned in a slow circle, taking in the neat cabin with its freshly raked yard, the cleared field beyond, and the two animals peacefully grazing behind the barn. "See you kept my gelding. Good horse. Better'n the one I rode here on. Niece, why don't you put together some supper while I have me a look around."

And then it dawned on her. Her uncle was looking at her farm the same way she had seen him look at a hand of cards—that same greedy gleam of anticipation. The wretched old man had come to claim her widow's portion. And even after all the work she had put into making the farm productive again, the law would probably let him have it.

Over her dead body! "There's nothing to see, Uncle Henry. The barn needs work, the house is drafty—the truth is, it's hardly worth the trouble of patching up, and as for the rest—" The disclaimer was an instinctive reaction to the fear that was beginning to settle in like a cold rain.

"Now, I wouldn't hardly say that. Place has got a lot of potential, way I see it. 'Course, I wouldn't expect a girl to see it that same way."

"I'm not a girl, Uncle Henry, I'm a woman. Who do you think patched the roof? Who do you think finished clearing that cut-over field out back?" She hadn't meant to brag, she'd meant to run the place down, to make it seem hardly worth his interest, but that blessed pride of hers wouldn't let her.

"That there breed you paroled off'n the county prob'ly did most o' the work, but he ain't going to be able to help you now, girl."

"Woman!" she corrected. "I'm not the green girl you traded to Darther to settle your debts, I'm a grown woman now."

"What you are is a widder woman. And as I'm your only kin, it's up to me to look after your interests."

Well, there it was. The cards were on the table, as she'd heard him say more times than she could count.

Carrie knew as well as she knew her own name that this man who claimed to be her uncle, but who had never shown her the least sign of affection, was far less interested in looking after her than he was in feathering his own nest.

"No," she said flatly.

"What's that? You ain't gonna offer me supper?" His smile reminded her of a vicious dog curling back his mouth in warning.

"You can take supper with us, but that's all you're taking. Boys, go and—" She broke off, glancing around.

"If you're looking for them brats, they took off through the woods."

Gone to Emma's, more than likely. She had all but told them if ever they felt threatened for any reason, to go to Emma. Evidently they felt as threatened by Henry Vander as she did.

"You can water your horse and give him a forkful of hay, but I wouldn't bother to unsaddle him, no longer than you'll be staying. While you wash up out here, I'll set out the food."

Torn between fear and anger, Carrie hurried inside, her mind going over every word that had been spoken since her uncle had ridden into the yard. He hadn't known about the boys, but he knew about Darther's murder. Hardly surprising, as they usually attended races together.

He obviously knew about Jonah—who he was and how he had come to be here, but then, Darther would've told him that much. *That there breed you paroled off'n the county probably done most of it, but he ain't gonna be able to help you now.* Only now did the words sink in.

He wasn't? Why not?

Not that she'd expected Jonah to help her any longer—he had his own land to work—but why would her uncle say such a thing? Did he know something she didn't?

The thought made her go cold all over. The minute he stepped through the door, his avid gaze taking in everything in sight, she pounced on him. "Uncle Henry, what did you mean about Jonah not being able to help me?"

"That ham I smell? One thing I missed since you left me, girl, is your cooking. You set a real good table, and that's the honest truth."

"Uncle Henry, you didn't come here to talk about my cooking, now what did you mean about Jonah? He just left here yesterday. Have you seen him? Have you talked to him? Is he all right?"

Henry lifted the napkin covering a basket of bread on the table, then turned to the range and uncovered the pot on the warming shelf. "Hmm, stewed ham and biscuits, a man can't ask much better'n that."

Carrie slammed the lid back on the pot. "You'll not taste a bite of my food until you tell me the truth. Now, what did you mean? Why wouldn't Jonah help me if I sent for him?"

"Well, first you'd have to send all the way to Curri-tuck Courthouse. Jailhouse is right next door, ain't it? I don't reckon they'll be letting him out on parole now that he's been charged with murder."

The breath went clean out of her body, as if someone had squeezed her lungs until she was limp as a rag doll. "No," she whispered, shaking her head in denial.

"Yep. Took him in first thing this morning. They come to me yesterday, sheriff from Princess Ann and the law from down in Currituck, wanting to know all I knew.

I'm what you might call a witness. Happens I didn't see the deed done, but I was the one that found poor Darther a-laying there, bleeding like a hog in January.''

Carrie sat down suddenly, then lurched up again. Grabbing her uncle by the lapels, she glared at him furiously. "You listen to me, Henry Vander, Jonah is *not* a murderer. Anyone who says he is, is lying!"

"Well now, I reck'n that's between him and the law. All I know is what I saw, and what I seen was them two arguing out behind the livery stable, where the body was found and later disappeared."

With her brain once more beginning to function, Carrie demanded the details. "What do you mean, the body disappeared?"

So Henry told her about seeing the two men arguing, elaborating as he went along. With all the telling and retelling he'd done the day it had happened, he'd discovered a real theatrical bent. He went on to describe his heroic search for the culprit, and then leading the sheriff and half the transient population back to the scene of the crime, only to discover that the body was missing.

"Jonah brought him home." Carrie stood, feet planted apart, arms crossed over her bosom, and glared at the man who might or might not be her relative—she had serious doubts about the matter. "He dug the grave, and we had a funeral and buried him out under the oak tree. More than a dozen people came. And then Jonah put up a cross and I'm planning to paint Darther's name on it. It was a—a real nice funeral."

Henry nodded, his avid eyes taking in every detail of the modest interior. "Only fittin', I'd say. Stab a man to death, you ought to have to dig his grave. Diggin' ain't easy, less'n you all have had more rain down here than we have up our way."

Carrie fought back a sick feeling, knowing she would
have to keep her wits about her until this matter was
sorted out. First of all, Jonah was no murderer. Anyone
who knew him would know that.

But who knew him as well as she did? She had seen
the way the people who had come to the funeral had
acted, watching carefully from a distance, only gradually
thawing enough to accept his help carrying the heavy
pine box. By the time they had left, several of them had
spoken a few words. She'd been so proud of his quiet
dignity she could've burst right wide open. How could
anyone believe he was a murderer? He was a noble gentleman from the top of his glossy black hair, right down
to his scarred ankles. If no one else would speak up for
him, she would be proud to do it.

On the heels of that thought came another. She could
yell it from the treetops until she was blue in the face,
but that wouldn't prove his innocence. She was only a
woman—she'd been nowhere near the scene of the
crime. And besides, it had been her experience that men
didn't put much stock in what a woman said.

"Leave that box alone, that's my clean linens," she
snapped, seeing her uncle dragging a wooden box from
under the bed. Meddlesome old fool, he'd even looked
in her sugar bowl!

She would go anyway. The minute she got rid of her
uncle, she would set out for Currituck Courthouse.
Somehow, she had to let Jonah know she believed in his
innocence. It would be late when she got there, even
riding flat out on the buckskin, but she would find someone to let her in the jail if she had to wake up the entire
community.

Nate and Zac would be safe enough. They were prob-

PART THREE: A GREEN SUNRISE

Chapter Five:
The Solar Threat

There was a parallel reality to the Peaceful Atom. Harry Truman's 1952 Paley Commission had promised a solar future. And the sun posed a greater threat to the IOU empire than even public power. If America could get its energy freely from above, who would need a private utility system? In the solar vision, the IOUs saw an end to their empire. A year later, Ike diverted the nation onto its tragic atomic detour.

But the idea of heating homes with the sun dated back to the Greeks. It wasn't exactly rocket science: face windows to the south; design overhangs to shade the heat of summer. To the south, plant hardwoods for shade; on the north, use evergreens for windbreaks.

The Paley Report envisioned 15 million solar-heated homes in the U.S. by 1975. Photovoltaic cells would convert sunlight directly to electricity. Wind power, used in Europe for centuries, would supplement or supplant the centralized grid. A windmill had operated on Manhattan Island in the 1600s. Tens of thousands of them powered farms of the Great Plains through the mid-century.

A post-war flood of subsidized coal and oil kept solar

Chapter Fifteen

"Uncle Henry, I hate to rush off, but you see, I promised to take supper with a friend this evening." Seeing his pale eyes shift to the pot simmering on the back of the stove, she improvised hastily. "I was going to take her the stewed ham for supper, but there's plenty in the pot. I can take out some for you—you can even stay here and eat it if you want to, but I'd better leave before it gets any darker."

She had to get away. Simply *had* to! Any minute now he would put down the gun, and then he would look at her and see the stark terror in her eyes and know that she knew. She *knew*.

Henry had murdered Darther and stolen his watch fob all because he knew his niece would inherit the property and that he, as her nearest male relative, could easily gain control of it. In the years she had lived with him she come to realize that he was mean, lazy and greedy, but she would never have thought him capable of cold-blooded murder. Now he was trying to cast the blame on Jonah, and that, in her eyes, was the worst crime of all.

Her mind seething with unfinished thoughts, she

snatched down a bowl, filled it with stew and plopped it onto the table. "It's almost dark," she said with a sickly smile. "Just leave the bowl on the table when you're done, I'll wash it when I get back from—from Emma's house."

She would saddle the buckskin and—

No, it would have to be the cart. She could hardly take a pot of stew with her if she rode horseback, but if she left it here, he might wonder. It would take forever to drive to Currituck if she had to rely on Sorry and the cart, but she had to convince him—

She would hitch the cart to the buckskin, then leave the cart in the woods and take the back road. She would have to do without a saddle, but if Jonah and the boys could ride without one, so could she.

Don't forget to take the stew. For Heaven's sake, don't forget that!

And a bridle, don't forget you'll need a bridle!

"You got any butter for these biscuits?"

"Butter? No, I'm sorry—my cow went dry and I traded her for—here's some preserves, though." She plopped a jar of wild peach preserves on the table. "I'd better hurry. I'm glad you came by, Uncle Henry—sorry I couldn't stay, but you see, I promised...."

She stepped into her high-top shoes, stomped her stockingless feet down inside them, but didn't bother to do up the laces. The things chafed her heels. She would take them off as soon as she was out of sight of the house, but she'd have to remember not to leave them in the cart. If she was going to stand up to the law of Currituck County she would need all the self-confidence she could muster. Bare feet wouldn't help.

Hurrying outside, she slid the heavy iron stewpot onto the cart, shoved the tailboard back into place and

wheeled the cart over near the paddock. After opening
the gate, she reached for the traces. It was a pity to waste
the stew, but if she'd left it behind Uncle Henry might
have grown suspicious, and if he had grown suspicious,
he might have murdered her, too, and then who would
stand up for Jonah?

She could take it to Jonah. They probably hadn't been
feeding him properly. He'd been far too thin when she'd
brought him home from that same jail the first time.
Dragged him home on a lead as if he were an animal,
she reminded herself, agonizing all over again.

Broken thoughts flickered through her mind like fire-
flies as she hurried inside the barn and snatched a bridle
off the wall. Jonah loved her stewed ham. She would
take him—

*On horseback? Without so much as a saddle? She'd
do better to concentrate on getting him out of that
wretched place.*

Thank God for the buckskin. Sensing her desperation,
Sorry would have plopped down on his behind and refused to budge. The mule had never once cooperated in
his entire miserable existence, until Jonah came along
and charmed him into behaving.

Jonah, oh, Jonah, I'm coming!

They had to believe her. She would simply have to
convince them that Jonah was incapable of murder, and
that her uncle had done it. *I saw with my own eyes,* she
would say. *Uncle Henry was wearing my husband's
watch fob, and Darther would never in this life have
parted with it, it was his good-luck charm.*

He hadn't been wearing it when Jonah had brought
him home. She'd been too shocked to notice. Jonah
hadn't known him long enough to realize the signifi-

cance, but she should have known even then that something was wrong.

Well, of course something had been wrong, the man was dead. Stabbed to death. He'd already bled all over his favorite shirt.

"Where's Darther keep his whiskey?" Henry Vander called from the open doorway.

Carrie hid the bridle she was holding behind her. "If there's none in the bottom of the pie safe, then you'll have to climb up in the hayloft. It's in the corner behind the stack of bales."

"Fetch me down a jug before you go."

Carrie slung the bridle in the back of the cart and pulled herself up onto the seat. "Uncle Henry, I'm sorry, but it's almost dark and Emma will be wondering where I am. G'bye now, come back again real soon." Stifling an irrational urge to laugh, she snapped the reins and clucked the gelding into a fast walk. By the time they entered the back lane, they were trotting.

The trip to Currituck Courthouse seemed endless. Once she reached Shingle Landing, it was only a matter of some ten miles or so, but it seemed to take forever. Her imagination working at feverish pitch, Carrie pictured Jonah, bound hand and foot, being dragged before a stern-faced judge. She pictured him being locked inside that miserable old jail that was more than a hundred years old and smelled as if it had never been scrubbed in all that time.

Leg irons. "They'll put him in leg irons again, and damn and blast it all to hell, he hasn't done anything wrong." She whispered the words, and would have shouted them to the high heavens if she'd thought it would help.

Here and there a few lamp-lit windows gleamed in the darkness. She had no idea of the time, she only knew it was late. She might have to wake someone up to let her in to wherever they were holding Jonah. If only she could have set out sooner...

If only it had never happened, she amended quickly, then Jonah and Darther would be off racing somewhere. Darther would still be alive, and Jonah would still be free. Of course, they could never be together in that case, for that would be a sin, and she already had enough on her conscience, thinking of him in a way that no married woman should think of a man not her husband.

But she could go on loving him and maybe not think quite so much about the sinning part, knowing that he was alive and well.

I'm coming, Jonah! I'll get you out of there if I have to confess to murder, myself!

"It was the watch fob, that's how I knew," Carrie said breathlessly for the third time. She had talked her throat sore, and that was only after she had threatened to burn down the jailhouse if that dimwitted deputy didn't let her in. Instead, he had left her on the jailhouse steps with an ugly hound that tried to sniff the back of her skirt while he shuffled off to wake the sheriff. Eventually—it had seemed hours—he'd returned, dragging the irate man back with him.

The sheriff, wearing a striped nightshirt, a pair of hastily pulled-on trousers and a pair of heavy boots with the rawhide laces trailing on the oyster-shell path, demanded to know what the bloody hell she meant, coming down here in the middle of the night and getting him out of bed.

Taking a deep breath, she tried to explain, repeating

what she had told the deputy. The young fool had kept nodding and mumbling, "Yes'm" until she'd flat out lost her patience and threatened to burn down the courthouse if he didn't fetch the sheriff. Shivering with a mixture of nerves and despair, she'd been given a choice of waiting outside or being locked in a cell inside.

She'd chosen to wait outside with the dog, a decision she had already begun to regret long before the two men showed up. Inside, even locked in a separate cell, she could have called out to Jonah and he would have heard her. The jailhouse was a two-story building, but even so, it was small enough so that she could have made herself heard.

The sheriff obviously didn't relish being wakened in the middle of the night by a strange woman with an incoherent tale to tell. Carrie tried her best to sound calm and rational, but her best wasn't good enough when she was out of her mind with worry. She'd forgotten and left her shoes in the cart—hadn't even thought to bring a shawl, even though the late September nights were downright cold just before daylight. Her hair must look like a hawk's nest, but then, it rarely looked much better since Emma had chopped it off.

None of which could be helped now. She was here, bare feet, wild hair and all, and regardless of appearances, she was in full possession of her wits, whether this man believed it or not. He himself was none too impressive. The first time she'd met him, when she'd come to rent a prisoner, he'd struck her as surly and condescending. She didn't know if he remembered her from before or not, but he obviously didn't appreciate being dragged out of bed in the middle of the night and having to come over to the jailhouse to hear some wild tale about an open-and-shut-case of murder.

"You want to run that by me one more time, ma'am. You say there was this here watch fob that proves the Injun didn't kill nobody, on account of he ain't got it. Is that what you said?"

So she went over it one more time. She would retell it a hundred times if that was what it took, but her patience was wearing exceedingly thin. "You see, it was my husband's good-luck piece because he loved racing above all, and the fob was shaped like a flying horse. He told me once when I was admiring it that it was pure gold, but I don't know about that." She did know he'd whacked her on the side of her head, knocking her senseless for daring to touch the thing, but she hardly thought that would interest this man, who looked as if he'd seen and heard it all, and didn't believe any of it.

"And now my uncle has it," she reasoned, "which means Jonah couldn't possibly have murdered anyone." She waited to see the dawn of understanding. From his tipped-back chair behind the scarred desk, the sheriff, who was every bit as thick-headed as she'd first thought, continued to study her. Whether or not he remembered her, he obviously didn't put much stock in what any woman said, much less a woman who turned up in the middle of the night with no hat, no shoes, and a wild tale about a watch fob that proved a murder.

But then, she had halfway expected that. In some parts of the world there were men who treated women as if they were intelligent creatures worthy of respect. The Currituck County sheriff was evidently not among them. "Well then, if you won't take my word for it, lock me up in one of your cells and send for the judge." Bone tired and worried sick, she had run plumb out of patience. Surely the judge who had listened to reason and given Jonah his freedom once before would do no less now.

"I'm tempted, damned if I ain't," he muttered. "Leastwise it'd get me off the hook." And then he bellowed, "Noah! Git yore lazy ass back out here!"

Carrie went home with the sheriff without being allowed to see Jonah, but with the satisfaction of knowing that the judge, who happened to be visiting his daughter only five miles away in Snowden, would be asked to come by and hear her tale tomorrow.

Fanny, the sheriff's wife, managed to smile when she was presented with a guest in the middle of the night. "Lord he'p us, child, what happened to you? Come inside—Julius, go an' open the window in the baby's room."

Julius the jailer. Carrie stifled a giggle. She was so tired she was ready to drop. "My horse—" she whispered.

"Jule, see to this young'un's horse. Come on inside, honey. My name's Fanny Smith, and you're that woman that rented out a prisoner. I told Julius, I said sooner or later, it's going to cause trouble. I said—"

The sound of a window squeaking open was followed by the slam of a back door. The house couldn't be much larger than her own, yet it was clean and comfortable, with a Bible on the table and a kettle on the range. Carrie's stomach growled, embarrassing her further. Before she could protest, Fanny Smith was pouring a glass of milk and setting out a plate of cold ham and sweet potatoes.

"Oh, I couldn't," Carrie said, and then did. She hadn't eaten in so long—hadn't even touched her own ham stew, which was probably feeding a family of raccoons by now. No wonder she was about to collapse. Fear, worry, hunger…and now this uncertainty, waiting for the judge to come and hear her story.

Sitting across the table, the sheriff's wife directed traffic like one of those men Carrie had read about who stood in the middle of a New York street and waved wagons and buggies and horsemen this way and that. Julius came in the back door and was promptly sent to bed. He went without protest. A battle-scarred tomcat was assisted out the back door with the side of a slippered foot. Then, in a softly scolding monologue, Carrie was instructed to drink all her milk, and to have another slice of ham, and what in the world was she doing visiting the jailhouse at this hour of the night, why it was practically morning.

Limp with fatigue, Carrie told her story all over again in response to a not-too-subtle inquisition from the plump little woman in the cotton wrapper, her stringy gray hair tied up in rags. "So you see, he couldn't possibly have done it," Carrie concluded, "but they'll think he did because he's a—that is, his mother was an Indian and his father was—well, I'm not sure, but I think he might have been a soldier."

"A breed, that's what you're trying to say, like his blood weren't red like everybody else's. I'm Scotch-Irish, myself, least so far as I know, and Jule, he's English on his mama's side, but his pa's folks were raised up in the Dismal Swamp, hunting, trapping, splitting shingles, making whiskey. No telling who-all's mixed up in that family. All kinds and colors lives in that swamp, most of 'em hiding out from the law."

Carrie's eyelids were drooping. She was drooping all over. Seeing it, her hostess rose and led her into a room hardly big enough to contain a narrow bed and washstand. "Daughter's room. She died of the diphtheria when she was just five years old, bless her heart. It like to tore Jule up so bad, I swear he's not been the same since. Now here's one of my nightgowns, it'll swaller you whole, but it's better then sleeping in your day clothes. Go on, now, get in bed. I'll wake you early—I reckon you'll be wanting to go see your young man."

A few minutes later in the other bedroom, Fanny elbowed her husband to make him stop snoring. When he choked on a snort and woke up swearing, she said, just as if they'd been in the middle of a conversation, "I don't know if that young feller did it or not, but I'm glad you had the good sense to bring her home. Poor child, she's all tore up about him."

"Young feller, hell—damn breed got no better sense than to—"

"Julius Cesar Smith, hush your mouth. You don't know the boy did anything wrong, so don't go setting yourself up as judge, jury and hangman, all rolled up in a bunch."

"Mmm...go t'sleep, woman."

"Did you send Noah to Snowden for Judge Powell?"

"Yes, ma'am, I did. Now can I get some sleep?"

"She's real pretty, but right now she looks like she's been dragged through a knothole."

A snore issued from the pillow next to her, and Fanny smiled in the dark. Folks might think he was a hard man, but she knew him better than she knew the face in her own mirror. Some of the ugliness he came across doing his job might stick to his outside, but inside where it counted he was as true as the north star, and not near as cold.

* * *

"Have some more eggs," Fanny Smith ordered. "Judge Powell won't be there yet. It's more than an hour's ride, and he won't leave Ella Mae's house without having himself a good breakfast first."

According to the wag-tailed clock on the kitchen wall, it was nearly half past nine. Carrie had meant to be at the jailhouse the minute the front door was opened, demanding to be allowed to see Jonah. "What's he like? The judge," she asked, rearranging the scrambled eggs on her plate.

"Fair man. He'll listen, think it over a spell and speak his mind. If he don't think there's a case against your feller, he'll likely settle it right there. You're lucky he was so close by, else you'd have had to wait weeks for a hearing."

She didn't have that much time. Jonah didn't have that much time. She couldn't have borne seeing him locked up in that awful place for weeks on end, with the uncertainty of a trial hanging over his head. It would be like caging an eagle.

Pushing her plate aside, Carrie stood and shoved in her chair. "Do you think your husband will let me see him now? Jonah, I mean. I need to—someone needs to—"

"Lor', child, you don't have to explain." The older woman glanced pointedly at her bare feet. "I don't reckon you've got a pair of shoes tied onto your saddle?"

"I don't even have a saddle. I was in such a hurry to get away—that is, as soon as I heard what had happened, I had to get here and straighten things out."

Fanny left and returned a moment later with a hairbrush. "Here, you'll want to look your best, seein' your young man. Pity my feet are so big, else you could borrow a pair of my shoes, but I don't reckon it's your feet he'll be looking at.''

Carrie did the best she could with her hair, and the jailer's wife brought her a blue fringed shawl. ''Put this on, it brings out the color of your eyes. He'll not look much beyond that, if I know young men.''

Carrie, too anxious to be embarrassed, was on her way out the door when the woman handed her a napkin filled with biscuits still warm from the oven, dripping with butter. ''Take him this. Tell him I'll send his breakfast over directly with Noah.'' And she muttered to herself, ''If Noah don't eat it first. That boy! If he weren't my own nephew...''

''Well now, straddling the state line the way it does, complicates matters some, I don't mind telling you.'' The judge, a man more impressive for the bright intelligence that gleamed from his eyes than for his rumpled suit and his slight stature, appeared to ruminate over what she'd just told him.

Carrie had wanted to see Jonah, but Jonah refused to see her, so she'd been waiting to collar the judge the moment he stepped through the door of the small, Tudor-style building.

''I remember your young man,'' the judge said thoughtfully, nodding his head.

Her young man. Why did everyone refer to him that way? Was it so obvious? Would it complicate matters? Would the judge think Jonah had murdered Darther in order to claim his wife?

''He's my friend, not my young man.''

''Now, you understand, Missy, that I don't have clear jurisdiction in this particular case, but I don't mind telling you I was right impressed by your young man's bearing. Happen to know he has an excellent reputation among those who've had dealings with him—mostly horse dealings, you understand. Still, it counts for something."

More nodding. More ruminating while Carrie fidgeted. "You say Vander from up Hickory way is your uncle? Storekeeper?"

Quickly, Carrie sketched in her own background, finishing with, "So you see, we're not sure, but we think so." Personally, she no longer thought anything of the kind. "At least he sent for me when I had nowhere else to go and provided for me, and that counts for something." She didn't see fit to add that he had worked her like an ox, repaid her with a pallet on the storeroom floor and barely enough food to get by on and then used her to settle his gambling debts. It wouldn't do Jonah's case any good to let it be known she had good reason to harbor a grudge against her uncle.

"Shame it couldn't have happened down here in North Carolina. As things stand my hands are pretty well tied."

Carrie felt like crying. Felt more like grabbing the man and shaking him until his suspiciously perfect teeth flew right out of his head, but she did neither. "But Darther—that is, my late husband, was from North Carolina, and so is Jonah. And the last time I saw my uncle, which was only yesterday, he was just a mile or so down the road from Shingle Landing where our farm is located, looking it over. That gives you all the authority you need, doesn't it, if you can catch him before he goes back to Virginia?"

"I'll study on it, that's the best I can promise. Whatsisname—Longshadow—he'll have to stay locked up, you understand, until I find out more about the matter."

It was too much to hope that Jonah would be released. All the same, Carrie's heart was as heavy as a cornmeal dumpling soaked in potlikker. The judge would hem and haw until Uncle Henry went home, and then the Virginia sheriff would come and get Jonah and carry him up north to Virginia, and she would never even get to see him again.

A sob shuddered in her throat. The tip of her nose turned red and her eyes filled and overflowed, despite her determination not to cry. "B-but it's wrong!"

Carefully, the little man in the rumpled suit unfurled a handkerchief and blew his own nose. "Well now, no call to get all weepy, little lady. Happens I know a few folks up in Virginia. I'll get to the bottom of it directly, don't you worry. If he's proved innocent, you can have him, but until then..."

She desperately wanted to believe him, but too many men had lied to her in the past. Henry Vander had claimed to be her uncle. She was almost sure he wasn't. He'd said that Jonah had probably killed Darther. Another lie. The sheriff had told her Jonah was dangerous. He wasn't. The judge might say one thing and do another. Or worse, do nothing at all.

Mopping her eyes with the tail of her borrowed shawl, Carrie glared down at his honor, Judge Alexander Hamilton Powell. At barely five feet tall, she hadn't a lot of experience in glaring down at anyone, but the judge was still seated, which gave her the advantage. "Henry—" She refused to call him uncle. "Henry's probably still at my place, adding up all the things he's fixing to claim now that Darther's dead. You just remember what I said—he was wearing that watch fob when he showed up yesterday, and Darther would never in this life have parted with the thing. You just bear that in mind."

If she didn't know better, she would have thought that was a gleam of amusement she saw twinkling behind the judge's gold-rimmed spectacles, but that didn't make a speck of sense. Before she could come up with any further demands, Julius the jailer strode past, muttering something about damn goats.

"Mornin', Judge, this here girl tell you what's got her all het up?"

"She did. I'd take it as a personal favor, Julius, if you'd let her see the boy before she leaves."

"I'm not leaving," said Carrie.

"Noah!" The sheriff yelled. And when the young man who served as caretaker and occasional deputy shuffled into the tiny office, dusting crumbs from his hands, he snapped, "Take Miz Adams to see the prisoner." To the judge he added, "Ain't got but one man in jail, business's been slow, but it's picking up some. Widder up the road says her goat's been stole."

Hurriedly, Carrie touched her hair, brushed at her shirt and licked her lips. She wished now she had taken the time to change to her best dress, but then Henry might have gotten suspicious. Jonah would just have to take her as she was. Lord knows, he'd seen her looking far worse, and right now the only thing that mattered was getting him out of this place and back where he belonged.

With her.

Chapter Sixteen

"Take her away." The words, spoken harshly in that familiar voice, broke her heart. Splintered it like a lightning-struck pine tree.

"Jonah, no—please. I've come to help you," Carrie pleaded. When he refused to turn and face her, she clenched her fists at her sides. "Dammit, Jonah Longshadow, you stop acting like a bone-headed mule and listen to me! Do you want to spend the rest of your life in a miserable place like this?"

She waited. He continued to stand here with his back to her, his arms crossed over his chest and his feet braced apart. Stubborn as a rusty nail.

"Well, all right, we both know that's hardly likely," she conceded, searching for another way to pry him loose. "People don't spend a lifetime in a jail. In prison, maybe, but jails are only for holding, which is awful enough."

Oh, God, and that was supposed to cheer him up? To give him hope? If by some miracle that weasely little judge got off his butt end and did as she'd told him, Jonah would be a free man. Free to return to his own home. If, on the other hand, he was found guilty of murder in spite of all anyone could do, then he would be hanged by the neck until—

Oh, God. "All right then, just listen to what I have to say." Gripping the bars, she ignored Noah, who was leaning against the wall, gnawing on a filthy thumbnail. "Henry—that is, the man I thought was my uncle, came to see me yesterday—or the day before—I've lost track of time. At any rate, he came to look over the farm because he thinks he can just walk in and take over everything now that Darther's dead. He as good as said so. He said a girl like me would need someone to take care of things, and I guess it's pretty plain he's elected himself for the job."

"Miz Carrie…"

She waved a hand behind her. "Hush up, Noah, this is important."

"Take her away from here, Noah," Jonah said without turning around.

"I'm not going anywhere until you hear what I have to say. Jonah, he did it! I'm certain of it, and so is Judge Powell." *'Scuse me for stretching the truth, Lord, but You understand, I've got to give him something to hang onto, or he'll just give up.*

"Go home and look after the boys."

"The boys are with Emma. They're fine, it's you I'm worried about."

"I don't need you to worry about me, I can take care of myself."

There, now that was sheer bravado speaking if she'd ever heard it. Taking heart, Carrie pressed her cheeks against the cold metal bars. "I know you can, but not in here. Once you're out of this place you can go your way and I'll go mine, but as long as you're locked up in here for doing something I know good and well you didn't do, I've got no choice.''

''Miz Carrie...'' Noah worked his hand inside his longjohn shirt and scratched his stomach. ''Miz Carrie, maybe you oughtened to—''

''Hush up, Noah. Go away and give us some privacy.''

''Stay where you are, Noah.'' Jonah spun around, his pale gray eyes alight with cold fury. To Carrie he said, ''I don't want you here. Can you understand that? I've been here before—I've been in far worse places and survived. It's what I do best. Survive.''

But they both knew that this time he might *not* survive. ''That's just too damn-blasted bad, because I'm here and I'm staying!'' Better to curse than cry.

The starch seemed to go right out of him then. From the far side of a cell no bigger than Peck's stall, he looked at her with eyes that had seen the past, too much of it painful, and now looked into a future that was no more promising. ''Carrie, I want you to go back home and tell Nate to take my horses back to your place. He'll need help. Ask one of the men who came to the funeral. I want you to sell my land and use the money to hire help with your planting. Add onto your house for the boys—they'll need a room of their own. And—''

''Hush up!'' It fair broke her heart all over again to hear him going on this way. ''If you're tired of living around here, and God knows I can understand it if you are, you can sell your blasted land yourself!'' She was yelling. She never yelled except when she was dealing with that damn-blasted mule.

''Will you just listen to me?'' Jonah shouted right back.

''Miz Carrie—''

"Hush up, Noah, I'm talking to Jonah." Irritated almost beyond bearing, Carrie turned to the boy and said, "Just what is it you're trying to say?"

"I, um—that is, Miz Fanny, she said to tell you, uh…"

"Well?"

"That you could sleep in her spare room and she'll feed you if you want to stay for the ha—that is, the trial."

Before she could think of a reply, Jonah crossed the room, his bare feet silent on the straw-covered floor, and covered her hands with his. Hers were cold as ice. His were warm and hard and dry. "Carrie—listen to me, I don't want you here. We both know what Noah meant to say. It might come to that, and if it does, I want you far away from here. I want you to remember the times we worked together in your cornfield. When your corn grows tall and green, I want you to think of all the words we never quite said, all the smiles felt, but never quite allowed to happen. I want you to remember—"

"Don't." If he had reached through the bars and wrapped his hands around her throat and choked the life right out of her, it couldn't have hurt any more. "You—I—" With a broken laugh, she pulled one hand free to smear the tears that drowned her eyes. "I know why you get on so well with that damn-blasted mule of Darther's. You're two of a kind. Dumb as dirt, stubborn as a stump."

"Don't cry, Carina," he whispered.

And at that, of course, she wailed and sniffled and threatened to take apart the jailhouse, brick by miserable brick, if that damn-blasted Julius Cesar didn't catch his damned goat stealer and get back here with his keys and unlock the damn-blasted cell.

Noah fled. Jonah did the best he could through the bars, stroking her hair, cupping her face, whispering broken words of endearment in both Spanish and Kiowa, neither of which language she understood.

Which was probably a good thing, for he found himself promising far more than he would ever be likely to deliver.

The sheriff didn't bother to hide his displeasure at finding Carrie seated at the kitchen table peeling potatoes and talking a mile a minute to his wife. She went on peeling and talking. It was not the first time she'd been forced to stay where she was not welcome, but there was just no way she could make the thirteen-mile trip to the jailhouse every morning and return home each night. There weren't enough hours in the day. She had vowed to stay close until Jonah was freed if she had to sleep on the jailhouse steps with Noah's flea-bitten hound. If the sheriff didn't like having her underfoot, that suited her just fine. Maybe he would get on with the job of bringing in the real murderer.

She saw fit to remind him of his duty, which didn't make him one speck happier. "Henry Vander might still be right here in your county, you know. He'll want to pack everything he can haul off with him, and Darther—my husband, that is—liked nice clothes—" Her face burned with hot color as the man's gaze wandered slowly over her patched blue poplin, faded to a colorless shade of gray everywhere but under the arms. She tucked her bare feet under the sagging skirt. "Well, he traveled around a lot, that's why he wore nice things. I was never much of a traveler, myself. I'm what you might call a homebody, so there was no reason for me to buy a bunch of fancy foofarolls."

"I ain't got enough deputies to go chasing all over tarnation for some man you say might've broke some law or another up in Virginia."

"Might have—!" A half-peeled potato rolled off the table onto the floor. Carrie ignored it. "Broke some *law?* Henry Vander killed my husband, I'm telling you he murdered him in cold blood, and then stole his lucky piece for good measure. Don't tell me murder's not against the law in North Carolina!"

"Now, hold yer water, young'un, I didn't say—"

"Julius Smith, mind your tongue."

"Then if you know there's a murderer loose and a man in jail for a crime he didn't commit, what are you still standing here for? Why aren't you going after him?"

The sheriff rolled his eyes. Until recently he'd led a reasonably peaceful life, or as peaceful as a man's life could be in his line of work. "I'm still standing here, *Miz* Adams, on account of I got crime right here in my own back yard that needs looking into."

"Lord in Heaven, what now?" his wife demanded.

"Somebody stole the widder Gilbert's goat. Woman claims she's got to have goat's milk, else her bowels'll seize up on her." Muttering, he stomped into the bedroom, came out with a pistol strapped to his waist, and left without another word.

Wanting to kick out at something, Carrie continued to peel potatoes, grimly paring them down to the size of marbles, while Fanny Smith spooned yesterday's stewed beef into a pie crust and slid it into the oven of the fancy cast iron four-holer with the nickel-plated trim. Time crept past with all the speed of a dying snail. Carrie wanted to march over to the jailhouse and force that sniveling caretaker at gunpoint to let her into Jonah's cell.

She wanted to shake that stubborn gray-eyed Indian until his teeth rattled and then hold him in her arms until this nightmare ended. And maybe do more than that, because who knew how much time they had left?

She wanted that damn-blasted sheriff to find his damned goat thief and then go after Henry before he left the state. The state line was only a few miles from Shingle Landing, and Hickory, where Henry's store was located, maybe twice that much farther.

She wanted the judge to reconsider and expand his authority. Surely the laws against murder applied in both states.

She wanted...something.

Anything! Never in her entire life had she felt so helpless, not even when she'd been swept up in the dead of the night and forced to flee the only home she had ever known. She'd been too young to understand what was happening then.

Now, she understood only too well.

By the time Fanny Smith piled a plate with steaming hot meat pie, boiled potatoes and pickles and covered it with a napkin, Carrie had worried her belly into a hard knot. "Here, child, take this to your young man. Make sure you hand it to him yourself, else Noah'll get first whack at it, and there's no telling how much'll be left."

Carrie took the covered plate and the pitcher of milk and hurried out the door. It came as almost a shock when she stepped outside to see that the rest of the world was still there. Two boys chased a half-grown dog down the road, their yelps and the dog's yaps a counterpoint to the sound of hammering as a carpenter took advantage of the fast-fading daylight. A woman rode past in an empty hay wagon and nodded to her. Numbly, Carrie nodded back. Half a dozen wild geese settled noisily onto the nearby Currituck Sound while a hundred more followed.

As the savory scent of herb-seasoned shepherd's pie drifted up to her nostrils, Carrie wondered how life could go on as if nothing were wrong. How children could play and men could go on working while not a hundred yards away, a man was being held behind bars, his very life at stake, for a crime he hadn't committed.

Noah met her at the jailhouse door and tried to take the food from her, claiming it was his duty to see that nobody smuggled in weapons that might allow a dangerous criminal to escape.

As luck would have it, the jailer's wife arrived with a plate of cornbread in time to prevent an incident. She shoved the dog aside with her foot. "Forgot the bread. Noah Gibbs, you're not going to steal that boy's supper and shame me by giving him leftovers the dog wouldn't touch." She turned to Carrie. "My own sister's boy. You'd think he was starving, the way he squirrels food away. Look in the cleaning closet, you'll likely find meals I cooked a week ago. I hate to think what these poor prisoners get to eat. Crumbs, more'n likely. Now, you move aside and let Miss Carrie take this in to her young man while it's still hot. If you're so all-fired hungry, you come home with me and I'll fix you some supper. Spot can have the scraps."

The caretaker brightened at the offer, but then his face fell. "Aunt Fanny, I can't go off and leave that there prisoner unguarded. Uncle Julius left me in charge."

"Is the poor man locked in his cell?"

"Yes'm."

"Then leave Spot to stand guard."

"Spot, he ain't too good at standin' guard."

"Then let him sit guard! Noah, just go pull up a chair to my kitchen table and watch the jailhouse through the window while you eat your supper. If you see any suspicious goin's on, you can borrow Julius's shotgun and come a-runnin'."

Carrie stared, both hands full, at the small, gray-haired woman wearing a ruffled apron over her neat calico gown. Obviously, Currituck County had elected the wrong Smith as sheriff. Fanny could run rings around her husband.

Jonah was waiting, the guarded hope in his eyes painful to see. His gaze went from her face to the covered plate in her hands, and back to her face. Carrie was suddenly self-conscious. She had taken the time to bathe, for while the Smiths' house might be small, the Smiths had a genuine porcelain indoor bathtub, a luxury beyond her wildest dreams. Not even Mrs. Robinson had possessed anything so fine.

"You look tired," was Jonah's comment. Not, *Am I free to leave? Did the sheriff go after the murderer? Did the judge believe your story?*

"Well, I reckon I am. I didn't sleep much last night— or the night before, come to that."

Fanny herself unlocked the door, handed the prisoner his supper, pocketed the key and then left them alone together. Swallowing her disappointment not to be allowed inside the cell, Carrie dragged a chair from the office and sat outside the barred door. She touched her hair, tugged her skirt to cover her feet, and said, "Well, go on and eat while it's warm."

He refused to look at her. She knew very well he didn't want her there, didn't want her to see him behind bars, but that was crazy. "The first time I saw you, you looked a lot worse than you do now,'' she reminded him. It got his attention. He glared at her. ''All I'm saying is, you don't have to be self-conscious.''

Jonah tried to ignore her, tried to ignore the savory scent of the beef pie, but in the end, he gave in. He knew the value of pride, but he also knew the dangers. Scooping up a shred of well-cooked beef with the spoon, the only utensil he had been given, he started to eat. No matter what happened in the days to come, he would need his strength.

''Jonah?''

He tried hard to ignore her, but he just couldn't do it. ''What?''

''I know you don't want me here,'' she said, as if hoping he would deny it.

He shrugged and bit off a chunk of cornbread. Remembering the stale remnants he'd been given the first time he had stayed in this cell, he knew he should be grateful, but it chafed his spirit far worse than the chains he'd once worn had ever chafed his flesh for her to see him like this—caged like an animal.

''I want you to leave.''

''Well, I don't much like being here, either, for that matter. If I'd known—if I'd thought—leastwise I might have changed into something decent.''

He didn't quite shrug, but it was there, nevertheless. The attitude that protected the small flame of pride that would burn inside him until it was finally snuffed out.

''Well, damn and blast if you aren't the stubbornest critter that ever walked on two legs. I'm not doing this for you, you know!''

''No?'' he asked with no real appearance of interest.

''I'm doing it for me! Because if you hang for Darther's murder, that means Henry will go free, and he'll swear he's my uncle and lay claim to my house and my cornfield—to everything I own. That's just the kind of scoundrel he is.'' She hitched her chair closer to the bars and thrust out her jaw in a way Jonah had come to recognize. She was hitting her stride now. ''You listen here to me, Jonah Longshadow, I'm not about to give up the first real home I've had since the blasted Indians murdered my family and damn near every other family in the settlement!''

''Those were Sioux. They were not Kiowa.''

''I don't care if they were Esquimaux, that's beside the point. I don't have time to live in the past, even if I could. What matters right now is that if I don't get you out of here and Henry Vander inside, he'll take everything I've worked for. Henry didn't mend that roof, and neither did Darther. I'm the one who climbed up there and nailed on those patches when I got tired of having to mop the floor after every rain. Darther didn't care if the fireplace threw off more smoke than it did heat, because he was seldom home once the weather turned off cold. I wouldn't see hide nor hair of him from January to April, once the real racing season got underway, and not all that much the rest of the time, what with all the nag races and such. And as for my cornfield…''

She sighed. It was all he could do not to set aside the plate and reach for her through the bars, but if he gave in to his own desire, she would know his greatest weakness, and that would do neither of them any good.

''If you're right about your uncle,'' he said carefully, ''then don't go home. Don't even go to your friend's house, for he would find you there.''

''I am right about him! I know it in my bones. Jonah, tell me what to do? We have to get you out of here.''

He set aside the half-finished supper, no longer interested in food. "Vander would have no cause to harm Emma or the boys. They're no threat, and the man didn't strike me as particularly vicious, only stupid and greedy."

"He's mean as a snake. He used to take his belt to me when I didn't move fast enough. At least Darther never used anything but his fists."

Something cold and hard solidified inside him, but Jonah knew better than to allow his emotions to overrule his brain. One man had already paid for his cruelty. The other man soon would. White, yellow, red or black, there were as many good men of all colors as there were fools. That much he had learned in his days of sailing with men of all races and nationalities. The sheriff was not entirely the fool he appeared to be, but he was a lazy man and not particularly intelligent. The judge he ranked somewhere below Lieutenant Pratt, but considerably higher than the sheriff. As for the caretaker who had stolen his food and shared his fleas during his last stay, he rated him not at all.

Carrie herself was the weakest link in the chain of circumstances that held him here. Seeing a wrong, she expected it to be immediately set right. Her own experiences should have robbed her of such idealism. Even he, a half-breed bastard raised on a reservation, knew better than that. Having been transported across the country from one prison to another, eventually freed only to be jailed twice more for crimes he had not committed, Jonah knew something about the workings of the white man's law.

He knew that the laws were no better than the men who enforced them, and therein lay their weakness. He would give the law three days, he decided arbitrarily, and then he would make his own law.

Meanwhile, Carrie must be distracted before she endangered both herself and any plans he might have to escape. "I remember the first time I saw you," he told her. "You wore that ugly straw hat smashed squarely on your head, but there was no mistaking the set of your jaw or the light of battle in your eyes. I was not at all sure I wished to leave the comfort and security of my cell."

Carrie scuffed a big toe on the splintery floor. "Yes, well...I hate to tell you what I was thinking."

"You don't have to. I heard the sheriff tell you to keep the chains on me and to shoot if I even looked like I was thinking about running."

"You couldn't have run far," she said, her voice soft with painful memories.

"And you could not have shot me."

"You knew the rifle wasn't loaded?"

"Not then, but I knew you wouldn't be able to lift it, much less to take aim, with only one hand."

After a while, she said ruefully, "You hated me. I don't blame you."

"I did. At that time I hated the world."

"Is that why you never once lowered your head? Every time I looked back over my shoulder, you were glaring at me fit to kill."

"Were you frightened?"

She nodded, her short, unruly hair, the top layer bleached by the summer sun, bobbing like a windblown thistle. "Scared half to death, but I'd borrowed money to lease you from the sheriff, and if I didn't get my field cleared, I wouldn't be able to plant my corn, and if I didn't get a crop in, I wouldn't be able to repay Emma the money. Darther would never in the world give me

money to hire help, even if I could've found a man willing to work for me.''

Several minutes passed in silence. Strangely enough,
it was not an uncomfortable silence. Jonah broke off a
chunk of cornbread and passed it through the bars. Ab-
sently, Carrie took it and nibbled at the crusty edge.
When it was gone, she brushed off her hands and said,
''I was scared you'd find out about the gun— I mean,
that it was never loaded.''

''You drew a line around your house.''

She nodded. ''Fat lot of good that would've done if
you'd wanted to come after me, huh?''

''I would not have crossed your line, Carrie. I will
never cross your lines, no matter what happens.''

No matter what happens. They both knew what those
words encompassed.

Thus the pattern was set for the next two days. Carrie
couldn't bear seeing Jonah locked behind bars like a
common criminal, yet she was powerless to change the
way things stood. All she could do was take him food,
water, soap and towels, and pray that the truth would
soon be discovered. By now Henry Vander would be
back in Virginia. Carrie knew he begrudged paying
someone to keep his store open when he was away at
the races, but he begrudged even more the money lost
when it was closed.

They talked through the bars, because when they fell
silent, too many memories rushed in. The wonder was
how so many memories could be created in so short a
time. Until the day she died, Carrie knew she would
remember the sight of her arrogant prisoner on that hot
August morning, standing on the bank of the creek without a stitch on his nut-brown body, his gray eyes mock-

ing, his manhood in full, glorious display. Even thinking about it now made her face flame.

"Come back," Jonah said softly.

"Back? I'm not leaving, I told you that."

"I meant come back from wherever you were in your mind."

Sheer mischief lightened her face. "I was down by the creek that first morning when you—"

He laughed aloud. Considering the situation and their dismal surroundings, the sound was shocking. But then something changed as his gaze held hers. It was as if the air grew too thick to breathe. As if lightning was poised to strike.

"Jonah," she whispered. They stared at each other while the ordinary sounds of the world outside faded away. Dropping to her knees, she reached through the bars and caught his hands.

Somewhere, someone called out to a neighbor. A mockingbird ran through his repertoire in a cedar tree outside the window. Jonah's hands moved up her arms, drawing her closer until he could rest his forehead against hers. The bars were maddening. She wanted to rip them out with her bare hands. Wanted him to take her far away, to a place where they could make love until this awful aching, itching urge went away. Their lips touched tentatively at first, and then eagerly, wordlessly expressing pain and longing, desperation and desire.

And fear. The fear that this was all there could ever be. Regret that they had not made more of their brief time together.

Jonah's hands moved over her body, frustrated by the limitations imposed by the iron bars. Cradling her breasts in his hands, he felt his body react as the small, hard tips nudged his palms, igniting all the pent-up long-ing they had tried so hard to ignore. "I want to make love to you, Carina, but not here—not now," he whis-pered.

They both knew that here and now might be all there was, all there could ever be. Hopefully, she said, "We could—I could—"

"No," he said quickly, for she would have done it, he knew. Shed her clothes if he'd asked her, with no thought to her own shame should someone discover them. "No, Carina, there's no way we can do what we both want to do through the bars." His low laughter held more pain than amusement, but she managed a smile in return. The sheriff had been gone all day. His wife had managed to distract Noah by asking him to help her bake and deliver pies for the church supper. Guarded only by the lazy mongrel, they had more privacy than either of them had dared hope for, but it wasn't enough.

By the time the sheriff got back that night after being gone all day, he still hadn't made up his mind whether or not to tell the boy what he and the judge had worked out between them. It wasn't entirely legal.

Legal, hell, it broke rules that weren't even on the books, but that was what came of living so close to a state line. There were times when busting through a few miles of red tape was the quickest way to see justice done. Spot was sprawled in front of the door, one long, thin ear dangling off the edge of the granite step. The mutt didn't even stir when Julius stepped over him. Noah was asleep on the cot, a plate and fork on the floor beside him. Boy ate like food was going out of style. Julius suspected he allowed his dog to sleep in the cells when they happened to be empty, which was most of the time, thank God.

The sheriff didn't even want to think about what he was going to tell his wife. Whatever he told her, she'd worm the rest of the story out of him and then hurry over to the jailhouse and repeat every word he'd said to the prisoner, adding a bunch more of her own. After nearly forty years of marriage, his Fanny was still a romantic at heart. Made a man proud, but damned if it didn't wear him out, keeping up with her expectations.

Tired and longing for his own bed, he nudged the sleeping caretaker awake. "Anything happen while I was gone?"

The boy jumped up, tripped over his boots, stepped in the empty plate and righted himself. "Um, no sir— that is, I helped Aunt Fanny with them pies and all. Nobody come in but Miss Carrie, she was here most all day."

Noah wasn't an official deputy, although Julius occasionally used him for simple duties when he couldn't find anyone else willing to be deputized. But the boy was Fanny's sister's boy, and to keep peace in the family, Julius had hired him on as caretaker and all-around errand boy. He'd never regretted it...leastwise no more than two or three times a day.

"Go back to bed, son, I'll make the rounds and go home."

Noah flopped back onto the cot, which was wedged between the chimney and the cleaning closet. The closet had been intended for guns and ammunition, but in all the years Julius had served as sheriff, guns had seldom been needed for anything more than hunting and killing snakes. From time to time he strapped on his Colt as a reminder that Julius Cesar Smith was fully capable of seeing that folks around these parts behaved. And for the most part, they did.

He carried the lamp with him. Noah had forgotten to clean the globe and refill the tank. "That boy," he muttered.

And then he stopped dead in his tracks at the sight of the woman lying on the bare floor, with the breed lying just on the other side of the cell door. They were both sound asleep, their hands linked through the bars.

He swore a little, but not loud enough to wake the sleeping couple. It was all Fanny's doing. She had already made up her mind who was guilty and who was innocent. Judge and jury all rolled into one, that was his Fanny, Lord love her.

Chapter Seventeen

In the sunny front parlor of his daughter's house between the railroad tracks and the bull yard canal, Judge Powell looked over his notes as he prepared for his meeting with the sheriff, the accused, and the accused's female cohort, widow of the deceased. Messy situation, any way you looked at it. He pondered which news to impart first—the good or the bad.

No firm rules had been spelled out when the judge had delegated the task of gathering information, but it was understood that certain jurisdictional lapses would be overlooked. The gentleman he had commissioned, a police officer who had seen fit to retire early after certain irregularities had come to light, was well-suited in this particular case, having a wide knowledge of gambling interests along the middle Atlantic states. Both Adams and Vander were known to be hardened gamblers, with the unsanctioned and unregulated nag races their preferred venue.

Before he left for the courthouse the judge took luncheon with his daughter, Ella Mae, newly wed and unfortunately not well versed in the art of cooking. The good news first, he decided, belching discreetly in his napkin. That should take the edge off the other.

Carrie sat a decorous three feet away from the cell door and watched while Jonah picked at the plate of sausage and cabbage she had brought over from Fanny Smith's kitchen. Noah had met her at the jailhouse door and offered to take it in for her, while Spot gazed longingly up at the napkin-covered plate, but she knew what would happen in that case. Between the boy and his dog, Jonah would be lucky to get a single bite.

"Tomorrow morning early I'll go home and see to things there. Nate knows to go home once a day and feed up and get the eggs. But what about your horses?"

"Two of the mares will soon be foaling. Other than that, they'll fare well enough." They'd been over it again and again. He'd wanted her to leave yesterday. She'd insisted on staying. Today they had reached a tentative compromise. She would go home and find someone to see to his horses. When a trial date was set, he would send word. He didn't want her here, but he knew better than to believe he could keep her away. If worse came to worst, he would ask that his punishment take place immediately, before she had a chance to get back.

Carrie Carina, hold me in your heart until the dogwood trees bloom again. Then it will be time to let go old memories and make new ones.

"Afta'noon, Judge, you come to see the pris'ner?" Noah's cheerful voice broke into Jonah's doleful thoughts. He welcomed the interruption. Setting his plate aside, he stood and braced himself for what was to come.

Carrie bristled defensively. "You listen here to me, Jonah Longshadow, no matter what anyone says now, it's going to come out all right in the end," she hissed as footsteps neared. "You didn't do it, and Judge Powell's got honest eyes."

He actually managed a chuckle, but then the caretaker was there, eyeing them both suspiciously. Eyeing the untouched plate longingly. With a sigh, he rattled his keys and unlocked the door. "Judge Powell says to let you go up front 'cause he don't like it back here, but Spot's standin' guard outside and the sheriff's on his way over from dinner, so don't go thinkin' you can run off."

It was a solemn group that settled in the cluttered little office. Carrie dropped onto one of the two chairs, then bobbed up again, too nervous to sit. Jonah remained standing, his face carefully without expression. Noah went on rattling his keys and scratching, and then the sheriff entered, nodded to the judge and said, "I reckon you got something to report, yer honor. Might as well set down and get started."

The judge cleared his throat. He glanced around the room. Carrie wanted to scream at him to get on with it, but Jonah only stared at a fly crawling up the wall. "Well then, here's the gist of it." He cleared his throat again, adjusted his spectacles and began to read from his scribbled notes. "First place, Miss, you're not married to the deceased. Seems the man who performed the ceremony is a well-known drunkard from up Hickory way. Never been ordained, never held any office—can't even read s'far's anybody knows."

Carrie caught her breath and held it as the words sank in. She wasn't married. Had never been married. She had lived with that miserable skunk, ruined her back and her hands doing his laundry, cleaned up his messes when he drank himself sick, slept in his bed—

Slept in his bed....

The sheriff spoke up then. "Then I guess that uncle you was so worried about can't claim your property after all, since it ain't even yours."

"But what about Darther's watch fob?"

"Probably never know. Adams might've given it to him. Vander might've won it from him."

Carrie sat down, then jumped to her feet and began to pace. As the small room was crowded with five adults, it was an ineffective means of working off her frustration. "Yes, but—"

"As for you, young man," the judge addressed Jonah, "On the weight of certain evidence, which has not yet been confirmed, mind you, I've decided to let you out on bond until a formal hearing can be set. A few of your neighbors put in a good word for you—said you were steady, hardworking, sober. Said you had an excellent eye for horseflesh," he added with a droll hint of amusement. "As for the other two principals in the case—"

"Principals?" Noah stopped rattling his keys to ask the question.

"Shut up, Noah, ain't you got a floor to scrub or something?" Sheriff Smith turned to Carrie and said, "He means the deceased and your uncle."

"I'm pretty sure he wasn't. My uncle, that is. Not that any of that matters now. Go on, Judge, what were you saying?"

"Seems neither man was especially well thought of in the community. Adams didn't seem to have a particular community unless you count the racetrack crowd. At any rate, son, if you'll put up the deed for your land and the bills of sale for your stock, that will serve as your bond. Meanwhile, I've set in motion certain inquiries in Virginia that might or might not bear fruit."

It was all Carrie could do not to hurl herself into Jonah's arms and stay there for the next fifty years. But as he had not even glanced at her, she managed to cling to her dignity by formally thanking the judge, the sheriff, and even Noah, who'd had nothing to do with anything. Lord help her, she even felt like hugging that wretched dog she'd had to step over going and coming.

Carrie and Jonah were allowed a few minutes of privacy to say goodbye. The others, including the sheriff's wife, who had been waiting outside, stood in a sunny patch between the jail and the courthouse, talking over the situation. Noah said it was even more exciting than the time he went all the way to Elizabeth City to see the Wild West Show and got sick on Saratoga chips and ginger beer.

Inside the sheriff's office, Jonah and Carrie were feeling an awkwardness neither of them knew quite how to overcome. "The sheriff will escort me to my land—" Jonah managed to smile "—to God Knows Where. I will give him my papers to hold until my hearing."

"When?"

He looked beyond her to the small, tree-shaded yard just as a shaft of late sunlight broke through the gathering clouds. Suddenly, gold brushed the tops of the distant trees, casting deep purple shadows across the fields. "I don't know when. A hearing is only the beginning. If it comes to a trial, it will be my word against Vander's word."

Jonah dare not allow his hopes to arise. As many times as he had been jailed or imprisoned, he had no real knowledge of how the system worked. He did know that it worked differently for different people, and in different parts of the land. He knew that there was too little time and far too much he wanted to say.

"I could go home with you," she whispered.

''No. Go back to Emma and the boys. When this is over, I will find you.''

When she would have said more, he gave in to temptation and silenced her in the way he had been longing to do since this nightmare had begun. The scent of her skin, the taste of her mouth, the feel of her small, firm body pressed against his made him want to weep, and he had not wept since he was too young to remember. Not even when his mother had allowed the blade to slip while she was scraping hides, cutting her wrist so that she bled out her life before anyone found her body.

Kissing her was not enough. Holding her was not enough. The urgency he felt was part desire, part desperation...and part fear that in the end, this was all they would have. A few stolen kisses. A few quick embraces. Not even words, for he was not a man who spoke of feelings. Nothing in his life as a warrior, a horse gatherer, a prisoner or a seaman had prepared him to speak words of love. The women of St. Augustine had taught him many things, but no words to describe what was in his heart.

''I love you.'' The words were uttered so softly he barely heard them. Lifting his face, Jonah closed his eyes against the pain. Holding her tightly, he willed her to feel what was in his heart. To know that if he could have been certain of a future, he would not have stood mute.

There was no way to control the response of his body. How many times had his flesh leapt at the sight of her briar-scratched ankles, her small, bare feet, the soft swell of her breasts against cloth worn thin with age? Holding her so close, drowning in the spicy scent of her hair, of her body—feeling the delicate frame of her hips crushed against his own, there was no way on earth he could prevent the thrusting erection, no way he could disguise it.

They both pretended to ignore it. Jonah knew she was waiting for a response to her words, but how could he tell of her of his feelings when he had nothing to offer her? The only sure thing in his future was uncertainty. She needed more than that.

"You folks better come on out, it's getting late," the sheriff called through the open front door. "We got us a ways to go yet."

Fanny Smith had put together two bundles of food, one for Carrie, the other for Jonah and the sheriff. Noah brought around the horses, and for the first time Carrie thought about the cart she had left in the woods with a cast iron pot of ham stew in the back. What had it been—two days? Three? It seemed like a lifetime ago.

They rode three abreast, silently for the most part, as far as the turnoff to Jonah's land. "I will come to you when this is finished," was all Jonah said.

The sheriff looked at them both, one after the other, and shook his head.

By the time Carrie reached the place in the woods where she'd left the cart, the truth of her situation was just beginning to sink in. She was not married. She had never been married. Which meant that she no longer had a home. No longer had a place to shelter the boys.

Methodically, she went about hitching the buckskin to the cart. She retrieved her iron pot which had been licked clean, and found the lid several feet away. The pot, at least was hers. She had made Darther buy it for her soon after they were married.

Soon after they had *not* been married.

Concentrate, Carrie, first things first and so on. You can do it—you've done it before.

The trouble was, she hadn't, not until recently. What she'd done was let herself be swept along with the tide, doing whatever, going wherever—accepting what she was told and trying to make the best of it. As a child, she'd had little choice. In the years since, it had simply never occurred to her that she could take charge of her own life.

But then one morning she had looked out at that barren field and thought of the waste. Next thing she knew, she was going at it from sunup to sundown, grubbing stumps, cursing and sweating and planning what she would do with her very first crop.

And then came Jonah. She didn't care what he was accused of having done, they belonged together. Something had happened to her the day she had brought him home with her in chains. Even when she'd been half afraid of him, she'd found excuses to be near him. To watch him. Even when she'd considered him a half-wild felon, he had fascinated her. She would find herself watching him from the house while he worked on the shed roof, admiring the way the sun glinted off his sweaty muscles. Soon, just being near him had made her feel a growing sense of—it was more than excitement, but she didn't have words to describe it. Whatever it was, she had never felt anything faintly like it before. He might not love her, but she was almost certain he felt something for her, even if it wasn't as powerful as the wild hot craving she felt.

At least when she wasn't feeling scared half to death.

Besides, they already had a ready-made family. There was no way he could hide the way he felt about Nate and Zac. It might take a while before he learned to love her, as well, but God wouldn't allow a woman to feel anything so powerful for a man without making the man to feel something in return...would He?

Without intending to, she turned toward her own place instead of going on to Emma's house to collect the boys. That could wait. The explaining would take a while, and she'd just as soon put it off until she'd had more time to think. Beside, she had packing to do. That is, she did if Henry had left her anything to pack. He might have taken Sorry, because a mule, even an ornery old bag of bones, had value. The chickens were probably still there. She would coop those up and take them to Emma.

As for her cornfield...

"Damn and blast the man all to hell and back." What on earth was she going to do? She couldn't ask Emma to make room for the boys, herself, her chickens and whatever possessions Henry had left behind. Although once she knew how matters stood, Emma would probably insist on giving them a home. Knowing the way gossip had of spreading like smoke on the wind, she might already know. But no matter how willing the older woman was, there wasn't room in her house for two women and two noisy, rambunctious boys.

At the same time sheriff Julius Cesar Smith headed back home with the deed to Jonah's land and the bills of sale for his livestock tucked securely in his saddlebags, a certain retired law officer was leaning against the hitching post outside Henry Vander's store, waiting for the man to finish relating his account of how the deceased Darther Adams had got that way.

"Now I can't say I saw with me own eyes who done it, but I'd be willing to swear there was bad blood between Darther and that Longshadow feller that rode for him. Argued over money, more'n likely. The breed didn't want to give Darther his share. Claimed he didn't owe him nothing as it was his own horse he rode, even after Dart spoke up for him, got him out of jail. It was poor Dart that set up the whole deal at the track. I declare, a man can't be too careful these days,'' the storekeeper said gravely.

Ex-lawman Purdy levered his rangy body away from the hitching post and turned toward the open shed tacked onto one end of the store, where several horses were kept. The place had not been cleaned out in weeks, from the look of it. There were two saddles on a makeshift rack, one with a plump saddlebag still attached. With seemingly idle interest, he wandered over to the shed.

Henry hurried after him. ''Come on inside the store, look around all you want to. He'p your self to a pickled egg and some crackers. I ain't been home long enough to cook up a meal, but I got plenty of canned stuff. Beans and all.'' Henry followed ex-officer Purdy inside the shed, started to touch his arm and thought better of it when Purdy looked pointedly at the pudgy hand hovering over his sleeve.

It was then that Purdy noticed that the gold watch fob the storekeeper had been wearing a few minutes earlier was nowhere in evidence. ''That your mule?'' he asked mildly.

''Well now, it is and it ain't. It come into my possession right recently— I took it in on account, so to speak, but the poor old thing's worthless. Won't cover half what I was owed, but ask anybody, they'll tell you Henry Vander's a soft touch.''

When the officer's hand fell carelessly on the plump saddlebag, Henry started to sweat. ''Come to think of it, I got some real good pickled beef inside the store. I could lay on some mustard, big slab o' onion and make us a right fine sammich.''

"You want to tell me about this here money?" Purdy's voice was soft as fresh-churned butter as he extracted a fat roll of bills from the saddlebag and peeled off the first few, appearing to study their denomination. It was then that he noticed the dark brown stains.

Purdy had worked both sides of the law long enough to recognize bloodstains, no matter how old they were. "We can talk here, or we can ride south. Either way, I reckon you got some explaining to do, Mr. Vander."

With only the moon to see by, Carrie could tell there wasn't a whole lot left. Sorry was gone. Carrie fervently hoped the mule had balked every step of the way, but in that case Henry would either shoot the poor beast or turn him loose to wander until he starved to death.

Inside the house, she lit a lamp. It didn't take long to discover that Henry had taken Darther's best clothes, leaving the rest bundled up by the door to be collected later. The Springfield was gone, too, but then she'd expected that. No doubt he'd even cleaned out the barn while he was at it, although how he would carry it all, she could only wonder. If the cart had still been there, he would've have piled it full and hauled off everything not nailed down. As it was, it looked as if he planned to come back for at least one more load.

"Over my dead body," Carrie muttered. She yanked open the doors of the pie safe. Empty. The box under the bed—empty. At least he hadn't dumped out her flour and cornmeal. Both bins were just as she'd left them, safely guarded from predators by half a dozen bay leaves.

The chickens had already gone to roost. It was too

dark by the time she'd driven into the yard to explore the barn without lighting the lantern, and besides, she was simply too tired. She had pitched a few forkfuls of hay into the manger and left the buckskin to fend for himself. The barn and the chickens would have to wait until morning. Meanwhile, if Henry had left her a sheet and blanket, she would sleep in her own bed tonight for a change, never mind that Darther had lain there dead less than a week ago, the conniving devil. She was mad enough and tired enough to sleep on his grave if she had to.

'Scuse me, Lord, but I don't reckon You liked him much, either.

Carrie was up with the sun, stiff and sore from having tossed and turned half the night, worrying about how she was going to take care of the boys. Even if she could locate a mission like the one that had rescued her up in Minnesota, Nate and Zac probably wouldn't be allowed to stay together, and that would break their hearts. Right now, all they had was each other.

And her.

And Emma, she added dutifully. Even so, it might not be enough.

Still wearing her worn muslin nightgown—it was a wonder that wretched old man hadn't stolen that, too— she stacked her meager supply of kitchenware on the table. Most of it had been there when she had come to live, but Darther owed her for three years of hard labor. He'd certainly never paid her wages. The linens had been bundled up along with Darther's winter clothes, to be collected later. She had untied the skimpy roll and taken what she'd needed to make the bed, now she folded it neatly and stacked it on top of the bundle.

Whether he knew it or not, Henry had done her a favor by doing most of her packing for her. If it hadn't started to drizzle during the night, she might even have loaded it onto the cart.

But she still had the barn to go through and pack up. That would take time, because she didn't intend to leave behind a single thing that could be useful.

It was midafternoon when she finished. She was of half a mind to set fire to the place before she left, but in this drizzle, it would only smolder and besides, she didn't have the heart to burn down a perfectly good shelter. Maybe someone would come along the way Nate and Zac had, who could make use of it. At least Henry wouldn't be able to claim it. There was some satisfaction in that.

The rain set in heavier as she stood in the door of the barn, gazing out at the place where she had spent the past three years. The horse trough she had toted countless pails of water up from the creek to keep filled. The chicken house with its leaning walls, its patched roof and mended wire fence, with the trumpet vine climbing up the gatepost.

She would miss it all. There had been good times to offset the bad times. For the most part she'd been left alone to do as she pleased. What would happen to it all now that Darther was dead? So far as she knew, he had no heirs. If the county stepped in and claimed his property, perhaps she could lease it against future crops.

"Carrie Adams, tenant farmer," she murmured, a smile dawning on her tired face. Independent as a hog on ice, as Emma would say.

Actually, she was still Carrie Vander, no kin to Henry Vander, although it had probably been the coincidence of the names listed in the newspaper that had given

Henry the idea of claiming her, and convinced the board of missions to let him have her.

She waited for the rain to slack off before trying to catch the chickens and stuff them into the battered coop. It wasn't a job she particularly relished—with the mud and everything else, she would need a bath afterwards, and she'd already bundled up all her clothes.

Then there was the house. She intended to leave it clean for whoever claimed it next. Clean, but empty of everything she could cart off. That was fair enough.

The rain droned on. Standing there in the barn beside an old wooden chicken coop, she was bracing herself to start catching chickens when she caught a glimpse of someone coming up the lane. Through the solid downpour, it was impossible to identify the rider. It would hardly be a neighbor. Even after the funeral, they weren't likely to come calling. Curious, she watched as the rider drew closer, and then the familiar set of his head and shoulders began to take shape through the downpour.

She caught her breath. "Jonah?" Disregarding the rain, she ran out to meet him, muddy water splashing up to her knees. "Jonah?" she shouted.

They were both drenched by the time the big bay stallion was led inside the barn, his body steaming as he was unsaddled, rubbed down and led into Peck's old stall. The sound of rain on the tin roof was deafening, making talk all but impossible. In their wet clothes, smelling of horse and damp cotton, they stood and stared uncertainly at each other until, with a broken cry, Carrie hurled herself into his arms.

Catching her, Jonah crushed her to him, burying his face in her damp hair that smelled faintly of soap, faintly of wood smoke from the cook fire. They clung together, speaking in broken phrases impossible to hear, but mostly just holding. For now, holding was enough.

But not for long. Carrie leaned back in his arms, her gaze moving hungrily over his face—the butternut skin, the cloud-gray eyes—his beautiful mouth and curved blade of a nose. Every feature was etched on her heart so that a hundred years from now, she would still remember the way he looked—the way he could melt her right down to the bones with a single touch.

It was Carrie who broke the impasse by reaching up and touching her lips to his. But it was Jonah who took over and turned the kiss into something that swiftly raged out of control.

There was fresh straw in the stall, but the stallion had already claimed possession. There was Liam's old cot, but it was narrow and rickety. As one, they turned and looked up at the loft. The light was fading fast, but neither of them noticed the darkness. The sound of rain was deafening as a true autumn rain, the first of the season, pounded down on the rusted metal roof.

Carrie went up the ladder first. Suddenly shy, she lowered herself to a pile of straw heaped up in the corner and tucked her wet skirts around her feet. Carefully, Jonah knelt beside her and leaned close to speak. "I came as quickly as I could."

She nodded, marveling at the warmth and hardness of his thigh. The instant she realized that she was stroking him through a thin layer of wet denim, she jerked her hands away. It was the sound of his laughter, barely heard over the rain, that broke the tension.

And then Carrie laughed, too. Her whole world might have collapsed but Jonah was here, and that made everything right.

"—boys?" Through the ceaseless din she caught the one word.

"Emma's." No point in trying to explain why she hadn't yet been to collect them, he wouldn't be able to hear her.

And then the rain stopped just as suddenly as it had begun. The silence was deafening. "Carrie?" he whispered. "I had planned to wait—to do this the proper way."

"To do what the proper way?" she whispered back.

Plink-plank. Rain dripped from the roof into the puddles. Jonah started to speak, broke off with a muffled oath, and caught her in his arms. They toppled sideways into the straw, and for a while there was only the sound of sighing, groaning, and sharply in-drawn breath, broken by a last brief flurry of rain.

As the late afternoon sun cleared away the clouds, allowing a golden light to fall through the opening, their lips met again, tentatively at first. And then Jonah drew back and gazed down at her as if he couldn't quite believe she was real. The blood racing recklessly though her body, Carrie took control, her inexperience no match for her eagerness. Her soft, damp lips swollen with desire, she kissed his mouth, his throat, his ears, sucking the small lobes between her teeth. She wanted to devour him, and didn't quite know where to begin.

It was Jonah who took the next step. Before she quite realized how it happened, she was lying naked on the straw, watching as he rose up onto his knees and peeled off his shirt. When his hands fell to the front of his trousers she caught her breath and stared.

This time it was going to happen. This time there would be nothing to stop them.

In the half light she stared at the shadowy area at the

base of his belly, where his powerful thighs came together. Her own thighs tightened instinctively, as if to
contain the tumultuous ache that started somewhere in
her center and spread throughout her body.

He touched her face, his fingers tracing the delicate
line of her jaw. "Stubborn," he murmured almost
proudly. "A woman of great bravery."

She wanted to tell him that brave was hardly the word
she would have used to describe herself, but by that time
he had moved on, his hands covering her breasts as if
they were fragile as hummingbird eggs. They were
hardly much larger. She didn't want him to touch her
gently, she wanted—

"Oh, ahh…yes," she whispered.

Moaning under the assault of a need more powerful
than anything she had ever felt before, she covered his
hands with her own and pressed hard. She could feel her
nipples tighten almost painfully, but it was a sweet
pain—sweeter still when he replaced his hands with his
mouth.

Never, if she lived to be a hundred years old, Carrie
told herself much later, would she forget the lessons she
learned that rainy evening in the hayloft. She learned
that a man could be both hard as iron and soft as silk.
She learned that touching a man in a certain way, kissing
him in a certain way, could make him whimper like a
babe.

She learned that there were many ways to kiss, and
the most intimate kisses of all were like being wrapped
in a rainbow and then hurled up into a whirlwind. That
the achy, itchy feeling she had known so many times
before was magnified a hundredfold when a man put
himself inside her body and moved in certain ways.

And oh, those many ways. Hungrily, feverishly, she

had twisted beneath him and shouted, "Yes, yes—oh, please, faster, faster!"

Later, lying spent, but still entwined, she whispered in amazement, "I can't stop smiling. Does that always happen?"

She thought he might have laughed, but it could have been that other sound he'd made when they were—when he was—when the earth was exploding all around them. "Does what always happen?" he asked.

"You know—like you're starving and feasting all at once, and you can't stop smiling because it's so—so indescribably wonderful."

"I think you just described the indescribable." He took her hand and carried it to his face, to his mouth. He was smiling.

When Carrie twitched and reached under her, pulling out a bit of straw, Jonah rolled her on top of him, still joined, and spread his shirt where she had been lying. "I wish I had thought to do this before. I wish instead of a wet shirt, you were lying on a bed of the softest, palest doeskin. I wish instead of barnyard smells, I had sweet leaves to burn outside my lodge, and stars to shine down and give their blessing."

Mesmerized, she stared up at him through the gloom, her heart too full to utter a sound. No one had ever spoken poetry to her before. Even if the words didn't rhyme, she knew poetry when she heard it.

"I wanted," he went on, "to come to you with my mares and their foals, for your bride price." There was pride in his voice, but even in the dim light she could see the uncertainty in his eyes.

"My...bride price?"

"It is how we do it, Carrie. I offer for you, and you decide."

"Yes."

"But my horses and my land are held in bond. I have nothing to offer except—"

"Yes?" This time it was a question.

He swallowed hard then. She could see the muscles of his throat working. "My heart. My hands. They are yours, Carina."

He wasn't going to use the word she ached to hear, but that was all right. She knew what was in his heart. It was love, and it was hers.

"Oh, yes," she whispered, and miraculously, felt him harden inside her all over again.

Outside, the storm moved out over the Currituck Sound, over the ocean. Slowly the red glow of sunset waned, closing them into a world of their own.

It was still barely midmorning when they neared Emma's house. They had risen early, and Carrie had finished gathering up the chickens while Jonah had loaded the cart with her belongings. He had taken a few things from the barn where they had spent the night, but left most of it behind. The air was as clear as crystal, though the trees were still dripping.

They smiled a lot. They touched frequently. It was as if they had stepped into a world newly created just for them. Jonah, driving the cart with the black-eared stallion following behind on a lead, said, "Does this remind you of anything?"

Carrie frowned, then shook her head. They had both been shy at first this morning, but with so much to be done, the shyness hadn't lasted. Carrie was eager to see the last of Darther's house. She had no notion what the future would hold, but as long as it held Jonah and her boys, she wouldn't ask for more.

"At least T'a-Kon is not wearing leg irons," he said with a chuckle.

And then, of course, she remembered. "You might laugh about it now, but I know I'll never be able to think about it without feeling shame."

Leaning closer, he covered both her hands with one of his, his eyes expressing what he was not quite ready to put into words.

The sound of wild whoops greeted them before they even drew into the clearing, and then two boys burst out from behind the trees, one black, one white, both wearing beads on their skinny chests, a dab of flour on their noses and chicken feathers in their hair. "Jonah, Jonah, we knowed you was comin'," Zac sang out.

"Miss Emma, she made 'lasses cake and yaupon tea wi' honey in it."

As soon as the big wooden wheels stopped rolling Carrie tumbled out of the cart and ran toward her two wild Indians, her arms held wide. Both boys piled on, nearly knocking her on her backside, and then Carrie wrinkled her nose. "Oh, my, what—"

"Nate got skunked on. Miss Emma, she used six cans of 'maters, but he still stinks. Hey, Jonah, come smell Nate, he got skunked," the youngest boy cried gleefully.

Later, they sat out on the front porch, although it had turned off cool after the rain. The boys set the chicken coop inside Emma's pen and let Carrie's chickens in with the others, then set to building a mud fort. Nate now smelled more like vanilla extract, which was some better, but not a whole lot.

"Well, young man, I reck'n you'll be taking my family down to your place." The boys had whooped and hollered some more when they'd learned that they were to live with Jonah. Zac wanted to be sure Miss Carrie would live there with them.

"Yes," Jonah said. "But first we must build her a house."

Emma Tamplin set her chair into motion, the words that went unsaid more painful than she was prepared to admit. "I've been thinking lately about moving into town. I reckon this is as good a time as any, while I can still get around." Shingle Landing could hardly be called a town. Still, it was a settled farming, hunting and fishing community, and Emma had lived in the area all her life. She had friends there.

"That would probably be better," Carrie murmured, and both women rocked and thought about it some more. Carrie could tell Jonah was itching to go, but he was far too polite to hurry her goodbyes. Emma had been her only friend for three years. How could she leave her?

Yet how could she stay? Jonah didn't even have a house, much less one large enough to hold two grown women and two children.

It was Emma who sent them on their way, with clean shirts for the boys and enough food to last several days. "Come back and get your chickens by 'n' by," she called after the lumbering cart.

There was another flurry of waves and goodbyes, and then Carrie turned to face forward. She would never forget the woman who had taught her courage by her own example. "One day soon, once we get settled, I'm going back for a visit."

Both boys promptly cried, "Me, too!"

"Every home needs a grandmother," Jonah said quietly, and Carrie cut him a sidelong glance, not daring to press for more.

Jonah pictured the way they must look, a weathered

old cart piled high with everything from feather pillows to a rusted plow, with a Kiowa warrior and a small blue-eyed woman, widowed barely a week ago, and two wigglesome boys, one pale, one dark.

His family. The gods might be laughing now, but surely they had known what they were doing when they'd had the Union soldiers sweep him up along with more than seventy other warriors and herd them to a prison in the East.

That had been only the beginning. Since then the road he had traveled had been fraught with danger, until finally, with the small, brave woman at his side, he had come home.

Epilogue

~~~~~~~~~~

Two weeks after Henry Vander, convicted of murder, cheated the hangman by dying of heart failure, Jonah put in a good day's work getting the young couple settled into Carrie's old house. He had a good feeling about them. They would not be asked to pay rent until the first crops came in, and then only a token amount. In exchange, they would clear more of the land. Once there was enough money coming in each year to do more than buy seed and equipment, they would renegotiate the lease. Headed home, he thought with satisfaction and no little surprise that since the county had awarded his wife the land she had once thought was hers by law, he was becoming a good businessman.

Carrie and Emma would be busy hemming curtains for the windows of the new house. As long as he had to live inside four walls, he insisted on having as many windows as the structure would support. Emma had told him he was crazy, that the place would be impossible to heat come hard winter, but both Jonah and Carrie had learned to compromise.

Emma's house, already being built on the other side of the garden, was taking shape. Several men from Shin-

gle Landing had ridden down one day last week to help
with the framing and roofing, bringing Emma along for
a visit. Both women were overjoyed to be together again,
but Jonah's generosity was not all it seemed. Nate was
determined to bring the new baby into the world next
April, saying he'd learned all about birthing from his
grandmother. If Jonah could make arrangements, the boy
would read medicine when he was old enough. But until
then, Jonah wanted Emma close by.

Their wedding had been held one month after
Adams's death. No one considered it indecently soon, as
the bride had not been legally married. Emma and Fanny
Smith, as well as a church full of friends and neighbors,
had been in attendance. Sheriff Julius Cesar Smith had
given the bride away, and Judge Powell, along with the
preacher, had performed the ceremony.

Now, as he turned in between the gateposts, several
horses trotted toward the fence. They numbered nine,
now. T'a-Kon, his three mares and their foals, and two
new mares. He was well pleased with these eastern
horses. For the first time in his life, Jonah felt as if he
truly belonged to a place and a people. Here, he had put
down roots. Here, with the help of friends, he was building a home for one crippled old granny woman who had
outlived a husband and five children. Here he had built
a home for two leftover boys, one black, one white—
for his beloved Carrie, survivor of a long-ago massacre
in a faraway place…and this half-breed warrior, once a
member of the Kiowa's elite Koitsenga. The Society of
the Ten Bravest.

Lifting his eyes to a cloudless sky, he gave soft voice
to a warrior's cry of triumph.

*   *   *   *   *

BRONWYN WILLIAMS

As the daughters of a major league ball player and granddaughters of a sea captain, it's easy to see where the two sisters who write as Bronwyn Williams, Dixie Browning and Mary Williams, get much of their material. The two grew up on the Outer Banks of North Carolina. After years of living away, Dixie, the wife of an electrical engineer, now retired, and Mary, the wife of a Coast Guard officer, also retired, have returned to their roots. As with many of Dixie Browning's nearly seventy contemporaries for Silhouette, most of the sisters' stories written as Bronwyn Williams have been set in northeastern North Carolina, an area rich in history and folklore. The two began writing historicals for Harlequin in 1988, and they also have published a number of mainstream titles.

HH553

Travel back in time to America's past with wonderful Westerns from Harlequin Historicals

ON SALE MARCH 2001

LONGSHADOW'S WOMAN
by **Bronwyn Williams**
(The Carolinas, 1879)

LILY GETS HER MAN
by **Charlene Sands**
(Texas, 1880s)

ON SALE APRIL 2001

THE SEDUCTION OF SHAY DEVEREAUX
by **Carolyn Davidson**
(Louisiana, 1870)

NIGHT HAWK'S BRIDE
by **Jillian Hart**
(Wisconsin, 1840)

Visit us at www.eHarlequin.com   HHWEST12

Thrilling Medievals? Racy Regencies?
Enjoy them both from
Harlequin Historicals

ON SALE MARCH 2001
THE HIGHLAND WIFE by **Lyn Stone**
(Medieval Scotland)
and
ANNE'S PERFECT HUSBAND by **Gayle Wilson**
(Regency London)

ON SALE APRIL 2001
ONE KNIGHT IN VENICE by **Tori Phillips**
(Medieval Italy)
and
GALLANT WAIF by **Anne Gracie**
(Regency England)

**Harlequin®
Historical**

Visit us at www.eHarlequin.com
HHMED17

Master storyteller and
New York Times **bestselling author**

HEATHER GRAHAM

weaves her magic in the Civil War trilogy

Summer fires

The war is over, but the
battle of life rages on in these three stories that
tell of the importance of family ties, loyalty and love.

Together for the first time in one special collection,
these stories will be truly enjoyed and treasured!

Coming in May 2001 only from Harlequin.

HARLEQUIN®
Makes any time special ®

Visit us at www.eHarlequin.com
PHSEASON

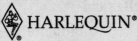

HARLEQUIN®

makes any time special—online...

eHARLEQUIN.com

your romantic life

●—Romance 101—

♥ Guides to romance, dating and flirting.

●—Dr. Romance—

♥ Get romance advice and tips from our expert, Dr. Romance.

●—Recipes for Romance—

♥ How to plan romantic meals for you and your sweetie.

●—Daily Love Dose—

♥ Tips on how to keep the romance alive every day.

●—Tales from the Heart—

♥ Discuss romantic dilemmas with other members in our Tales from the Heart message board.

HINTL1

Silhouette
bestselling authors

KASEY MICHAELS

RUTH LANGAN

CAROLYN ZANE

welcome you to a world of family, privilege and power with three brand-new love stories about America's most beloved dynasty, the Coltons

Brides of Privilege

Available May 2001

Where love comes alive™

Visit Silhouette at www.eHarlequin.com
PSCOLT

HARLEQUIN®

bestselling authors

Merline Lovelace
Deborah Simmons
Julia Justiss

cordially invite you to enjoy three
brand-new stories of unexpected love

The Officer's Bride

Available April 2001

HARLEQUIN®
Makes any time special®

Visit us at www.eHarlequin.com

PHOFFICER

REGENCY ROMANCE

Visit the elegant English countryside,
explore the whirlwind of London Society
and meet feisty heroines who tame roguish
heroes with their wit, zest and feminine
charm, in...The Regency Collection.

Available in March 2001 at your favorite retail outlet:

TRUE COLOURS
by Nicola Cornick

THE WOLFE'S MATE
by Paula Marshall

MR. TRELAWNEY'S
PROPOSAL
by Mary Brendan

TALLIE'S KNIGHT
by Anne Gracie

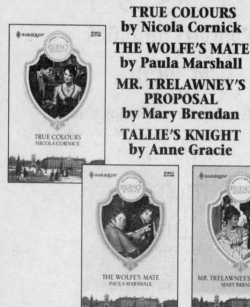

Visit us at www.eHarlequin.com

RCREG2